His thoughts turned inwards.

Luciana learned something new about Max Rivington then. It would be infinitely dangerous to pry.

But she wanted to. She could barely take in how much she wanted to know this man.

So she said, very carefully, 'But you know us now, sir, and you *will* come to see the boys, won't you? They would so enjoy it.'

Somehow she had got things right again, for when he turned back to her there was only that so familiar, all-pervading smile.

'If you'll have m

Louisa Gray was born in England of Scottish-Irish parents (with a little Spanish and French thrown in). She was educated in Wales, ran off to Italy, but has now concluded that she can never live anywhere where they have never heard of digestive biscuits. The chocolate ones. She now lives happily in Somerset with her haughty and ill-disciplined Labrador, Cressie.

THE STANDISH INHERITANCE

Louisa Gray

© Louisa Gray 1996

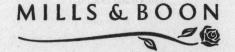

MILLS & BOON

All the characters in this book have no existence outside the imagination of the author, and have no relation whatsoever to anyone bearing the same name or names. They are not even distantly inspired by any individual known or unknown to the author, and all the incidents are pure invention.

MILLS & BOON, the Rose Device and LEGACY OF LOVE
are trademarks of the publisher.
Harlequin Mills & Boon Limited,
Eton House, 18–24 Paradise Road, Richmond, Surrey TW9 1SR

© Louisa Gray 1996

ISBN 0 263 79527 6

Set in 10 on 12 pt Linotron Times
04-9603-84218

Typeset in Great Britain by CentraCet, Cambridge
Printed in Great Britain by
BPC Paperbacks Ltd

AUTHOR'S NOTE

BECAUSE this story is set firmly in Somerset, it needs to be said that the settings, Somerton Prior and Somerton Parva, do not exist, and have nothing whatsoever to do with the actual town of Somerton. Everything—and everybody—are entirely imaginary (except two lawless mongrels). And maybe the hero—which is why this book is for:

The Clan in memory of Grandpa Alessandro

CHAPTER ONE

'*Are you my father*?'

Until Freddie flew past her, alight with excitement, his voice reckless with hope, Luciana had not known the man was there. Lost in the warmth, the security of this summer afternoon, cool in the shadow of the ancient trees, she had been dreaming. Of nothing in particular, just the pleasure of it all as the boys clattered and splashed and fought their way upstream, makeshift nets trailing in the water, their attendant groom yelling after them that they would terrify every last fish out of the county the noise that they were making. The boys ignored what they didn't deride, up to their sodden knees in weeds and twine, fierce with concentration, while Cass and Polly did what mongrels did best and made a spectacular nuisance of themselves amongst the rushes.

Luciana trailed her feet in the water, soothed by its gentle flow, remembering two other boys, so long ago, playing where hers played now, while she watched, directing operations from this very place beneath her favourite willow. Remembered, too, that Freddie had been conceived here. . . .

Remembered all she longed so helplessly to forget.

Yet the stab of loss, always new, always brutal, did not spoil the day.

'Freddie, please don't drown your brother; I am oddly fond of him. And Carlo, *not* in your pocket if you don't

mind. . .no, I don't care, it *wriggled*, that's all I need to
know, put it back where it came from. And when you've
done that—oh, *Polly*!'

The once silken mongrel shook its dripping red coat
all over her—people sitting on rugs were themselves for
sitting on to Polly's mind. Not—Luciana wrestled him
off—that this latest damage could make much difference now. Her muslins were stark devastation. Hugged
in turn by Carlo, Freddie, Cass and Polly (only the
groom had spared her), she had long since been ren-
dered a mass of gluey pawprints. Her hem trailed in
the water. . . Cass plunged across the stream to tug at
it. . .

Of course she never heard the man coming. Or even
the horse she now saw through startled eyes as she
turned at Freddie's hectic plea, 'Are you my father?'
and her heart stood still.

So still it was as though it had never known life at all,
that she never had. Her whole body soaked to ice with
shock—real, raw, unexpected—rigid with it. She felt the
last of her blood drain away.

He. . .the man. . .just for a second—longer, as she
fought to hold on to what she knew was the truth,
failing—he *could* have been. *So* like! Standing so tall, so
powerfully at ease against the sun as a small boy tugged
at his sleeve, just as Carlo had done the last time Philip
came home.

Dear God, but for one punishing, dragging second he
could have been!

Then it was over. Philip had never laughed like that.
No more would Philip have had the first idea what to do
in a situation as delicate as this. This man was a stranger,
yet instantly he made Freddie his ally.

'Your father? Do I want to be? You're a disgusting specimen.'

Freddie, still hoping, never really understanding his father could never come home, recognised the tone, so like his mother's teasing manner. He felt completely safe with it.

So he argued. 'Am not! Well, not as bad as Carlo, he's. . .' Freddie was only four and his vocabulary was inadequate to his sneer.

'Very likely. I can smell him from here!'

The man had not moved and Luciana knew in that moment that he was aware of everything, acutely attuned; unused to children yet instinctively letting Freddie take the lead, his gaze quickly summing up the wariness in Carlo, holding back just as the older boy held back, knowing somehow that the child would eventually trust his laughter.

Carlo seemed to, though he stayed mid-stream and Luciana's throat clenched with pain. Carlo remembered, too—the last time Philip had come home, equally a stranger to be unsure of until he saw his mother's radiant smile. Carlo understood death, but he had kept hoping. She could not bear it. She didn't know what to do, or say.

The man saw that and spoke for her.

'Forgive my creeping up on you in such a villainous fashion, ma'am, but I could not help it. I didn't want to disturb you. It is so long since I heard such liberating sounds as these.'

That was when Luciana knew she was no stranger to him, that he knew all about her and the children, and she knew, as her heart slowly began to breathe again, why he seemed so familiar. His very stance, and those quietly regretful words, were enough. Another soldier. She knew where he had come from and why.

Toulouse. Where her brother-in-law, the Marquess, had died not four months since in that last unnecessary battle. From Rory's regiment. Philip's, once. . .

Slowly she unwound her frozen limbs and stood. Which was when the stranger moved, careful not to let go of Freddie's hand which clung to this prize captive so determinedly. Close enough for him to see her clearly at last, and Luciana to see him.

'Max Rivington, my lady.' He did not bow, or even smile, and never had she felt such intensity as was in his eyes. Dark eyes, unreadable. Her heart stilled once more.

She found her voice, just, husky with effort. 'Oh. . . but, yes, of course. . .but I had thought. . .'

'I am recovered now.' He spoke almost reflexively, she thought, as if he were no more aware of what he was saying than she was, just as dazed.

'I'm so glad, sir. Rory. . .he spoke of you so often. My husband, too.' Rory, with the mature affection of the fiercely independent man he had become; Philip, with all the hero-worship of the boy that was all he was granted the time to be.

'And they spoke of you.'

Strange, Luciana thought, how taut his voice is, how it seems hard for him to speak. Perhaps it was. That was when she really saw his face.

Her eyes flared in shock — so ferociously handsome, so hurt! That scar, ripping into his cheek, twisting down into his neck, was brutal. Hideous. It should have destroyed his beauty but it did not.

She fought to control her response, the expression in

her eyes as they flickered to his hand—the hand Freddie
was holding as if nothing were strange about it at all.
Even gloved as it was in thick, worn leather she could
see. . .

It was Carlo who saved the day, hearing the man give
a name he knew from all his Uncle Rory's most exciting
stories, puzzled by his mother's drained silence.

'Did you *really* lose your hand at Talavera, sir?'

Straight to the core of her dilemma—Luciana smiled
in pain—and through it with all the frankness of a child.
Just as Lord Rivington needed.

'Not all of it; I'm sorry to be so dull. Just two fingers.'

'Ohh. . .' Freddie suddenly became aware of what he
was holding and his delight boiled over. 'May I *see*?'

'Freddie!' That was too much. Luciana moved to
recapture her son. Too late. Even as she laid hold of his
collar—in an all too ominous and familiar manner—
Lord Rivington obligingly tugged off his glove and
bared his hand to the revealing sunlight.

And by a miracle Luciana said the right thing.
Because she was little more than a child herself, after
all, and the widow and daughter of soldiers—

'Well, I must say I don't think much of that. How
unimpressive!' As she said it, her stomach settled; saying
so—lying—really did make what she saw seem not so
terrible.

'Isn't it? I'm not doing very well, am I? Perhaps I
should go back to the village, co-opt the blacksmith into
removing my leg, then hobble back and try again.'

It was easy to offer her hand to him then. What was
not so easy was understanding the instant, penetrating
shock she felt as that jagged skin met hers. Nothing to
do with her wariness of maybe hurting him. . .

So much to do with those eyes that fixed so keenly on hers, so dark against his sun-gold skin and flecked with amber, almost a mirror to the true, warm bronze of his hair. . .and with the way that punishing scar caught at the corner of his mouth, trying to twist anger into that easy smile. Failing. His smile was electrifying.

'That would be cheating.' How was she speaking at all? She was beyond thinking, and not because he was so unexpected and a stranger, but because he did not seem to be and never would. She knew so much about him, this man who detested garlic and tobacco, loved dogs and Mozart, rode as if born to the saddle, who had fenced his way out of at least three duels he had never wanted in the first place, and caustically derided Rory's inevitable gambling losses—whilst bailing him out from equally undernourished pockets. I feel I know you, she thought, and yet. . .

Carlo intervened again. 'You haven't even *really* lost any fingers at all!' he accused.

'Not whole ones, no. I had my mind on other things at the time.'

'Why is your hand so strange?' Freddie touched the shiny skin with awe.

'Burns. My sleeve caught fire.'

So matter-of-factly spoken, and suddenly Luciana realised what she was looking at and why it had happened. He had tried to save her husband's life. The spell that had made him such a normal part of this gently ordinary afternoon was broken. He had come to talk with her, answer hard and painful questions, to bring Rory's possessions home. Both her husband and his brother were gone now. Tears stabbed at her eyes and she fled behind the familiar routines of motherhood to hide them.

'Well, now you have thoroughly inspected your victim, Freddie, perhaps you will let him go. It is about time you two returned to the house to get clean.'

'*Clean*. . .!'

'Urrgh!'

'*Why*?'

'Now.'

'But—'

'I am convinced his Lordship feels quite scrutinized enough.'

'But we want to stay and talk to him!'

'No. But perhaps—' Luciana turned as composedly as she could to her visitor '—Lord Rivington will dine with us? I feel sure, sir, you must be exhausted after your journey. . .' Then realised what she had said, and to whom.

Men like this had slept in their saddles, in mud, in snow, in their comrades blood, hunched against their horses—living or dead—anything for warmth and shelter, to keep off the freezing rain that would kill the weakest of them. . .one less man to worry about in the morning, to share out his rations, hope to the hell they were living through that he had a blanket that might keep someone else from joining him in oblivion, and on and on for days, unthinkable miles at a time.

She was never more grateful to Lord Rivington than in that moment when he kept the contempt out of his eyes and smiled without any irony at all.

'I did not come to impose, my lady, and it is later than I thought. I was watching you longer than I realised. But if it is no inconvenience. . .'

Watching. Yes, of course he had been. Maybe for as much as half an hour. She knew it without ever knowing how. She should hate it, but she did not. Which was when Luciana knew that he was different, special in some way. She would have minded profoundly had anyone else been prying here, this was their private place, for their private nonsense, not for strangers. But she was glad he had seen them and drawn such heartening amusement from what he saw. And not because of who he was or what he had once risked his life to do. She liked him.

'How could it ever be, sir? You have heard the boys; you are quite the most exciting prospect to come their way in an age. I only hope you can stand up to the barrage of insalubrious questions—'

Carlo's quick wits translated for Freddie before Luciana realised the full import of what she was saying and had time to take it back. 'I knew Mamma would never spoil sport!' Cunning little demon!

Freddie assimilated the most interesting part. 'Oh. . . so we can have *proper* dinner, too?' A hungry one.

For a second, Luciana's sense of domestic preservation rebelled. Carlo and Freddie loose in the dining-room? But they were staring at her so sternly, and she had all but unthinkingly promised, so she had no option.

'Yes. Just this once. And only—'

'If we're good, *we* know!' Really, Freddie was getting very impertinent; she tried to regret it. The trouble was, he had his father's smile.

'I'll keep Freddie in order,' lied Carlo, who never had been able to, even had he not been the orchestrator of a good three-quarters of the trouble in the first place.

'Of course you will.' His mother saw through him

sweetly, and Carlo had the grace to flush. 'Now go and find poor Liam. I think he is being molested by the animals.'

As indeed the groom was, cornered up a straining tree, his game leg dangling, a dog hanging from its mangled boot. His roars of, 'Ah, divil hounds!' had an all too familiar and despairing ring.

'Sounds as if the cavalry is required.' Max Rivington dislodged Freddie from an experimental dig in his pocket. Freddie came loose with an interesting collection of objects his Lordship had quite forgotten he had put there. 'Yes, that *is* a musket ball. And yes, I did dig it out of my anatomy, you ghoul.'

'And no, Freddie, you may not keep it!' Luciana lapsed into maternal weariness.

Freddie gave it back, grabbed Carlo's elbow and hauled him off to Liam's rescue, loudly informing his senior that the musket ball was thick with blood. One or other of them yelled, '*Charge!*' and, muffled by his fall through the branches, Liam was heard to damn Polly — on whom he fell— to vulgarly expressed perdition.

Luciana watched her boys go, not really knowing what to do next.

Nothing ever seemed to unsettle her companion. 'Well, plainly I'm not a total disappointment after all.'

'It *was* blood?'

'Pints of it, if I remember, which I don't, since I made anodyne use of brandy before ferreting that ball out with what my batman later berated me were his sewing scissors!'

Oh, he was *so* like Philip! Rory, too. So insouciantly careless of his pain, the touch of death coming too close again, it was impossible ever to tell with men like this if fear existed for even a second behind the self-mocking laughter.

If that had been all he said she would have held back, shied from what needed to be said but she dared not face yet. But he added so drily, 'I'm not very brave!' and Luciana knew she could not let him joke about it.

'Don't ever say that, sir, even in jest! Least of all, *ever*, to me!' Then she tried her best. 'I tried to thank you. . . for your letter when Philip died, for all the truly comforting things you said that helped me so much. It could have been so different, you see, a clumsy duty letter from his commanding officer. I have always been grateful that officer was you. And afterwards, when Rory told me what you did—trying to save Philip, though nobody could—I so much wanted to say. . .*so* much, but I didn't know how. I'm not very. . .' She meant articulate.

He said simply, 'Not very old, my lady. And your husband was my friend.'

'He thought the world of that friendship, and of you, my lord.'

'And I loved him, too. What more have either of us to say than that?'

She never was to know who reached for whose hand first. Only that their fingers met and held, saying everything. She found that she was crying. . .

And that he was stroking away her tears.

'About time, I think. Why do I think you have been far too brave for far too long, my lady? Oh, but dear God, I never really understood what a baby you are! Even though Philip was just a boy, I never realised. And nobody to take your tears to now Rory's gone!'

'No.' The tears were unresisted now. Held back so

long because of her sons, they overpowered her, cool and clean.

His voice was so tense, remote suddenly, that Luciana knew he had looked away from her. He said it so quietly.

'And you loved him, too.'

Which was when she finally admitted the truth of it and faced the real impact of her loss. She had loved her husband's brother so much—her dearest friend, *her* brother. When Philip was dead and Rory came home, so protective, so guilty at his own survival in the face of her loss, she had tried to help him, and wished and hoped that he would never go away again and that something, at least, would always be the same. Only it wasn't. Wild, kind, irreplaceable Rory was gone, too.

She could only nod her assent.

Very gently Max Rivington caught her hands between his own and said, 'That is why I came here, my lady. Not because of Philip, though I will answer anything you ask me. Not to bring Rory's possessions home. I came to keep a promise.'

'A promise?'

'That I would come and tell you just how completely Rory loved you. No. . .' This as she flung back her head, eyes bleached with shock, almost understanding. 'Not as the brother you never had, as you loved him. I came to tell you that you were the very heart of his existence.'

CHAPTER TWO

LUCIANA sat for a very long time on the fallen willow where the rushes grew, unable to speak or even think. Only sense, somehow, through eyes sealed with unshed tears, that her precious afternoon had faded and shadows had crept up on her. Shadows from deep within herself.

She felt it utterly. Stunned, dazed, without the smallest connection to the world about her or to the self she had been not a second—or was it a lifetime?—before. The self who was coping, adjusting; who had come through the fight against loss and anger, ready, if still reluctant, to accept bereavement and move on.

This frozen, shaking creature, racked by shock as cold as it was pitiless, wouldn't begin to know what acceptance was.

Or truth. Because that was what Max Rivington had spoken. A truth too appalling to face.

So how strange that, needing to be angry with him, Luciana found she couldn't be. He had shattered her fragile regeneration as if it had never been and yet he comforted her.

Strange, all of it. . .

For with the tact that was instinct in him, Lord Rivington had withdrawn from her, leaving her private but not alone, coaxing his horse across the glade to drink at the stream's edge. She could not see him but she knew he was there, and his presence warmed her.

Something about his laughter. . .so patient with the reluctant mare. . .so calming. . .

Luciana faced at last her overwhelming need for comfort and cried again. Shameful tears—she raged—soaking her through with guilt, because this was just how she had clung to Rory. Clung with such selfish gratitude to his strength, his care of her. Never seeing him, his suffering, blinded by her despair at losing Philip. She had never even begun to guess that Rory loved her. Now it was as if she had never known him and, when she felt less numbed, she would despise herself. How could she have been so self-concerned? How could it be that she was still so utterly self-centred that even now she was doing the same again, crying for herself? Desperate for Rory's friend to come to her, help her. . .

She needed to feel human comfort as she needed to breathe.

And for a brief, bewildered moment, Luciana wondered if she had cried her need aloud. Because even as she hugged her arms about her, vainly trying to stifle her pain, Max Rivington came back to her, unhurried—everything about him seemed that way—calm, assured, infinitely reassuring. Luciana looked up at him, a shadow against the clouding sun, and thought, It is as if compassion can be a physical force, a touch. He was yards away still but his sympathy reached her. Began to work on her.

Not since she was the tiniest child, frightened of the dark, had she felt as she did now, that another human creature could push the dark away, keep it from her. But Max Rivington did. Yet all he did was smile.

Then he said, 'There is rain coming, my lady. It's time to take you home.'

Which was when Luciana cried in earnest—knowing she must not, knowing she had no right to inflict such intimate unhappiness on him. . .what kind of helpless child would he think Philip had married, Rory wasted his love on? She was not like this! She never cried. She hated it, it frightened her. It could overwhelm her utterly.

She realised she was shaking, rocking herself deep into protecting shock when he came to her, his still unhealed voice strained, almost harsh, yet so powerful. 'Good girl. . .brave girl!' He took off his coat, slipping it about her shoulders, holding it there. 'Brave, *brave* girl!'

'I'm. . .sorry! I. . .please. . . I don't mean to—'

'Sshh.' He sat beside her then, careless of the damp and the mossy willow bark. 'It is I who am sorry, my lady. Sorry there was no other way in this world I could tell you, no way to make it less terrible a shock. I would almost wish I had not—'

'Promised Rory?'

'But I did.'

'And—' she knew it was true '—you always keep your promises, I think.'

He was keeping one now, she knew it as if she could read his mind in this strange calm that invaded her as her tears ended. She had known Rory well enough to know Max Rivington had promised to look after her, Rory had made him swear it.

She ought to mind, fight it. After all, she had managed alone for so long now she could manage again. She should reject this protection Rory had bequeathed her. But that was impossible. She did not want to. Not close

as she was to Lord Rivington now. Not while the heat of
him, the already so familiar, so clean scent of him,
diffused from the silk that lined his coat deep into her
veins, and made her shiver again, not quite from the
cold any longer. Not while he spoke. . .not quite to a
lonely child any more but just as gentling.

'Will you let me say something to you now, my lady?
Because I know what you're thinking, how much you
wish the truth of what I told you would go away. Will
you listen to me, because I knew Rory better than
anyone else ever had the chance to? I was *there*.'

Luciana knew she tried to speak, but her voice had no
strength in it. Lord Rivington's, too, seemed forced and
a very long way away. As if he was and did not want to
be. God forbid, she thought, and felt a wrench of
sympathy, that I ever understand the half of what he is
remembering now!

'Rory needed to love you. He needed to talk of you
and read your letters, remember you and all you meant
to him. Think what you represented for him, my lady.
Everything he had left home to fight for, everything we
who were out in the thick of the fighting had very real
reason to fear would be destroyed. We didn't *know* we'd
defeat Bonaparte, there were times when only a
madman would have believed we ever could. Thank the
gods we were led by such a madman, but it was bad, my
lady! Worse than I ever intend to tell. . .'

Worse than she would ever want any man to remember. With no thought to stop herself, Luciana tucked her
hand into his, not for her own comfort this time. Absurd
that she should feel he might need this solidarity, his
strength seemed absolute. Then she felt his broken
fingers lace with hers and began to understand a little

just how ruthless with themselves these soldiers had had to be; how hard, how cold, and that they did not like what they became.

'We fought through on hope and rage. Hope that Bonaparte would be blasted into the oblivion he came from and England would be safe. That we could come home again and find everything unaltered and know it had all been worthwhile. When Rory read us the few of your letters that got through, it was like the lifting of a siege. Just to know there were lives, places, in which children could run wild without fear, and there were women waiting who cared what happened to us.

'I've seen brutal mercenaries weep with laughter at the exploits of Carlo and Freddie, and your own—I'm sorry to have to say this, ma'am!—quite helpless efforts to keep their unruliness in check! You made men laugh when they needed laughter more than anything. Men go into battle on memories like that, my lady. So don't rage at yourself for Rory's loving you, don't feel he shouldn't, don't wish he never had. You were everything that was clean and innocent and worth the fighting for. You *were* his hope!'

Hope. She—Luciana Standish! So important to someone. So undeserving! She began to shake her head in denial and sensed, so unexpectedly, his anger.

Heard it in the sudden harshness of his voice. 'No... *no*, my lady, it can't be run away from! It's *true*. Even if Rory had no hope to win you—he knew you'd never love him as anything more than your brother—'

'But—'

'But gaining one's Promised Land is not the point of hope, my lady. You, of all people, should know that!' When he got to his feet, then, and released her Luciana felt she had died. Or he had. He seemed so remote. So changed. Hard. 'The only point to hope I know of is that, even in the teeth of Hell, one still can!'

Luciana was left staring up at him, a puppet with strings all broken, needing his support, knowing he had withdrawn it. And then she really looked at him, caught the brief sting of bitterness in his eyes, and found her own strength. After all, she was not really the weak, shivering creature he had comforted. Not completely, not ever again. She had had four hard years in which to learn her capacity for overcoming even the Hell he spoke of.

So it was with calm dignity that she rose to her feet, his coat still held close about her fragile body, and said, 'I think you would not have spoken such difficult things unless you truly had to. I'm sorry—more sorry than I can say that my stupid weakness made it necessary. I shan't cry again. Nor shall I ever forget what you have done for me.'

And—it felt like a miracle to her—she saw the bitterness leave him. The change in him was so dramatic it appalled her. There was so much more behind that lazy, intimate smile of his than she—maybe anyone— could penetrate. So much behind his lightness of manner, his humour. Something dangerous. Something harmed.

That was the moment Luciana began to really see what Rory had left to her, and that if she owed Rory anything, it was to help Max Rivington, as he was helping her now. But how to help—even why she sensed he needed it—she had no way of knowing. And this was not the time for it, as he made plain with a glance of purest disgust at a sky now weighted with cloud and the chill, electric threat of a storm massing.

'I knew there was a reason I hated England! We really must hurry you to the house, ma'am, this storm won't hold off much longer.'

'Please, my name is Luciana.'

His scarred throat really must hurt him very badly, she thought, for he sounded in real pain. 'Yes... Luciana. Thank you. Now, come!'

It seemed the most natural thing in the world to Luciana to be swung onto the great mare's back. The animal, unsure of a stranger, shifted angrily and Lord Rivington's hand, reaching out to steady her, brushed Luciana's bared ankle.

It seemed a very long time before he murmured, almost to himself, 'No shoes—now why doesn't that surprise me?' and Luciana felt a shivering of heat run through her and could not look at him.

Only struggle to laugh as lightly as she could. 'Oh, but surely Rory didn't read out *every* foolish thing I told him! Despicable!'

And he laughed, too. 'If you mean that the whole of the Peninsula now knows those misbegotten mongrels of yours like nothing better than to raid your wardrobes and eat the contents...' Then Lord Rivington swung himself up behind her, lapsing into a silence so concentrated it was as if he was no more able to manage idle social converse than she was. As if this sudden, engrossing new awareness was in him, too.

Maybe it was. Or maybe it was only the coming storm that made Luciana feel so electrified as they rode, still in silence, the two miles home to Somerton Prior. Not an easy silence, yet not strained either. Intensely private and yet somehow shared.

Time and peace lost their reality for Luciana. It became as if every sense, so long dead and glad of it, was warming back to life. So long missed she could only feel excited as her eyes took in the familiar sights of home and she understood she hadn't really seen them since Philip died.

No more had she breathed, and really scented, the rich summer grasses that met them as they at last rode out of the woods onto Somerton Rise. It was as if not just she, but her whole world, had been sleeping and even as her reawakening calmed her she thought, Why, *why* do I feel so elated? Resurrected. I couldn't be further from happiness if I tried.

So why was it that now she could *feel* as she had never felt before? Luciana tucked her feet into the warm, breathing hide of the mare and marvelled at the thrill of it. At herself, as she relaxed into Lord Rivington's arms where he held her so protectively, listened to his quiet breathing and felt, as she lifted her eyes to the screaming flight of birds above them, the brushing of his hair against her forehead before he looked so sharply away.

Her eyes stung—trying to remember Philip, the only man who had ever held her so closely as this. Finding that, somehow, just for this brief journey home, he was gone and she did not mind it.

It felt so right to be here with Max Rivington. Here, for the very first time, she understood that life goes on— not dragged on, effortful and empty; life *lives* on.

So how right it was that, as her spirits soared, there in the valley below was Somerton Prior, its soft gold stone the most fragile etching against a black and hostile sky,

its languid parkland acid-bright beneath the storm. Then
the clouds parted, and the old house blazed, dazzling
against the darkness in one piercing shaft of sunlight,
and the rain came.

With an instinct born of half a lifetime's campaigning,
Lord Rivington kicked the mare into a canter one split
second before the lightning struck earth around them;
his arms tensed, shielding Luciana, as he raced them the
final half mile across the deer park through the stinging
rain. Luciana, held so safely, revelled in the wildness of
it all.

And so, quite plainly, did her outrageous children.
For as the mare reached the stable yard, the boys came
racing, falling over one another, jumping puddles, their
nurse raging ineffectually as usual in their wake. Lord
Rivington caught the mare to a stamping halt in the
shelter of the stable's arches; Carlo and Freddie slewed
to a far less elegant standstill in a pool of mud.

'Oh, Freddie!' blamed Carlo.

'Oh, Carlo!' mimicked Freddie.

'Oh, lord!'

Their mother buried her face in her borrowed coat,
knowing it would not do to show her laughter. She could
feel Lord Rivington's powerful body quite shaking with
amusement, especially when Carlo accused so sternly,
'Mamma, you're all *wet*! Whatever can you have been
doing?'

'Wet*ter*.' Luciana had not forgotten that her boys had
soaked her with their fishing nets, even if they so very
much hoped that she would.

Freddie deflected the implied threat very grandly.
'Now you'll have to go and get clean. *We* are.'

'*Were*,' put in Lord Rivington more than drily. Carlo

and Freddie grinned proudly at one another and Luciana gave way helplessly to laughter.

It was a full minute—during which her sons exchanged men-of-the-world glances with Lord Rivington—before she could manage so much as a shaken, 'Oh, dear! I'm *so* sorry. . .but, well—oh, lord! Small boys. . . really, my lord, you cannot have the least idea!'

She felt that electric current of amusement run through him again as he murmured, 'Oh, but yes I can, my lady!' And just as Luciana felt the shock hit her—of course, he must be married, have children of his own!—he added innocently, 'I was one once, remember!'

And Luciana discoverd her heart must have stopped, for it started again, and she heard a breathless voice manage, 'For some reason I find that quite impossible to believe!' and realised instantly that she had said the wrong thing.

Something that had brought down the shutters made him withdraw from her and move away, jumping down from the mare. Yet he seemed to be smiling when he raised his arms to lift her down, saying, 'You wouldn't find it so difficult if you had seen me in the heat of campaigning!'

Even so, very real restraint was there. What in the world had she said that could be so wrong? Something about his being a child? For the second time, Luciana felt an inexplicable stab of pity and rushed into speech to cover her embarrassment.

'Well, I have to say you can't have appeared much more of a wreck than you are now!' If wreck was quite the word for how Max Rivington looked at this moment, shirt clinging damply to his gilded skin; so powerfully strong, so in his element. Luciana lowered her eyes

hurriedly and caught Freddie out in a puzzled frown at
Carlo, sensing something in the air, a constraint that had
not been there between the grown-ups before.

She would do anything in the world not to unsettle
her children, so she forced the polite words out. 'I think
we're both very much the worse for wear, Lord
Rivington. I'd be pleased to have you make use of. . .of
Rory's things. . .' Dear God, this was getting worse and
worse! Yet common civility meant she must go on. 'His
man will show you. . . I'm sure his clothes must fit you.'

Philip's wouldn't. Philip, who had been little more
than a boy when never had anyone seemed more a man
to her than Max Rivington.

Who yet again was astonishing her with his tact. 'I
shall dry out, my lady. And what would *my* man have to
do if I were to turn up without a full complement of
grass stains! If I promise not to sprawl upon your
furniture. . .' and he began to smile that warm, penetrating smile that so calmed her. 'Carlo and Freddie can
show me how to behave in civilised surroundings in the
very likely event that I've forgotten!'

And as swiftly as it came the tension vanished. Carlo
smirked in a *some*-people-treat-us-like-grown-ups way
and Freddie laid hold of his lordship's sleeve, determined nobody else should have the training of him.

'*I'll* show you!' Then he drew himself up to his full
knee-height for lesson one. 'I *suppose* we should show
you where to take your horse first.'

Carlo wasn't having his seniority usurped by the likes
of Freddie.

'*I'll* lead him,' he said, then directed a swift glance at
the shivering mare. '*Her*,' he amended hastily.

Luciana was left to watch the three of them disappear

across the stable yard, her heart tumbling. It should have been Philip, Rory... She watched Max Rivington take the mare's reins from Carlo, who could not manage them. It shouldn't have been a stranger, yet it was the most hopeful sight she had seen in years.

These reassuring thoughts were shattered by a blood-curdling yell of recognition. Liam, dragging his game leg across the stable yard as if he was yet again hurtling into battle. '*Sir*! Colonel Max, sir! *Is* it you? An I'd thought the devil'd have you in his toils long before!'

Luciana turned away, a hard lump in her throat, as she saw the men clasp hands, greet each other, a long, long way from where they had last set eyes on one another.

Max Rivington had saved Liam's life. And—in quite another way—he had begun to save hers, too.

Luciana stood in front of her looking-glass, her maid standing warily back, not used to seeing her Ladyship look at herself, or care.

Luciana did care. Suddenly, and for the very first time since Rory last came home and she had tried so hard to hide her misery, she really cared. Not that Max Rivington should think her pretty—it never entered her head—just that he had called her brave and she wanted to look as if she deserved it.

But she was so pale! Not the warm, glowing ivory of the portrait Philip so loved, now mocking her from across the room, but tired, drained, defeated.

Then she looked again and saw that this was no longer so. Something had happened. She could not say what it was except that the shroud of unhappiness that had enveloped her was gone and her violet eyes were clear, alight, alive. Even her hair seemed to have spun from straw back into gold. She might no longer be Philip's Botticelli angel, she was too frail, too bruised about the eyes, but she had dignity and this strange new sensation of hope and her appearance pleased her.

Luciana draped a white lace veil about her hair and shoulders and smiled. Her family, though Irish, had lived for generations, soldiers of fortune, in Italy, and Luciana, in real defiance, had clung to the old Italian ways. She was in mourning, but she was young and so she was all in white. It was the way Philip... Rory, too...had so jokingly said they wanted it.

Luciana slammed shut her defences against that thought, and shaking out the fluid fall of muslin about her still fragile form, she hurried down the great oak staircase towards the normality and laughter of the sunlit salon.

Here she found Max Rivington, the centre of eager, ebullient attention, smiling down at her impossible boys, so amused, yet—it struck her instantly—almost puzzled, as if he found himself so much at ease with them but did not know why. She hesitated, suddenly not wanting to disturb them, only wanting to watch. . .

There was something of a riot in progress.

'Well, you don't breach defences like *that*!' scorned Carlo, armed with an early Michaelmas daisy for a sword; the daisy had bent in half. Freddie was raiding a painfully valuable Meissen urn for a fresh one.

From behind the defences in question—the most fragile Louis XV sofa—Max Rivington commanded, 'The only thing breached will be my patience if you clamber on the furniture again!'

Carlo scrambled backwards in awe and scrubbed a muddy footprint off the rose-wrought tapestry.

'Mamma's going to...string you from the battlements!' gasped Freddie.

'We haven't got any battlements!' sneered the owner of Somerton's Elizabethan splendour, hurrying to place a strategic cushion over a smear that wouldn't come out. Then, hugely embarrassed, he pretended airily that he hadn't noticed. 'Please, sir, aren't you going to tell us what happened next?'

And Luciana, particulary fond of that sofa, interrupted dampingly, 'What happened next *was*—'

'Oh, *no*!'

'*Mamma!*'

'My lady!'

Luciana wondered however she was going to control the urge to laugh at them, all three so very sheepish, if defiant.

Max Rivington looked almost more guilty than the two boys put together. 'The storming of San Sebastian,' he explained in mitigation.

'And almost as much disaster left in your wake here as you left behind you in Spain, my lord!' Luciana absently picked Freddie's shoes out of a delicate porcelain bonbonnière. 'After all I've ever told you boys about playing sensibly!'

And again—the most fleeting impression—she sensed she had said something deeply hurtful to Lord Rivington. Something...no, she could not pin it down, and when he smiled so ruefully she was sure she was mistaken. He was almost as amused as she was.

'Well, you cannot expect me to manage children,

ma'am. After all, I'm used only to mad Irish mercenaries—'

'Grandpapa was one of those!' Carlo pounced on the
means of distracting his mother from mud on sofas.
'They called themselves the Wild Ducks,' he finished
proudly.

Never had Luciana admired Max Rivington more
than when he controlled his choke of laughter and
murmured, 'I think you'll probably find it was geese,
Carlo.'

'*I* knew that! Carlo's *stupid*!' crowed Freddie. Carlo's
elbow administered a savage thump. Freddie rubbed his
side, glaring murder, then added helpfully, 'Not Papa's
papa, *Mamma's* papa—'

'Now who's *stupid*?' Carlo sneered down at his so
much smaller brother and Luciana, recognising tired-
ness, hunger and real violence in the making,
intervened.

'I think, you know, that you are both becoming rather
silly. So what I want you to do is go away—yes, Carlo!—
and clean yourselves up, *again*! And don't say "urrgh",
Freddie; it's a horrid noise. No—go along and be quiet
and sensible until you're called for dinner. You've been
very lucky to play with his Lordship at all when you
should have been resting. Say thank you and—'

'Um. . .thank you!' This in wariest unison.

'Sir!' added Carlo, still miserable about the ruined
sofa.

'Not at all, I enjoyed it,' returned Lord Rivington,
forcing his tones into a semblance of sobriety, and
failing badly.

Which made it harder than ever for Luciana to keep
her own voice steady. 'Go *on*! *Straight* to Nurse—and no

loud noises for the next half an hour or you're sent to bed, cold and hungry. No dinner!'

Which was going too far ever to be believed. Carlo grinned and Freddie started to giggle; Mamma would never do anything one half so uncivilized. And then it struck them. Today was different and, in some sense hard for a child to understand, it was momentous. Carlo and Freddie sobered instantly. But they couldn't be expected to leave without the final word.

Or the grand performance. 'Very well.' So great was Carlo's dignity and condescension his mother nearly choked. Then feet dragging, shoulders hunched, explicit of disillusionment, the boys made for the door, where they hesitated, casting looks of such anguish and hurt from eyes as huge and brown and pleading as any puppy's.

It was too much for Max Rivington. As the door closed with a thud redolent of final disappointment, he laughed out loud and said, 'How in the world do they manage that? To look so exactly like two starved and neglected orphans cast cruelly into the rain!'

Then he stopped, stunned by his thoughtlessness, and turned fiercely to Luciana. 'I'm sorry, my lady! Dear God, I deserve... I should never have said—'

She could not bear to see him falter. 'Never have said exactly how they meant it to seem to you? Victims of their cruel and unfeeling parent! I could be fearful of every last word and action, my lord, but it comes to nothing in the end. I can't protect them from the truth. I can't pretend it hasn't happened. What would I do? Never utter one spontaneous word again?'

'No.' She had not reassured him. 'I thought perhaps you were angry.'

'*Angry*?' Luciana could not take it in. Angry—with him, who had never done anything but what was kind and reassuring! 'I could *never* be—'

'That I was telling them about the war.'

Never had Luciana felt so much that her next words must be the right words. Almost the most important she had ever spoken. She wondered for a moment if it was her own voice at all when she felt his regret so badly, and yet she sounded so assured.

'If I'm angry about anything it's the ruining of my sofa; if I'm annoyed with anyone it's Carlo. He knows so much better than to be so careless. But *angry*—to see them play with you, as boys should play? How could I ever be angry at that?'

It mattered so much that he believe her, she had to turn away; it was her own intensity scared her now.

'If I stopped them listening to you, asking questions, what would they think? If every time the war was mentioned I silenced them? They'd start to believe the war was not just something terrible—which, God knows, it was!—but something shameful. That everything their father did was in some way inglorious and wrong. How could I want that? All I want is that they be proud of him, as I am.

'One day they'll be grown enough to understand why I'm angry with him, too, for leaving us. But he'd have been less than the man he was if he'd stayed—he *was* a man, for all you all thought him so young. He was a good and strong and loving husband and I could never regret his courage!'

Luciana only realised she was shaking when she felt the steadying of Max Rivington's hands against her veiled shoulders. Even through the lace she could feel those shattered fingers and yet she never for one moment thought to reject his touch.

It was a real struggle to go on. 'I loved Philip and maybe I shall never quite forgive his leaving me. He was all I ever, *ever* wanted. So I want you to tell his sons what you know about him, my lord. Everything. All the things he kept from me, the things I never knew. Help them to know him and share my admiration. So they want to be like him, as I pray every day that they will be!'

'*Luciana!*' It was but the harshest breath ripped from his damaged throat and Luciana found the courage to look at him. To turn, almost as if he turned her towards him. He was holding her with such gentle intensity she wanted to look away again but never could.

Her voice was just the barest whisper. 'I'm a soldier's daughter, sir, and a soldier's widow. Maybe—though God pray it never happens—the mother of soldiers, too. So don't ever apologise to me for anything you say or do. For what you are. Why—*why* don't you seem to understand, my lord? I'm *glad* you've come. My children needed to know you. Why won't you see?'

And it was *would* not, not just that he could not. She reached out her hand, a tentative, almost pleading touch, needing to make him heed her. '*Please* believe me. Please understand how hard it's been for me to do what's best for them, feeling it so badly that they have no father to ride with them, and hunt and fish, and come home covered in mud, to break my windows playing cricket. Philip would have revelled in it. It was—oh, magical, to watch him with Carlo that last summer! And Carlo remembers. . .not clearly but he *does* remember!'

'Of course he does.' It seemed Max Rivington could

always find his voice to comfort her, and she needed it, for all she suddenly felt so strong. Her fingers tensed into the still damp linen of his shirt, urgent to explain.

'I used to watch him run out onto the steps whenever horses came—just as Freddie ran to you—longing for it to be this great, strong, laughing creature come home again. He just wanted to have his papa to play with. A mother. . .a mother *isn't* the same!'

Which was when he stopped her, as if suddenly it had become too much for either of them. With just the gentlest resting of his fingers against her lips, Max Rivington silenced her.

'I won't believe that—and you, of all women on this earth will never make me! Believe *me*, Luciana, Philip would have been so proud of you! God knows, he loved you. No, it was more than that, you were his every thought and reason! Do you know how we all envied him his beautiful young wife to worship? To dream of, who made him so happy! And Rory—how do you think he was ever able to leave you to go back to war, except that he knew no-one could be safer for the boys than you are? No.' This as he sensed her fighting him. 'No, Luciana! We're friends, I think. I *know* we are.'

His eyes demanded the truth of her. 'We barely know each other, my lady, and yet you *do* know to trust me. . .'

'Yes.' Oh, yes! She had no doubts at all. She had completest faith in this man she had known but two extraordinary hours.

'Then, believe me, no mother on this earth could have done better by her children. Your boys—they could have been so different, so timid and clinging, but you haven't let them be. You've had the courage to let them alone to risk their necks as any other children. They're boys, my lady, as tiring, embarrassing and impossible as they should be, and they owe everything that they are to you!'

'But they still needed. . .' And suddenly it became the hardest thing she had ever tried to say, because she meant it. 'They needed a friend like you and I'm so glad you're here! I hope—lord, but I don't even know where you live, sir! I'm trying to say, please visit us, as often as you can bear it but, for all I know of it, you may live—'

'On the moon?' And she heard again raw anger in his voice. 'There have been times when. . .but no matter! I live, I suppose, not seven miles from here, at Rivenal.'

'Rivenal?' The estate that marched with Somerton and, of course, Rory and Philip had told her! His father was the Marquess of Rivenal and Max himself had been so long at war he had probably never set up an establishment of his own, save perhaps the usual rooms in Town. 'But so *near* and yet. . .you didn't know Rory when you were children?'

He turned from her then so abruptly and where his hands fell from her shoulders she felt the acutest cold. He moved to the window, but she knew he saw nothing beyond the glass. His eyes and all his thoughts turned inwards.

'No. I never did.'

Luciana learned something new about Max Rivington then. It would be infinitely dangerous to pry.

But she wanted to. She could barely take in how much she wanted to know this man. As if she had always wanted to. . .

So she said, very carefully, not wanting to anger him, 'But you know us now, sir, and you *will* come to see the boys, won't you? They would so enjoy it.'

Somehow she had got things right again, for when he turned back to her his anger was gone. There was only that so familiar, all-pervading smile.

'If you'll have me.'

And Luciana could not help herself. She had had four years in which to learn the harsh restraints of widowhood, but she abandoned them now. She held out her hands towards him, saw his surprise—pleasure—and felt him take them so firmly in his own.

It was so easy, the most natural thing in the world, to smile back at him, her eyes blazing into happiness at the knowledge she had pleased him.

'How could we ever not? How could we ever be anything but glad of any time you find to share with us?'

And Max Rivington drew her closer. One more breath and their bodies would touch. As if they should, as if they always had. . .

Luciana closed her eyes against his quiet breathing, listening to the calm of it, the comfort in it, as if she had always needed it. She began to sense that she was recognising something, something from deep in her past that she had thought destroyed. Something to do with Philip. . .

But he was not here. Because Max Rivington kissed her, the barest benediction of a touch against her brow, and Luciana's heart stilled. Accepting the truth. 'I could trust this man with my life, even with the lives of my children. I could give myself into his care and know that I had come home'.

It was as if there had never existed a time when she did not know this.

She had no word for it, no way of understanding what it was, this diffusing, undramatic feeling. She only knew

it was the most redeeming moment of her life. The most
wanted and the most calm.

Intensely important, as she looked up and realised at
last that her whole world had changed from the moment
he walked across the glade to find her. It was true, then,
that one only really knows how bad things have been
when they are over. She felt it absolutely. All fear was
gone. It was as simple, as irrefutable, as that.

Max Rivington lifted his hand to her cheek, stroking
aside a strand of hair as if he had done it a thousand
times before, and she felt such promise in his touch.

And heard it as he spoke. 'I hope, my lady, that one
day I deserve such welcome.' His voice was so low, so
unsteady, she thought his injured throat must really hurt
him.

Until she heard her own, more shaken still. 'How
could you ever not?' She was bewildered by the bitterness in his smile. Gone the moment she sensed it, having
no place here. Not now.

One day she would understand it. If she had to fight
him every inch of the way, she would know the cause of
it.

But not now, as he laughed at her, amused, almost
indulgent, and she sensed real excitement in his smile.
'You've done the impossible, Luciana. You've made me
glad I came home!' And he drew her finally into his
arms as he whispered. '*Thank* you!'

Luciana curled her head into the hollow of his neck,
safe and hopeful and shielded from grief, sensing that he
was, too. The past and the future were held at bay. She
no longer feared what that future was. This stranger—
this lifelong friend—was here now. That was everything.

It was a long, long time before she realised that it was

not Max who broke their healing silence, but another voice, so jarring it caused actual pain. Not even through the door yet, but inevitably condemning.

'Cousin, it is intolerable! It is above, it is *beyond* the insupportable and I will not stand for it!'

Lysander Standish, all silken, all scented, all intolerance, striking up his pose of outrage in the doorway, a whining poodle clenched ruthlessly to his lime-green waistcoat and his quizzing glass all but screwed into one eye.

Luciana saw him too late, just one whit too dazed by all that had happened to her, to withdraw from Lord Rivington's embrace. Cousin Lysander froze, opened his mouth then shut it again, words failing him, and stared as if he would never again believe his eyes, let alone comprehend what they were so forcefully inflicting on him now.

Luciana began to see what it was Lysander thought he had burst in upon; he was so utterly wrong, it appalled her. She would have broken free then, but Max Rivington held her and she needed it. Because there was something about Lysander Standish. . .

She felt the threat of him like a fog crawling along her veins, yet never had she seen anything more ridiculous than this puffed up and perspiring dandy, his neckcloth starched into a stranglehold, his ludicrous little dog dangling like a duster, the padding of his calves slipped relentlessly round to join his knees. He was a mockery of all the other Standish men had ever stood for, and yet her blood ran cold.

Because, despite Cousin Lysander's theatrical incursion, Max Rivington was anything but laughing. Just silent, intent. Sensing trouble. As if he knew. . .

Lysander had begun to harrass her from the moment Rory died. Luciana had faced him out and always would, refusing to be afraid of him, to be as belittled and grateful as he meant her to be. He had no right even to be here, this was not his home. Carlo was the Marquess of Standish now, the immense inheritance that came with Somerton was his and Freddie's, and Luciana would protect it for them if it killed her, as Rory would have expected her to do.

If only she'd told Rory the truth about Lysander. But she had not wanted to worry him. Besides, she could cope, she would fight anybody, was she a Standish, too.

So it was unsettling to realise how much it mattered that Max Rivington was here. How much a relief it was that she and her children were no longer so undefended and alone.

CHAPTER THREE

'You do not know our cousin, my lord.' Luciana was astonished at the calmness of her voice as she moved away from Max Rivington at last to make this most unwelcome of introductions. 'Allow me to present Mr Standish, sir. Cousin, you will have guessed, perhaps, that this is Lord Rivington, come from Toulouse.'

Lysander would have guessed no such thing, but it did no harm to remind her tormentor that her brother-in-law had had a wealth of friends and here was the very best of them.

A fact to give even Lysander pause, for the contrast between the two men could not have been more glaring had they tried. Max Rivington so cool, so commanding, despite his coatlessness and grass stains, so utterly unembarrassed. Yet he must realise what Cousin Lysander was thinking.

Luciana knew for certain that he did when he smiled, a polite and distancing smile explicit of the suggestion Mr Standish unthink his ideas pretty smartly, and he returned Cousin Lysander's elaborate genuflection with a bow so courteous it was rude.

Luciana had to turn away—not even Rory would have delivered such a shrivelling verdict on Lysander's unwarrantable intrusion! In the unholy innocence of Max Rivington's eyes, she saw that he was laughing now—laughter she could so disastrously catch if she were not very, very careful, for as Cousin Lysander

straightened, so tight-lipped and resentful of his instinct
to bow at all, there came the most sad little sound from
the poodle. It had the hiccoughs.

Luciana hastily adjusted her veil to hide her smile and
concentrated desperately on tidying a space for herself
on the sofa. If she so much as looked at Max Rivington
she would never be able to control herself. Luciana sat
with her back to him, demure as the cinquecento
madonna she so resembled and prayed that Lord
Rivington would stay safely where she could not see
those mocking eyes.

Folding her hands in her lap, she nodded to Mr
Standish to be seated and managed to say, 'You will be
as pleased to see Lord Rivington as I am, Cousin.'

Happily Lysander would not have recognised malice
in her if it smacked him. Besides, he was busy stifling the
poodle.

'Delighted, Cousin, delighted!' He couldn't have been
more delighted had he been poisoned. 'You. . .er. . .had
a tolerable journey I trust, my lord?'

'As tolerable as I ever find the Plymouth crossing,'
returned his lordship, so amiably Luciana dug her nails
into her palms to stop herself from choking.

'And you. . .um. . .you?' Lysander and the poodle
were now neck-and-neck in incoherence. 'You've come
to. . .erm. . .?'

'Ensure all is well with Lady Philip and her children,
as your late cousin the Marquess charged me.'

'Ah, capital,' winced Mr Standish. 'Capital!'

'Yes, I'm glad to find it so.'

And Luciana recognised at last that Max Rivington
was at his most dangerous when he was smiling.
Lysander knew it—no man could fail to—and it threw

him off his stride. Enough for him to indulge in a quite
unnecessarily fussing performance as he perched as best
he could in pantaloons designed for a much younger
person and cooed urgent threats at a poodle on the
verge of turning green.

Contemptile coxcomb! But Luciana had come to
know Lysander only too well, and he was anything but
the fribble he appeared. She knew him well enough to
hear the calculation in his question.

'And you are. . .er. . .home for good, my lord, now the
war is so happily ended?'

Lord Rivington had heard it too, Luciana could
almost feel his lack of surprise at it. He had read
Lysander with unsettling accuracy.

'I was undecided, sir.' But not undecided now. If he
had spelled out the warning in letters ten yards high, he
could not have made his message more plain. Until he
added, so very lightly, 'I have outlived my effectiveness
on the battlefield, but perhaps I have my uses here.'

He so plainly meant *here*, at Somerton. Luciana
watched Cousin Lysander take this in and felt a surge of
healthy anger, so frustratingly kept in check these past
four months. She had had to be so careful in her dealings
with him. Until now.

Revenge was as sweet as ever she had been promised;
Luciana turned a smile of shining innocence on Mr
Standish and twisted the knife in as far as it would go.

'Lord Rivington lives not seven miles from us, at
Rivenal. Is that not wonderful, Cousin? It is the greatest
comfort to me to know that so *dear* a friend of Philip
and Rory is close by. The boys are quite silly with
excitement about it. Indeed, I fear we shall become
quite a plague to poor Lord Rivington.'

'Not at all.' His lordship took his cue and Luciana
heard again that underlying laughter, appreciating her
anything but madonna-like behaviour, encouraging it
with the same devilment she had known in the Standish
men she had lost. So like them! So *safe*. Allowing her
her recklessness, and her vengeance. . .

And how she had earned it! So she finished delight-
edly, 'Oh, I have just thought, Cousin—Rivenal! Lord
Rivington is to be your neighbour, too!'

And—Mr Standish now but marginally less sick to the
stomach than his poodle—she smiled composedly.
'Now, you had some complaint to lodge with me,
Lysander?'

This composure was all but overset by Max Rivington,
who leaned over the back of sofa to adjust her cushions,
murmuring, 'Allow me, ma'am.' Then, so softly that
Lysander could not hear, 'Oh, fight clean, my lady, the
poor devil!' Luciana could happily have strangled him.

Lysander was certainly on the point of strangling her.

'Indeed—*indeed*, I have, ma'am! But. . .it is so. . .
so. . .well, I am hard put to it to know where to begin!'

But you'll find somewhere, Luciana thought wryly,
and behind her, she heard an answering breath of
laughter as if she had spoken out loud and Max
Rivington had heard her. Luciana felt a shiver of
excitement tease her heart and drew her veil closer, as if
lace or anything on this earth could come between her
and the touch of his smile.

She was never going to concentrate on what Lysander
was saying.

'And now, *now* I discover that she is in the. . .in a
most *unfortunate* condition and I hold that. . .that
unconscionable mongrel entirely to blame!'

Luciana came round from the spell of Max Rivington's closeness utterly bewildered.

'I. . .um, forgive me, Lysander, but I cannot at all see. . .?'

'I'm sure you cannot, ma'am! I'm sure you should be too ashamed! I am speaking of the *violation of Antigone*!'

At which the poodle was cast into the arena, whimpering evidence of the crime.

Evidence completely lost upon Luciana, who was struggling with the wildest visions of mutilated Theban women, not helped in the least by Max Rivington's choke of laughter, which he turned into a cough just in time, as, goaded beyond endurance and sensing someone meant him to be, Lysander finally lost grip on both his temper and his poodle.

'*This* is Antigone!'

Luciana caught the frantic animal into her arms—as if she had any choice, the force with which Lysander thrust it at her—and finally grasped the connection.

'Oh—*oh*! You mean *Polly* has impreganted your *poodle*!' She bent her head comfortingly towards the nauseous and confused Antigone. 'Is that not just too bad of him after fathering all Cass's puppies!'

At which Max Rivington could not be expected to control himself. 'Castor and Pollux? But I thought they were both—'

'We made a mistake about Cassie,' Luciana returned austerely, then wished she had not looked at him, because her eyes flared into delight she could never disguise. Least of all from Mr Standish, who was now watching for it with all the friendliness of a ferret.

'I expected this!' he denounced, his case critically

flawed by the behaviour of Antigone, who curled happily onto Luciana's knees, licking her hand, flauntingly unconcerned at the smirching of her pedigree.

'Well, I should imagine you would, really,' agreed Luciana practically, 'for you know what Polly is like.'

'*I*? Are you saying that *Antigone* is to blame? You permit that. . .that *animal* to rampage about the village like some marauding Hun, leaping—I repeat, ma'am, *leaping*—upon every unguarded female! I. . .what possible example can you imagine this to be setting for the boys?'

'One that hardly need trouble us quite so prematurely,' came the dry interjection from Lord Rivington, whom Lysander had made the mistake of disregarding, and Mr Standish exploded.

'Sir, you will forgive us but this is, as must be quite plain to you, a family concern!'

'Aired so publicly?' smiled his lordship. 'I must have been in the Peninsula longer than I realised. . .and left my manners behind me.'

Luciana held her breath, almost frightened, yet flooded with excitement at support so powerful she no longer had need to fight for herself at all. Something passed between them in that moment, some subliminal solidarity that pushed Lysander so far beyond his minimal endurance Luciana could almost pity him.

Until he raged, 'Cousin, this is the. . .the. . .' and she ran out of her own not unlimited patience.

'Outside of enough? Indeed it is, Lysander! I will not have you speak to me in such unbecoming tones!'

Too used to her rigid self-control, Lysander reacted viciously. 'I speak to you as you deserve, Luciana!'

And suddenly it was not funny any more. For

Lysander, little real threat before, had just thought of
something that made him very dangerous. He might just
as well have said so out loud, so crowing was his smile.

'After what I have witnessed this afternoon, ma'am, I
marvel that you are surprised at my revulsion!'

Which was Mr Standish's worst imaginable mistake.
Even where she sat, her back to him, Luciana sensed the
change in Max Rivington. Instantly, icy and more
dangerous than anything Lysander would ever dare to
challenge. He was furious. So angry, Luciana found
herself flinching from the cold of it, until he reached out
for her, a calming hand against her veiled shoulder, and
her own rage died. For the first time, perhaps since
Philip died, she admitted to herself, I've had enough of
this, I'm too tired. Let somebody else handle it, let
someone else cope.

And yet never in her life had she felt stronger than
when Max Rivington spoke, so very, very quietly.

'I marvel, Mr Standish, that you can be so indecent as
to find one single thing to disgust you in the sharing of
so recent a grief! I find myself astonished at how readily
you disregard Lady Philip's feelings. This house is in
mourning, yet you enter it with all the consideration of a
charging bull.'

Luciana wondered if Cousin Lysander would ever
find words to express himself again. In a surge of real
gratitude she made her most serious mistake, though
she could never know it. She lifted her hand to where
Lord Rivington's held her and let it rest there. The most
natural thing in the world.

Which somehow even Mr Standish comprehended.
Luciana saw his eyes flare with excitement and it chilled
her. Lord Rivington saw it, too; knew, as she did now,

just how intimate her gesture had appeared. Luciana would have drawn away, expected him to; instead Max's fingers laced with hers and she felt her throat go dry at the pity of those shattered bones.

Cousin Lysander watched them, his mind racing, calculating, meaning her harm and soon. If he could find a way past Max Rivington.

He tried. 'Yet again, sir, I fail to see what possible concern it is—'

'Of mine?' Luciana heard the amusement in Max Rivington's voice as he sensed Lysander's fear of him and took merciless advantage. 'You make comment upon how Lady Philip and I conduct ourselves and then would have it that it is not my business to object? It could not be more my concern, or less yours, Mr Standish, and I trust Lady Philip will not be subjected to your unedifying speculations again!'

'I'll...' Lysander was helpless and knew it. If he had hated her, Luciana knew, it was as nothing to how he now hated the Earl of Rivington.

One more thing to be grateful to this precious new friend for. . .her first victory. Luciana lifted her head in a gesture as imperious as it was cold and ordered.

'Leave, is what you will do, Lysander! At once, if you will have the courtesy. I did not invite you in the first place!'

'You *dare* to—'

'And unless you can conduct yourself in more civilized a manner, Cousin, my servants will be instructed that you may not enter the house at all!'

Which was the root of all this ugliness, after all, Somerton and how Lysander felt about it. That it should have been his and she had cheated him by bearing the

Standish heirs. No harm in reminding him. 'I have the right, Lysander. You really are going to have to understand this. This is Carlo's house. Carlo is the Marquess of Standish and as his mother I direct his household as I choose.'

If she had not been so elated by her anger, her first ever freedom to express it, she would have seen the warning; she might have guessed what Cousin Lysander was planning. She missed it. Even when he said, so speculatively, 'And yet it need not necessarily be so.'

And—while he had advantage—Lysander rose to his shiny patent feet and picked his portly way towards the exit, only to be stopped in his tracks by an unimpeachably polite Lord Rivington.

'Your dog, Mr Standish?'

Cousin Lysander was obliged to traverse the whole room again, his toes pinching, his hands so literally shaking now, the poodle reacted with all the instincts of her kind. Antigone bared her teeth and bit him. Before Luciana could protect her, Lysander lashed out at the cowering animal, but his painfully ringed fingers never reached her.

His arm was snapped back by Max Rivington, whose broken hand belied a strength that could break a wrist bone and think nothing of it. Luciana felt her breath still; she could not take her eyes from the men, their own eyes locked on each other, Max Rivington's so contemptuous, Lysander's inimical. Inevitably Mr Standish was the first to look away.

Max Rivington released him, but, as Lysander reached the door with the quivering Antigone, Max called after him so innocently, 'I should attend to that bite, Mr Standish. We should be sorry to hear your blood is poisoned.'

And as the door slammed behind Lysander, Luciana felt his hand come imperatively back to her shoulder, keeping her sitting, keeping her quiet until Mr Standish was quite gone. Luciana felt the power in him and discovered she actually could not move. Weak with rage. . .and something much more disabling.

She was glad when Max Rivington let go of her and came round to face her. Until his eyes met hers so intensely she felt branded to the sofa.

His voice was rasping with the effort it would always cost him to speak since his injury. 'That was well done, my lady. And yet—' she saw a fleeting frown disturb his brow '—not so well done, either.'

Luciana tried to laugh away her breathlessness. 'I? Why, you. . .you *encouraged* me!'

'I know I did, and more the fool it makes me!' Then he added grimly, 'How long has this been going on?'

'I don't know what—'

'Don't give me such nonsense, Luciana! How long has that creature been tormenting you?'

Tormenting. . . God knew he had, but suddenly Luciana did not want to tell it. Almost she did not know how. It had all been so much part of the misery of Rory's death that she had in many ways been oblivious to the worst of it. Certainly she could not say exactly what it was Lysander had said or done, only how she felt about it.

How to explain? Especially to Max Rivington who was looking at her now as if he would burn the truth right out of her. And could. It was the ease with which he could take her over Luciana could not handle. Yet she knew as she looked up at him, half defiant, suddenly desperate for her old autonomy, that she was going to try to tell him.

'It's just that I don't know where to start, sir.' And instantly she sensed impatience in him.

It was the reason for it that astonished her. 'Oh, have done with this formality, Luciana!'

'I'm sorry!'

'And I'm sorry, too!' Lord Rivington reached out a hand to her face and felt the heat of her blush steal into his palm. 'I'm sorry, Luciana. I've been away too long. Among men too long. I would not bully you for the world!'

Luciana felt again that creeping helplessness, her absolute longing to give in to the comfort he gave her. 'I know you wouldn't, and I'm sorry —'

And wonderfully he smiled, his dark, gilded eyes blazed with it. 'Are we to keep apologising, politely in turn, like anxious diplomats, my lady?'

'Now who is being formal!' She found she could laugh back at him. But she could not use his name yet. That would be one step too far from Philip; too close. . .to what?

You would have thought he knew, the way he took his hand away, withdrawing not his friendship, not his comfort, just that much too much intensity.

'So, what has this most unlikely repository of the Standish values been doing to you, Luciana? Dear God, it is impossible to believe he —'

'Can be of the same blood as Philip and Rory? Believe me, you are not the first to wonder at it!' A memory made Luciana smile. 'I'm afraid Philip questioned it rather more. . .um. . .imaginatively than was to

Lysander's liking! They did *not* treat well together. In fact—oh, this is so complicated! How much do you know about us, sir? About the Standish inheritance?'

'Very little—Philip and Rory rarely spoke of anything but you. We never spoke of things that troubled us.'

'No. No, of course, you wouldn't. Besides, Philip and Rory took not the smallest notice of Lysander even when he was with them. They never did. I suppose that is the root of everything.'

Luciana looked up, to see if she was making sense to him, only to look away again. It helped nothing at all to have him tower over her like this, his arms folded, his smile edged with amusement, so intent on her.

'It all goes back to the time they were very young, long before I came here—perhaps even further, to the expectations of Lysander's father. He was younger brother to Philip and Rory's father, the fifth Marquess. The Marquess married so very late in life, his brother had every reason to believe he never would. Certainly he hoped it; he was a very bitter man by the end of his life. So very like his son, really. He unquestionably brought Lysander up believing he should inherit the Standish titles. He went so far as to buy a property just across the river from Somerton, the Rivenal side. I'm surprised you didn't know him. Lord Strafford Standish?'

It had happened again, as it happened every time she mentioned Rivenal. Max Rivington looked away, briefly, but she sensed again that he was hiding something that went painfully deep.

So she hurried on. 'Lord Strafford was quite. . . I truly think *broken* is not too strong a word by his brother's marriage. The Marquess fell in love with a girl young

enough to be his daughter. Strafford had no hope at all
that there would be no children. Lysander was eleven
when Rory was born and he simply never got over
feeling cheated by it. Philip was born five years later and
Lysander hated him, if anything, more than he hated
Rory. As if Philip were the final straw.'

'Until you came?'

'Yes,' she answered wearily. 'Until I came.'

'Philip told me a little about that.'

'That my father and Marquess Charles. . .we all called
him that. . .were the closest imaginable friends? They
truly were. They campaigned together for years and you
know how important that is. My family were Irish
mercenaries, Carlo told you, driven into exile—a price
on almost every head—oh, centuries ago. They went to
fight for whichever Italian state would pay the greatest
reward. There was untold opportunity for a man who
could prove himself. We made a name for ourselves
keeping peace between Florence and Siena and became
the Counts of the Montefalco. The Fitzgerald of
Montefalco, if you will believe it!'

She was laughing, but he heard the pride in her voice
and smiled. 'I can believe you come from anything but
ordinary stock, Luciana!'

It was the first real compliment he had paid her.
Luciana bit her lip, a little disbelieving, and tried not to
blush beneath his teasing smile.

'Anyway, that is how the family went on, fighting
other people's wars and farming olives, until Papa
offended against Bonaparte's toadies at the Tuscan
court, acquired the price on his head no Fitzgerald
seems able to do without and took it so much a personal
affront he joined the hated British army! I need hardly

say he was looked on very much askance until Marquess Charles spoke up for him. . .they had been friends ever since the marquess was a young man on the Tour. He was so very like my father, I think that is why I came to love him so much. Papa was killed when I was eight years old and Mamma died when I was only a baby so I was all alone, the last Fitzgerald of Montefalco, until Marquess Charles came for me. I came to Somerton—' the memory lit her face with happiness '—and found a family again.'

She could almost not go on when she saw Max Rivington's face then. Family. Always it was the mention of family, family as something good, that hurt him. Yet she needed to explain so he would see just how precious a thing it was Lysander was set upon destroying.

'I'll never forget how I felt when I first saw Somerton. Uncle Charles brought me home over Somerton Rise, the way we came today—'

'You don't need to explain.'

'No, I don't, do I?' She had felt it in him as he first saw this gilded valley, the same recognition, as he too sensed what a healing place it was and always had been.

'It was the loveliest summer day and I'd been a terrible plague to him, crying after such a long journey. Missing my home. Then. . . Philip came running out to meet us. He was ten years old—and the most beautiful thing I ever saw!'

'And you brought up among all the glory that was Rome!'

'Oh, I know it sounds foolish, but there was not a moment in the rest of his life when I didn't love him. It was the way he smiled at me, not at all disgusted by a snivelling girl! He just saw me as another brother, I suppose.'

'Which is why he begged you, on bended knee, to marry him on his eleventh birthday!'

'Oh—' Luciana felt a sudden threat of tears '—did he tell you that?'

'Of course he did. And how cruelly you spurned him!'

'I did no such thing! I—'

'Laughed, you heartless little devil!'

'But only from joy! You cannot imagine how proud I was. Or how desperately, all the time we were growing up, I wanted him to mean it.'

Luciana was looking down at her hands, tensed together in her lap, so she did not see Max Rivington look away, as if he could not bear it. When she looked up he was still smiling so she managed to continue.

'So you see how it was, sir. First Philip and Rory, then the two of them and me, *contra mundum*. That's the Standish motto, sir, *against the world*. It was like that, we were always together and the lord help anyone who meant harm to any one of us! They were the most magical family in the world and I loved them all. The Marchioness, Aunt Anne, was so kind, she never once grudged having an extra child thrust upon her. We were so. . .oh, I just *can't* explain how good it was, my lord!'

'You don't have to. I've seen you with your boys, remember?'

'Thank you. Truly, *thank* you for saying that! It's what I'm trying to give them. Everything I had. Such fun and encouragement—even from Rory, who seemed desperately huge and grown to me! He was almost fifteen when I came, but only ever patient and kind.'

'And outside it all was Lysander, watching them inherit all he would never have?'

'Yes. It must have been terrible for him, I hope we weren't so smug and horrid we did not *try* to include him, but he was so much older, a man while we were just children, and so consistently disapproving. It just seemed easier that we all avoid each other, seeing the trouble it caused. Then when Rory was twenty, he went into the Cavalry. I think Philip would never have followed if there hadn't been a war. . .he was only just nineteen.'

'And Lysander hoped again?'

'Yes.'

'Which is why he hates you so terribly, my lady? Because Philip married you before he went and left you with child.'

'Yes.' Luciana felt a shudder of memory chill through her. So young! She had been only seventeen. 'When Lysander knew I had a son. . .'

'It explains much I hadn't properly understood before.'

So Rory had suspected. Max Rivington confirmed this. 'Rory knew, my lady. He knew you mustn't be left alone if anything happened to him.'

And for the first time Luciana felt fear that was quite primitive. 'Lysander cannot do anything! He *couldn't*!' Could not hurt her sons? That was the fear she had refused to admit to herself, the one fear too many. She would kill him if she so much as thought it was true.

She was so intent on her fear that she barely heard Max Rivington say it. 'No, Luciana. He can do nothing and never will. I'm here now.' But she felt the truth of it.

So why did this very truth that should be so comforting suddenly make her a thousand times more afraid? Of losing control, of losing the strength she had forged for herself out of losses almost too great to be consoled, if ever she gave in to this craving to lean on Lord Rivington. . .who seemed to want it of her.

Or maybe he didn't? Maybe it was just that he expected it and accepted it only for Rory's sake. It was her first moment of doubting her new friend and more damaging than anything that had happened all day. He *was* her friend, she knew that. But why he was. . .

Luciana looked up at Max Rivington then and wondered if he felt the barest atom of what she was feeling and always had been going to feel about him. She looked into those eyes now fixed so steadily on hers and wondered if he knew that she would love him.

Luciana was so certain that she would it might as well be that she already did.

And in this first moment of knowing, and fearing that he might not want it, Luciana knew without any doubt at all what Rory had done. Rory had known her so well. He had loved her so much he had sent this man to her, knowing what would happen.

Only, just because it was happening to her, didn't mean it was happening to Max Rivington. Luciana found she was searching every line of his damaged face, needing to see just the smallest echo of what she was feeling. Yet would she know it even if she did see? After all, she had never known with Rory.

Luciana lifted her hands to her cheeks as if to hold her fears inside her. Thank God that just as he moved, bent close and whispered so urgently, 'What is it, Luciana?' the door opened; Walpole, the butler, with

Lord Rivington's coat now pressed and clean, saving her from God alone knew what disaster!

'Dinner is served, my lady.'

And there, behind him, rowdy, wrangling and so very reassuring, were Carlo and Freddie, chanting 'dinner' over and over again in an utterly infuriating manner.

Luciana got to her feet and hurried from the room without another glance at Max Rivington. But even as she dealt with her offspring—'Will you *please* be sensible?'—she knew that he never took his eyes off her, not even for a single second.

Dinner must have been eaten; the boys must have behaved as disgracefully as only they knew how; Max Rivington must have quelled them. Luciana could remember nothing of it. Shock had come back at her like a ricocheting bullet. Today—everything—was all too much. Rory gone, Max Rivington come, Lysander suddenly so dangerous. Luciana gazed out into the softly fading sunlight and bled, 'I want Philip! I want him and he left me!' Everything used to be so simple, now it was confused. She ached to have her old world restored.

'Mamma?'

Luciana somehow managed to pull herself round at Carlo's worried question. Carlo was looking from his mother to Max Rivington and back again, trying to decide if he should be angry that their visitor had upset her. Carlo was only seven and this was the only possible explanation for her remoteness he could find. Mamma was unhappy and since Max Rivington was the only difference about today, Max Rivington was responsible.

Carlo frowned; he liked Lord Rivington, he liked him almost as much as Uncle Rory. But not like Papa. He *sort* of remembered Papa. Carlo's austere young face closed down, turning all his attention to the apple he was peeling, and Luciana's heart screamed.

He had been like this ever since Rory died. So responsible, so protective, so quiet. So subdued, it was not until this afternoon she had seen even a glimmer of the old Carlo, the boy instead of the would-be man. He was so aware of his burden, the seventh Marquess, and the greater part of that burden was his mother's sadness. Luciana pulled herself together and thanked God for the insensitivity that was Freddie.

'Freddie, have you got a *dog* under the table?'

'No,' came back the far too swift reply. Which meant he was both telling the truth and lying.

'*Freddie!*'

'Sorry!' Freddie dived his tangle of tawny curls under the table, reappearing—after a protracted struggle— with a puppy. 'Well, it isn't a *dog. . .*'

'That one's a bitch. I *think*,' Carlo added carefully.

No one could quite forget their blunder over Cassie, least of all with Freddie clutching the resulting offspring, an extraordinary mop of fly-away hairs, reflecting its unhappy parentage.

'I wonder,' smiled Max Rivington, 'what Antigone's puppies will look like?'

'Urrgh! That horrid—'

'Stupid—'

'*Poodle!*'

And Luciana could not take it. Simple as that. Could not cope a second longer. Not and not shame herself and the boys with a flood of tears. She rose, barely knowing she did so, and fled the room. She might have apologised for her unforgivable behaviour; she did not know.

Behind her, just as the door closed, she heard Max Rivington calm the boys' uncertainty. 'Put the puppy down now, Freddie, or it will eat your supper. Your mother is just tired, that's all. It's been a very long day for her. Now which one of you will tell me how you came to be so clueless about poor Cassie!'

Damn him! Damn him for getting it so right! For getting everything right. For making her so glad that she had found him—glad that he had found her. Damn Rory for doing this! Damn Rory for loving her and leaving her with so much guilt!

But damn Philip most of all, for not being there as she closed the door of their chamber behind her and looked at the bed, so irrevocably empty. So lonely, still, even after all these years. Luciana turned her back on it, curled into the embrace of a tiny silken sofa and cried.

Just let me sleep. Please God, let me sleep! Let sleep unconfuse me.

Let me wake and find Philip never left me. Most of all, let me wake and find Max Rivington never came!

Of course, she felt dreadful in the morning as she woke to the first stirrings of the birds beyond her window and the bright insistence of early August sunlight. As dreadful as one can only feel when one has cried all night and it has got one nowhere. Luciana sat up, her head complaining; she had not been to bed at all. Her bones ached terribly, the sofa was not designed for sleeping. Luciana unravelled herself and rang for her maid. She had to be ready for her early morning conference with Carlo.

Charles Lorne Fitzgerald Standish, taking his responsibilities so gravely. Since just after Freddie was born, Carlo had taken to coming to join her as she drank her morning chocolate, nibbling at the sweet biscuits he still had not guessed she only ordered for his sake. He would sit curled on the bed beside her and watch for every sign that she was well and that he was getting things right, being the man of the house and looking after her as Papa had told him to.

Carlo came in, far too quietly for a boy of only seven, and took up his place against her pillows. He did not kiss her this morning, however. She had been right to think she was in the deepest trouble.

It took some delving to discover what that trouble was.

'Lord Rivington was very good with Freddie,' Carlo tried out her mood. Luciana fought not to smile at his pomposity.

'Did Freddie do something dreadful after I left?'

'No, not really. He was just Freddie, you know.'

Carlo was picking at his sugared biscuit, not eating it. That was serious. But Luciana knew to let him take his time. 'He just had the puppy on the table and Lord Rivington made him put it down.'

'I should hope he did!'

And Carlo grinned suddenly. 'Lord Rivington was very rude!' Carlo always thought profanity warranted a medal. 'But I think he was a bit. . .well. . .*why* did you run away, Mamma? Did I do anything wrong?'

And Luciana suddenly saw it as clearly as anything; Carlo, weighing up whether or not to be hostile to Lord Rivington, not knowing what she expected of him. Luciana defied the great maturity of seven whole years

and ruffled her son's curls as if they were not rumpled
enough already. 'Are you going to eat that thing or just
shred it?' And as Carlo didn't shrug her away she pulled
him close and kissed the top of his dark head.

'No, sweetheart, you didn't do anything wrong. It was
I who was rude and silly and I shall apologise to Lord
Rivington as soon as ever I can!'

Carlo, not even pretending he was too big to be
hugged by his mother, cuddled closer, shedding crumbs
unpleasantly down the front of her gown, and said on a
mouthful, 'You'll have to be quick. He said he goes to
Rivenal today.'

'Rivenal!' Luciana came close to panic. Leaving! He
really might as well be going to the moon.

Carlo felt her shock and added quickly, 'Not till later,
though. He's still at the Cat and the Moon, I should
think. . .'

The village inn. Of course, he had broken his journey
home to come and see her.

Luciana was already sliding off the bed when Carlo
brought her up as if he had shot her.

'He said he couldn't start out too early because his
little girl wouldn't like it. He said if we like we can take
her a puppy to play with and—can she have one,
Mamma, please? We've got so many and Lord
Rivington says—'

'His *what*, Carlo?'

'Can he have a puppy for his little girl?' Carlo didn't
understand, how could he? She didn't. Luciana had
thought she had suffered all the shocks there were left in
the world for her to feel. But this—impossible! Surely,
impossible? No-one had ever mentioned that Max
was married.

She had grown so certain that he was not.

Luciana killed that thought before it had chance to undermine her. She could not cope with the reason she had been so sure; she had spent all last night fighting to deny it.

'His *daughter*? I'm sorry, Carlo, I'm being quite witless, I know, but. . .'

'Didn't he tell you?' For some reason Carlo liked this idea. 'He told *us*.'

And that was what made Luciana so very angry. She had no right to be, it was none of her affair if Max Rivington had a score of daughters. That did not stop it hurting that he had not told her.

She had been going to apologise to him. She still must apologise—hurry to the inn and hope he understood her embarrassing behaviour of the night before—and yet she was so angry with him she could barely move.

Because she had felt so much that she knew him and the feeling had given her such heart. Now reality struck with the full force of its contempt for fairy-tales. Really, she did not know him at all.

'Come along, Carlo!'

'Umm—' a mouthful of biscuit was hastily gulped down '—where?'

'Round up Freddie and whichever puppy you mean to take to Lord Rivington's daughter, we're going for a walk!'

'*Now*?'

'Yes, now!' Or she would grow so angry she would never go at all.

Needless to say, the boys brought all the puppies they could muster. Having argued and come close to blows over which puppy was best suited to a mere girl, they weighted down Liam with the largest of them and, Cass anxiously twining about their heels, took off across the deer park towards the road from Somerton to Rivenal, their arms full of yipping animals.

At the crossroads with the new post road to Exeter stood the Cat and the Moon, its aged inn sign being re-painted by its burly owner. Jake Blackmore fancied himself a Michelangelo and today, despite the early morning sleepiness of Somerton Parva, he had all the audience he could desire. As Luciana pushed open the iron gate that led from the cornfields onto the bridge over the mill stream, she saw Max Rivington and his groom shaking their heads in disbelief as Jake rolled up his sleeves and set to again, to make his Cat's violin a little less like a 'cello. She could hear their disparaging laughter from here.

Of all things it made her angrier than ever, to find Max so light-hearted when she was so utterly confused. Jake's daughter came out of the inn to defend her father—and to smile not quite as demurely as she should at the dark Irishman with Lord Rivington. Another soldier, of course. Luciana saw Max's sardonic grin at his smitten groom and burned with misery. It was like watching Philip and Rory again, the way Rory had so tormented Philip for falling in love with her. Maybe even then he had loved her, too.

'Come *on*, Mamma, you're getting in the way!' Freddie brought her back to earth with a thump in the ribs as he puffed his way through the gate with an armful of squirming puppy.

'Oh, did you have to bring them all!' She came close to snapping at him.

And was firmly put in her place by Carlo. 'Well, of course we did! If we didn't, how would Catalina know she's got the one she'd like best?'

They even knew the child's name! Feeling as close to murder as she had ever come, Luciana caught Freddie out of the path of a passing pony cart and reached the forecourt of the inn just one bit too angry to apologise.

But it was happening all over again—the sheer magic of Max Rivington just being here—as she watched her boys yell out in greeting and race to meet him; saw Max catch Freddie as he began to fall, puppy first, towards Jake Blackmore's pail of scarlet oil paint.

'Mind yerself, ye girt donkey!' Jake got between his picture and annihilation.

'Aye, steady!' The Irish groom.

But Luciana was aware only of Max Rivington. How could she ever fight the simple power of his presence just to please her? This stranger—who kept secrets from her. Wanting to rage at him would never be enough, not while Max had Freddie fast by the seat of the grown-up breeches he was so proud of and was laughing at Carlo, as if he knew Carlo was the one who must be won over.

'Lord, *all* of them?'

'I thought your daughter would like to choose for herself,' explained Carlo again, with a gravity that was utterly disarming. Freddie might have the hectic lovability of Philip, but Carlo was set for Rory's lazy charm.

Max Rivington let go of Freddie, who had recovered his balance enough to shrug off adult interference. 'That was kind of you. Of course, she would. How many are there?'

'Thirteen, sir. Only. . .well, there *were* but three died.

Mamma tried to feed them from a bottle but they were too small.'

'Did she. . .?' Which was when Luciana understood that he had been aware of her even before he saw her and knew she had only herself to blame for his so very careful restraint in greeting her.

Because she was trying still to be angry, when, in truth, she was only bewildered that she ever felt threatened by his hold on her at all. A hold so powerful she needed him to smile at her, almost as if she could not breathe until he did. . .

As he did now. 'My lady, I seem to be making off with all your puppies, what can you think of me!'

Which made it so easy to apologise. 'No worse than you must think of me, sir.'

'You were tired, Luciana.' At last he came up to her, wiping paint from his hand onto his breeches, reaching out for hers which had already reached, unquestioning, for him. 'And don't you ever apologise to me, *ever* Luciana!' It was said so softly, yet she knew the whole forecourt heard.

She saw Max Rivington's groom look at him as if he had just struck gold—Jake Blackmore, as sentimental as his sorry painting, beamed—and Luciana could not mind it. Not even Freddie, nudging Carlo, who hissed him to silence. 'Be quiet, you dratted little fool!'

It was not yet eight on a high summer morning, but the sun shone down and Luciana found herself thinking, Let this be what he came home for. I hope he's still glad he came. Here, to this middle-of-nowhere Somerset village where the mill-wheel creaked with age above the millrace and the apple scent of cider welled up from the cellars down below. So far from the carnage he had lived through. Luciana looked about her, aware again of how little she had taken in of this world that was her life since Philip had died. It was beautiful.

Somerton Parva was tiny, just a hamlet of cottages round a church dating back to Saxon times. It was a happy place. Marquess Charles had been a good patron of his lands, Somerton had been safe in Standish hands and always would be. The workers knew it; if they had a grievance it would be attended to; when the estate prospered they shared.

Luciana had worked herself into the ground over the past years, deputising for Rory since his father died three years ago. Marquess Charles had trusted her enough to run Somerton during his final illness and to manage it for his son when he was gone. It had given her the blessed distraction of sheer hard work. She looked about her this morning and knew she had done well. Rory would be have been satisfied.

The medieval inn belonged to Jake, however, and, independent as its owner, it was the only building in the village falling down. The fact that it was the most comfortable, the most patronised inn for miles around was lost on the observer of its shabby old shutters and stonework blackened by the smithy fires.

Light glinted off the leaded windows and for a moment blinded Luciana. Then she saw that all the time she had been observing, she was herself being observed. There in the doorway, hesitant—no, frightened—was the tiniest child. Too tiny, too fragile, pale as a shell, eyes dark and huge beneath black, black hair.

She was like him. Just a little. Just enough. Catalina.

Luciana smiled.

The child was so utterly terrified she ran away.

CHAPTER FOUR

THE first thing Luciana noticed as she swung back to Max Rivington was his weariness. It blanked out his eyes as if his laughter had never been. She had never seen any man so tired as he seemed now.

'I'm sorry, my lady. She can't help it. I can't blame her, God knows, I can't!' He was so tired he didn't even know how to explain, or so it appeared to Luciana.

Of course, she should have realised Catalina was Spanish, and what she knew of Spain would have explained the child's behaviour even if her own compassion had not.

'Of course she's frightened! All these new people all at once and in a strange country. After all, how long has she been here? Three days?'

'Four.' She sensed in his terse reply that he was grateful. It redressed for her a balance she felt she had been losing; the equality she had sensed between them from the start. She had been drowning in his commanding personality, it was important for them both that she surface now.

'What happened to her mother?' Did he even know? Spain had been as turbulent as that.

'Killed. Her whole family with her.' He was not going to talk about it. And not just because they were not alone here; he did not want her to pry.

Luciana understood that. 'I'm so sorry. I didn't know.'

Her reward was that he opened up to her. 'I never

69

told anyone. Even Rory didn't know until the end that I had married. I didn't know until a month ago that my daughter had survived.'

'Where was she?'

'In a convent.' Max Rivington ran his hand through his hair in a gesture very close to desperation. 'Sometimes I think I should have left her there, safe among her own people. What was I to her but another soldier? She didn't know me. I might have come to kill her for all she knew!'

Luciana knew how badly it was hurting him; simply, he would never have spoken in front of others if he had been able to stop himself. She might have seen that the boys, the grooms and Jake Blackmore were engrossed in rescuing puppies from the millpond, but Max Rivington hadn't, his mind was locked on Catalina.

Luciana tried to imagine what it must be like to have your child run from you in terror. Just imagining was too horrible. 'But she knows you now.'

'No. No, that's just it, she doesn't. She won't. I do understand, but I... God damn it, Luciana, I don't know how to help her! I'm a soldier, I only know about war! I...my own family was so poisonous a thing I have nothing, not even one good memory to tell me what to do for her.'

So she had been right. Luciana's heart stilled. She had been right and he was beginning to confide in her. It mattered more than anything to be able to help him, so she did not feel so overwhelmed by him, so useless.

'Max, you *do* know.' She could use his name now; it came so naturally that she wondered that she had ever found it hard. 'You know as well as anyone! Look how well you manage the boys.'

'Yes, but they're boys.'

'No different—' and suddenly she was teasing him '—except that girls are by far the rougher, by far the more militant to manage!'

'They certainly grow into women who are, at any rate!' And Luciana felt her heart kick into hope just knowing he was believing her. He was going to trust her experience and listen.

'She needs time, that's all. Time and your company, just seeing you every day and learning to depend on you. Believe me, that's not difficult.'

'Am I so very autocratic?'

'You know that's not what I meant!' Something had been said, she knew it. Something that could never be taken back. She didn't mind it, but it committed her. 'Maybe at first she'll only turn to you because you're there, the only grown person who is a constant for her—'

'She has my groom's wife; Kitty is doing all she can to be a nurse to her.'

'Not the same, Max. Truly not the same. *You* make decisions for her, you make the rules she must live by, all the things she needs to feel secure again. She'll trust you—'

'You don't say she will love me.'

Something profoundly important was being asked. So intimate Luciana almost fled from it, but she had no right to.

'She will. You really must understand, it wouldn't be hard.'

Committed absolutely.

So committed his next words physically hurt. 'Even like this—this monster with half a hand and half a face?'

They were not talking of Catalina now and they both knew it. If she deserved to keep her friend she must not lie now, although where the truth might lead was overwhelming.

'You'll never appear anything but what you are, however hurt, however torn your face appears. You have only ever been good and kind to me, how much more kind and gentle have you been with your child? There's not one thing in you to frighten her once she forgets her past.' Catalina was not the only one with that to do. Luciana fought on against reluctance to give too much, knowing Rory would expect it of her. Maybe even Philip would have, too. 'Give her time, that's all. Time to know you for her friend.'

Give *me* time. She began to believe. Whatever it was she wanted—she did not know yet—he could want it, too.

Her thoughts were safely interrupted by a soaking Cassie, desperate that Luciana come to the aid of her puppies.

'Oh, Freddie, what are you doing? Poor little things!'

'I'm only washing them. They got dirty.'

Luciana turned from Max as if she were fleeing for the safety of past.

'Carlo, how in the world did they get paint all over them? Oh, for *heaven's* sake!' Luciana focused on her children as if they could ever shield her from those gold-dark eyes that followed her, searing through her as if skin and flesh were no barrier between them at all. Luciana felt the heat of them flare so hotly inside her she almost fainted.

Thank God for Polly—ever unpredictable—after all his irresponsibility now playing the anxious father, too.

If only it were as easy to sort out Max's problems as it was to sort out Polly's. 'Here you are, silly creature. No, *gently*, Polly! That's right, you dry him for me.' She nudged the rescued puppy close enough to be licked clean by its father; watched the puppy recognise and trust.

Poor Max. What a way to find out that children scare you senseless and make you bleed! How had it been for him to see Catalina for the first time? Luciana could picture it so clearly, the child hiding behind the skirts of the nuns, the nuns trying to coax her out, equally unsure what was for the best. Poor Max, poor Catalina!

Because she was thinking of the child, Luciana looked back at the inn and surprised a look on Max's face that cut her through. Catalina trusted somebody, but it wasn't him. The innkeeper's wife had come out, drawn by all the barking and shrieking, flour spilled down her apron and clinging to her cheeks and nose. A pretty, rounded, homely woman, and Catalina was quite content to hold her hand. Even to come out into the forecourt with her.

Carlo was the first of the boys to set eyes on her and Luciana almost cried.

She had never forgotten that first moment Philip saw her and decided, one way or another, that she was his. Or he was hers. Anything so long as it was his concern to look after her and no-one else's. Carlo had all his father's instinct for the frightened and the lonely. He was going to do something about it.

She saw Max move towards his daughter and shook her head. He understood at once. Maybe he remembered what she had told him last night; at least, his eyes smiled.

Carlo was a mess. Tall, handsome, utterly Standish, but a mess. Paint on his knees and mud on his elbows, his jacket and shirt front sodden by wet dog. Yet he seemed so very much the Marquess. . .even Freddie stayed quiet and chewed his thumb.

Carlo, shy himself, approached the girl very carefully.

'Um. . .hello,' he said, and when she did not back away from him he smiled.

And Catalina responded with all the gravity of the convent child. She was not a day over four years old but so very dignified. She dropped Carlo the most immaculate curtsy. Then, as if just remembering how, she smiled too.

Luciana caught a hand to her throat. Now Catalina was all Max! She had the most mesmerising smile. Slow, sleepy, turning mischievous at the edges. The perfect little *femme fatale*. . .

Her son had not the smallest chance from the very start.

'Hello,' tried Catalina. She spoke confidently, as if she had been practising, though her father had never heard her. She had the soft breathy 'h' of the Spaniard and Carlo was utterly enchanted.

Enough to plunge right in. 'We've brought a puppy for you. Well, lots, actually. You can have any one you like.'

Of course, Catalina did not understand a word of this, but when her father moved a little closer and translated for her she did not draw away. She did not look at him, and held Jess Blackmore's hand more tightly, but she wasn't frightened any more.

In fact, Luciana suspected she had never been quite so afraid as Max imagined. So careful not to frighten

Catalina he had probably been too careful and she must
have sensed the restraining of his usual easy manner,
known he wasn't being himself. He may inadvertently
have fed her unease himself. He was relaxing now and
Catalina liked it.

She repeated one word, then tried it in English.
'Puppies?'

Max laughed, shocked into pleasure, and teased her,
'Not *all* of them, kitten!' It didn't seem to matter that
she had no English.

She plainly liked him laughing at her. Catalina tucked
herself close against Jess Blackmore's skirts and dared
to look at him as he knelt down closer to her, cradling a
puppy that had scrambled on cue to greet her. Luciana
caught Mrs Blackmore's eye and the woman nodded;
Max was doing very well. The village had already taken
to him, but this will to know his daughter was unexpected in a man of his station and it earned respect.

Luciana fled from questioning why that should matter
to her so greatly and turned as Freddie, left out and on
the verge of sulking, rallied his usual boiling-over
friendliness and skidded over the stones to join his
brother.

Carlo stiffened, jealous and possessive. Freddie, sensing and not liking it, backed away again.

Max caught him, drawing him in. 'Here, help me keep
hold of this foolish creature.' Freddie complied, feeling
important again. Carlo only had eyes for Catalina.

'Do you like him?' He pointed at the puppy.

'*Her*!' Max and Freddie burst into the most derisive
laughter and Catalina buried her face in Jess
Blackmore's skirt and cried.

Luciana could bear it no longer. She had no idea if she

was any use with nervous children. Just because she could manage her own meant nothing. . .but she thought children generally trusted her.

Catalina seemed to. Certainly she looked up as Luciana held out a handkerchief and Mrs Blackmore said serenely, 'Now here's someone for you, little one. Here's her ladyship come 'specially to see you. Isn't that nice?'

Catalina was not sure, either of the words or of Luciana, but she trusted Mrs Blackmore enough to risk the smile that was so obviously expected of her.

'Good girl,' returned Luciana briskly. The less fuss they made of her fears the better. '*Do* you like the puppy, Catalina?'

Max translated.

Catalina listened, then thought hard. '*Bonito.*'

'She say's it's pretty—but I hear a reservation!'

Max was right. Catalina had inherited a great deal more than his smile. There was real decision in the way she pointed at quite a different puppy, by far the least agile and the least robust.

'You want that one, *niña*?'

Catalina nodded. There seemed to be something that made her unwilling to actually speak to her father but she always answered him.

Carlo went at once and fetched it for her, the reddest, the silkiest, the most obviously Polly's of all the puppies and by far the most beautiful, courtesy of the sleek elegance of Cassie.

Max said as much. 'She'll be a beauty.'

Luciana smiled suddenly, looking at her smitten son and remarked, very drily, 'Yes, indeed she will!'

Catalina was already beautiful, or as close as anyone

can come to it who has been crying and sleepless and hungry for maybe months on end.

It was the second time Max paid her a direct and very intimate compliment. 'Carlo has all his father's instinct for the finest, my lady.'

Only yesterday she would have flushed, unused to flattery, so cut off from the world she rarely met any man to flatter her in the first place. Now Luciana just smiled, and murmured, 'Fool!'

Freddie wasn't having that. 'No, he isn't, it's a lovely puppy!' Then he beamed at Catalina. 'Are you going to call it something pretty, too?'

Freddie and Catalina were the same age, but the contrast—even aside from the difference between boy and girl—was painful. He was twice her size. Luciana felt a shiver of rage at what the child had been through and thought, That's a brave little thing! She could be so much worse. She has real courage.

Catalina—*femme fatale*—decided charming Freddie was shooting outsize fish in tiny barrels. 'Hello,' she smiled, but never took her eyes off Carlo.

Freddie thought girls a bore, anyway, and returned to puppies.

'So what *are* you calling it?'

'*Her*!' Luciana and Max.

'Call it Poppy.' Carlo brought them briskly into line.

'Puppy?' Catalina plainly thought he was mad.

'It's how you say puppy, it sounds like poppy. And besides she's going to be as red as anything, like Polly. . .'

'Carlo, you're confusing me let alone anyone else!' put in his mother, and this time when everyone laughed Catalina smiled too.

'Poppy?' She put Carlo in his place by pronouncing it perfectly. She could be a haughty little madam when she chose. Luciana liked her.

Max? She was not sure yet if Max loved this difficult child of his, but it was written all over him how badly he wanted to. She was the second chance he had never expected. He had nearly died trying to save Philip at Talavera. He had nearly been killed beside Rory at Toulouse. He was useless for a soldier any more—his hand shattered and his voice so damaged—but he had a new life here that had real hope in it.

Now it was as if for the first time he believed it. He was still kneeling, a little outside Catalina's adoring circle, but he had hold of Poppy and was rubbing her plumy ears, being licked to pieces for his kindness. Catalina looked at her puppy and wanted it. To get it she was going to have to take it from her father.

The air seemed very still then, as everyone waited, even the children seeming to sense something important was happening. Catalina let go of Mrs Blackmore's hand. Then, as if she had done it a hundred times before, she went over to her father and tugged at his sleeve.

'Mine!'

'*Mine*!' he teased back and Catalina started laughing.

Dear God, if I cry I'll never forgive myself! thought Luciana. Just how sentimental can one be! And yet this was what life was built from. Little things. Mundane, ordinary things that the great and the intellectual would sneer at. These were what everything came down to in the end. The only things that were important. This *mattered*.

Catalina went so far as to lean against Max's arm as

she rather clumsily wrestled the puppy into her own. It was the least muddy of the brood, but quite the wettest.

'*Urrgh*!' she squealed as the puppy shook itself in her uncertain hold and soaked her muslins. Then she showed again whose child she was. Gently but firmly she controlled the little creature, whispering to it, soothing it, stroking her cheek against its silky ears. Then she turned her back on everyone and walked away. Crying, of course, and the child had already learned the hard way not to show it.

If ever Luciana had not understood the evil of the war, she understood it now. She had thought her own children had suffered, but they had suffered from what had been taken from them, not from all the misery they had seen. Thousands of children, all like Catalina, displaced from their homes, cut off from their families, never knowing if they would ever be safe and loved again. Thousands dying. . .

Luciana moved quickly and rested her hand on Max's shoulder.

'She's as happy as anything, the best thing you did in the world was bring her home. Stop worrying!'

His broken hand came as it always did to cover hers. 'I'm not.' Not now.

And yet as he watched his daughter and listened to Luciana agreeing readily to Jess Blackmore's offer of a glass of milk for everyone, he wondered what, in the name of God, he was doing here.

Time would come pretty soon when he would have to face up to himself. To all of it—his responsibility for Catalina, his betrayal of her mother.

What in the name of all the saints did Rory think he

was doing, bequeathing the protection of his family to the one man he knew could not be trusted?

What had he, Max, let happen, to himself and to Luciana Standish? It had. No doubt at all that something irrevocable had passed between them. Something that, if they spent every day of the rest of their lives apart, they could never end.

He didn't want to. He had come to Somerton ground down by the burden of all he had to do to make a life for Catalina and himself in England. Luciana had taken that burden away. She had taught him how a man should feel to come home.

But this wasn't his home and she wasn't his. Damn Rory to an eternity in Hell for forcing him to see this!

Be damned most of all himself for wanting it so badly! If only for what she had done for Catalina today. It *was* Luciana who had done it. Something about her presence that set the whole world easy with itself and made her boys so friendly and so self-assured. The villagers adored her. He had heard them say it often enough over the short day and a half he had been here, now he could see it. He knew more about why they would fight to the very last ditch for Luciana than she ever could imagine. So much more about her.

Max stood up and looked over to where Luciana sat in the shade of a sycamore on a peeling old bench that Jake had once recklessly painted an iridescent green. His groom Gabe had the boys well in hand and was swapping stories over their heads with Liam, old comrades in arms—and frequently in custody.

It was as if half his old life, the best half, had come with him, making this civilian world more welcoming, and at its centre, madonna-gold and just as serene, was

Luciana, teasing poor Jake about his creative aspirations while Jake's wife threw up her eyebrows and ladled fresh milk into tumblers from a pail.

Philip had once told him about Luciana; that the eldest Fitzgerald girl of each generation was given this name, meaning light, from the motto the family took when they became Counts of Montefalco. *Ad lucem*, towards the light. It suited her so perfectly it hurt.

What would hold him back from her, if anything could now, was the knowledge he could lead her into darkness.

She thought he was safe. She trusted him. He would work every last atom of his being until it bled to deserve it. But Catalina's mother had trusted him, too. . .

Max had had enough. He had lain sleepless most of last night, fighting with himself because he wanted Luciana Standish. He always had. From the very first moment Philip ever spoke of her. He had listened, disbelieving anyone could be so gentle, so inspiring. He had come here hoping all he'd ever imagined of her was real—and hoping to Hell it never would be.

Anything to set him free from all she had come to mean to him as the war dragged on, as much his talisman as she had ever been to Philip and to Rory. When he had told her that her letters sent men into battle laughing he had meant himself. He had come here hoping nobody could be so perfect as he dreamed her, but he was here now and she was the most beautiful woman he had ever seen.

Enough! Today was a good day and if he had learned anything over the years of losing his friends with merciless regularity, it was to take each day as it came. Luciana was smiling and contented and only the most selfish bastard would spoil it for her. Max rolled back his sleeves, all covered in paint and dog hairs, and pleaded for Jess Blackmore to take pity.

'And a proper mess you are too, m'lord!'

'Shocking,' tormented Luciana. 'You make me feel quite clean!'

Max looked at her so hard then she wondered what terrible thought was half killing him. Just knowing that it was, half killed her.

So—she already loved him. So instinctively, so completely she could almost convince herself Philip would have wanted her to love him.

Philip must want it. Or he'd stop her, wouldn't he?

That was the trouble and had been for so very long a time. Philip had felt so near and she had clung to that nearness for the strength to get her through. He was far away now and she was so happy, so released, that guilt must surely come and overwhelm her.

But not now. What she had never once imagined had happened to her, she had fallen in love. And God willing—could any God be so cruel as to let her know him and then lose him?—Max Rivington could want her. He wanted the peace and gently disordered domesticity he had found here, she was sure of that much. It was enough.

'Nurse would make you go and wash with smelly soap,' chimed in Freddie at Max, snapping his mother from her thoughts before they grew too troubling. He had none of Carlo's ambivalence towards Lord Rivington. He liked him. He had no other father, uncle, mentor, so Max would do.

'I'm adequately sure I'd make myself! Do you suppose we shall ever meet when we're clean and tidy? And

don't say "urrgh", Freddie—yes, you *were* going to!—
it's an unspeakable noise!'

Such an echo of Luciana's own vain plea. It was all so
calming, so typical of life at Somerton, that no-one
noticed when Catalina came back, still cradling her
puppy, her eyes a little swollen but that was all. Without
hesitation she came straight to Luciana and without
hesitation Luciana hauled her onto her knee.

'You're getting heavy!' Luciana complained.

'Poppy?' Catalina smiled helpfully.

'Probably! Max, that's going to be a very large dog
you've taken on, are you quite certain that you want to
keep her?'

'Have I any choice?'

They both knew he hadn't and just smiled.

Once Catalina had found Carlo she wasn't letting go.
Luciana remembered her early days at Somerton, trailing after Philip who was so patient with her. Carlo was
so like him. Carlo was also flattered and surprised and
showing off and it settled their parents' plans for the
day. It would be spent together.

Leaving Jake and Jess hunched over the Cat and the
Moon masterwork watching paint dry, Max and Luciana
went ahead with the children and the older dogs, across
Somerton's park on foot, leaving the two grooms to
follow on with the carriage laden with exhausted puppies. Rory's possessions, too.

It could have been so sad a homecoming, for Freddie
found his uncle's sword and dragged it after him for the
first quarter mile so very proudly. It got too heavy for
him, so Max took it and idly scythed the nettles and
grasses as they walked, close together, silent but for the

odd weary admonition to the children. Catalina, trying to keep up with an ebullient Carlo, stumbled and muttered something that made her father smile; Carlo hauled her to her feet, after which he held her hand.

'If you say "urrgh", Freddie!' Luciana warned her youngest. And there at last was Somerton again, its ancient stones soaked through with sunlight to the deepest gold.

'This place is paradise,' Max thought out loud.

Luciana stopped as he had done, taking in the resonant beauty of the house, so much part of its surroundings.

'I think it always must have been, long before any house was here. The Standish who found it chose well.'

'You really do love it, don't you?'

'Yes, I love it.'

She wanted more than anything for Max to feel at home here.

Everything was going so well. . . . Catalina was almost as lively as the boys, Max tangibly relaxing as each minute passed. Luciana knew about taking each day and making the best of it. Today that would not be hard.

She was so wrapped up in planning how to entertain the children that at first she did not see Freddie, bounding on ahead, just freeze. Carlo, too. Luciana came round to the fact that something was wrong when her sons ran back to her, half protective, half alarmed. Freddie went so far as to take her hand and Carlo did not sneer at him.

'Visitors.' Max's voice had taken on an edge of caution.

Visitors? *Please* not today! thought Luciana. She

shaded her eyes with her hand the better to see against the sunlight.

A smartly polished landau was slowing to a halt on the carriage sweep, careless of Somerton's lone peacock pacing his dog-tattered way across the gravel. Luciana's spirits rebelled. Would she *never* be rid of him? Worse, them. For Cousin Lysander, the owner of this showy equipage, had not come alone this morning. He had a stranger with him, a woman Luciana had never seen before, which could only mean the most trying confrontation.

Without realising she did so, Luciana drew closer to Max and was glad when his arm came so protectively about her.

His breathing altered, quickened, but it must have been his anger for he said, an order not a request, 'Catalina, angel, come here!'

And when the child came, he took her hand very firmly in his own. Luciana watched the tiny fingers curl around the broken stumps of his and ached for him.

Can't the fool see she doesn't even care that he is hurt, that his hand is ugly, so long as she may hold it and feel secure? As I do. Luciana felt so safe just to be held by him it was undermining. It was so easy to lean on Max and lose her hard won strength in his. She did not want to lose it, but she could not fight him.

So it was together, so like a family, that they crossed the final stretch of the deer park onto the carriage drive. The Standishes, *contra mundum*, had quietly come to mean Max and Catalina too.

It gave Luciana the strength she needed to face the carriage party. Cousin Lysander had come with very definite purpose, she knew it the moment she saw him hurrying his companion's descent from the landau, with an impatience that made Luciana sorry for the woman, until she proved so snappishly impatient in her turn.

'You are standing on my hem, sir!' A middle-aged woman, all soft and buttery blonde and pretty, her voice as soothing as nails dragged ruthlessly on glass.

Luciana watched as the woman glared Lysander's tight-gripped assistance away, and wondered how, in the name of anything, the world could contain such unpleasing people. Lysander was still young, only just forty-three; Max could be no more than five years his junior, but you would have thought them generations apart.

Taut, tight-lipped, fanning away the heat and the dogs with his lavendered handkerchief—how could anyone hate so passionately as Lysander hated the contentment and solidarity he was seeing now?

Hated and meant to harm. Lysander was so sure of himself, even in the face of Max Rivington. He must be very certain of what he had come to do.

Luciana had long since learned never to run from confrontation. Learned most of all that taking on Lysander before he was ready was the very best way of spiking his guns.

'Good morning, ma'am.' She nodded to the stranger with all her natural civility, knowing her irreproachable manners were just one more thing to make Lysander's cold blood boil.

'My lady,' came the serenly ice-edged reply and Luciana felt Freddie's hand tense in hers, frightened by such lifeless indifference. The anger gathering in her veins froze cold.

'Cousin!' Luciana's voice was chill with warning. She

already had Lysander seething. He had been all for launching his attack on her at once.

Luciana frustrated him further. 'It is growing very warm despite the early hour.' Too early for a morning call, which meant afternoon to anyone but Mr Standish. 'I should like to get the children indoors and cleaned up. . .and don't say "urrgh", Freddie; you know you are quite horribly dishevelled!'

But Freddie, tucked childishly against her side now, didn't want to let her go. He seemed to sense something even she did not. It worried her, but she managed to say, 'What I want is for you to take Catalina to see Nurse, wash your hands, and then you may come down to the morning room.'

The blow when it came was so unimaginable, so wicked, no sane person could ever have anticipated it.

'That is a most excellent idea!' Lysander's voice had an edge behind its coldness, a cruel, cutting edge of laughter. 'And while they are there, Charles will ask Nurse to begin their packing.'

'*Packing*?' Luciana gripped Freddie's shoulders so hard she must have hurt him. Freddie was too upset to care.

Lysander was relentless. 'Surely this is not unexpected, Luciana? I have warned you and I have *warned* you but not one whit have you attended! I have engaged Mrs. . .er. . . Mrs. . .here—'

'Hastings.'

'Hastings, to look to their welfare. I really cannot permit the boys to remain beneath this roof a minute longer.'

At last Luciana saw it. 'Not remain in their home, Lysander?' There was a warning so explicit in her tones she felt Max stir beside her and realised he still was holding her. He was trying to govern her anger, but this was her fight—these were her children, no one else's. 'I find your notion of your authority bordering on the eccentric, Cousin!'

'And I find your attitude only as I expected to find it, madam! I have been patient, the Lord knows, with your. . .*lax* foreign ways, but you cannot imagine I would allow it to continue. After yesterday—'

'Yesterday, Cousin?'

Luciana's tone was so dangerous now that Freddie turned and flung his arms about her, burying his face in her skirts. Carlo saw it and glared murder at Lysander.

'It's all right, Carlo.' Luciana thanked him for his defence of her. 'Our cousin is just leaving.'

Carlo was not the Marquess of Standish for nothing. 'He should never have come!' he stated bluntly. 'I didn't say he could!'

'There! *There*,' pointed out Lysander. 'Is that not the most perfect example of what I have been saying! These children are running quite wild in your care. *Care*! I never encountered a woman less careful of her children! They are become as insolent as gypsies and I will not have it! This is not how the Standish heirs should comport themselves—'

'I'm not an heir, Freddie is! I'm the Marquess!'

'You are a seven year old boy with not a shred of manners, that is what you are, Charles!'

'Carlo! My name's *Carlo*!'

'This is insupportable! The Marquess of Standish and he insists upon a foreign—'

Carlo was game for anything and Luciana's heart

twisted in pride. 'Papa called me Carlo. And so did
Grandpapa.' He meant the Standishes who mattered.

'From now on you will answer to Charles, young man,
and not answer back to your betters at all!' Then
Lysander, feeling he had quashed rebellion, turned back
to Luciana. 'The boys come with us to Graveney. This
morning, ma'am! I shall not leave them to your influ-
ence. When and whether or not you will be permitted to
see them—'

'Permitted to see my sons. . .' Luciana repeated the
words so quietly she felt Max Rivington's hand tense at
her waist in warning. But he was letting her fight alone.
Knowing that on this one issue she would fight Lysander
to the last drop of blood; his, not hers. Carlo and
Freddie stayed with her. She had no doubts about that
at all.

Until Lysander said, 'If in time you can prove yourself
to be suitable as a. . .well, I will not say *mother*, for really
you—'

And she exploded at his inhumanity. '*Suitable*! Suitable company for my own children? You must finally
have let go your senses, Cousin, if you imagine I should
allow them from my sight for one single second, least of
all to endure the custody of a monster such as you!'

But he had won, she sensed it. Somehow he had won.

For the one reason she had never thought of. The
most obvious.

'But then the law of this land says that you have no
choice, madam! As their senior male relative, I am—
and remain—their guardian until Charles' majority.
You have no say whatever in the matter! If you were to
dispute me, what court in the land would allow wardship

of the Marquess of Standish to the daughter of an Irish mercenary? The guardianship of these children is mine!'

No court in the land. It was true. It had happened a thousand times before, widows left defenceless in the face of their husband's grasping families. But it could not happen to her! She would not let it. Rory *couldn't* have left her so exposed!

He hadn't.

It was quite extraordinary the capacity Mr Standish had for disregarding Max Rivington's presence. Like an ostrich with its head rammed firmly in the sand.

Max's voice, so long silent, came as the greatest shock of all to her reeling senses.

'I think you will find yourself in error, Mr Standish. Very much in error.' Then he went so mercilessly for the kill. 'You overlook the late Marquess's intentions most recklessly, sir. His brother's sons have a guardian already. And that guardian, Mr Standish, is me!'

CHAPTER FIVE

'WHAT? *What* did you just say?'

The most extraordinary part of this incredible confrontation was that Luciana was furious with Max. For not telling her before and letting her go through one second of this torture.

'*Why* did you not say? Oh, damn you, Max! *Damn you*!'

And suddenly it was as if no-one else in the world was there, because he took her by the shoulders, so gently, and rocked the rage right out of her. Fought her for control, of herself and of the situation. Calming her and yet she was reeling beneath the onslaught of emotions.

'What urgency was there to tell you, Luciana? Carlo and Freddie are yours, why in the world would I ever change that? I'm their guardian in *law*, their trustee, but that's all. Rory just didn't want you bothering with all that—'

'But I'm their mother and I've been *bothering* with all that, as you call it, for years! I've managed Somerton single-handed and you know it! You *must* know it!'

'I know, you little spitfire!' And in those simple words Luciana understood what was happening to her, that this unstoppable torrent of rage was the most intense relief. The boys were safe. Lysander could not touch her. But he made one last try.

'I need proof of what you claim, sir.' Lysander

91

sounded stunned, barely able to take in this final
frustration. 'It seems the most unlikely—'

Max turned on him then, so swiftly Lysander flinched
away as if he expected violence. But the only threat lay
in Max's flaying tone. 'No more unlikely than that Rory
would leave these children to you! Good God, man, did
you really expect to get away with this? Did you really
think you could harass and bully and threaten until you
had your way? Did you truly imagine you could ever
grind Lady Philip down? What kind of man does that
make you, if not the worst imaginable guardian for any
child!'

'I...I—'

'Will you remove yourself from Somerton this
instant—and I mean *this instant*, Mr Standish! After
what you have done today, even you would not imagine
to return.'

And as if Lysander had already gone, Max turned
back to Luciana, his hands calming her flaming cheeks,
soothing her back to the fact her sons were safe, stroking
her fears away. 'Come, my lady. Let us take the children
inside, you're right about the heat and Catalina is tired.'

It was what she needed, to put the children first. In a
minute she was going to flay herself alive for losing her
temper in front of them and scaring them so badly.

She need not have worried. Freddie looked up at her,
his eyes glowing and squeezed the breath right out of
her. Carlo merely flung a look of dismissal at Cousin
Lysander of which even his father would have been
proud. It would take more than Mr Standish to frighten
these boys of hers. With luck, they were both so angry
they had not really taken in what could have happened.

'Yes, come along, you scruffy creatures.' The sooner

they forgot this episode the better...'Take poor Catalina to Nurse and see if you cannot find her some lemonade.'

It was Catalina who almost swept her poise away. Shaken to the roots of her new found security, aware of violence, yet the child gazed on Lysander with an hauteur that paled Carlo's disdain to insignificance. She was aware only that the nasty man had been dealt with, by her father. That was all she needed. Catalina took hold of Max's coat; Max pulled her against his side, close into Luciana's skirts and Luciana thought, I could almost thank Lysander for this.

It was certainly time to dismiss him, and his familiar, with the most annihilating courtesy.

'I'm sorry you should have been subjected to unpleasantness, Mrs Hastings.' Though any woman who could witness so coldly what this Hastings creature had witnessed today was beyond any sympathy, however desperate she might be at her lost employment. 'Nevertheless it has served a useful purpose if Mr Standish has at last comprehended that if he trespasses here again, I shall not answer for the embarrassment it causes him!'

And with that Luciana left. She had had enough, her brain was punch-drunk with shock. She wanted Lysander gone, the children safely with Nurse. She wanted time alone with Max Rivington.

They had such a lot to say. It was almost, as she followed the boys and Catalina into the cooling welcome of the panelled hall, that her whole relationship with Max must be altered. Maybe it had always been misunderstood.

Now she knew that he was legally the boys' guardian it made things different somehow. It made it easier to leave things to him. . .and yet it made it harder. She had felt more in balance with him while she had thought his support was just his friendship. She had always known Rory had sent him to look after her, but now she was left to wonder just why he had agreed to come. Was it only because the terms of Rory's will said he had to?

She needed to know. It mattered. *He* mattered.

Luciana was sunk exhausted into the ivroy silk cushions of a morning-room sofa when Max came to her. He had taken his time. He had collected Rory's papers from among the belongings brought home by Gabe and Liam. Luciana felt a stab of pain as she saw the box he carried them in. She had given it to her brother-in-law the last time he was home.

It had been her most prized possession, an Indian inlaid box of mother-of-pearl and sandalwood. A girlish thing, but Rory hadn't minded. He may even have understood that she gave it to him because she had told herself she would never give it away and not expect to see it again. While Rory had it—she believed it with the passionate convinction of a child—he would come back to Somerton. Now it was hers again. She could not bear it.

Max saw her exhaustion and rang at once for a servant to bring her some refreshment. 'Tea—as hot as the devil! Don't look at me like that, my lady, it's what you need.'

'Yes,' Luciana rallied, 'but I detest it so!'

'Then you must suffer bravely, ma'am!' With which he set the box down on the sofa beside her and added, 'Don't be quite so angry with me, Luciana.'

'I'm not!'

'You are. I don't blame you. God knows, it must seem

the final insult that the law deems a widow not fit to guard her own children. You should be raging at the injustice of it all! But Rory understood, Luciana. He chose me for their guardian because I wouldn't interfere, because I would see you for the good and loving mother that you are.'

'Max, please!' She could not take his kindness. Because she had been angry—angry with him for being a man. For being judged superior by a law that was so much an ass it was beneath the contempt of the meanest intellect. Yet it could have taken her boys from her. 'Oh, God!' Luciana buried her face in her hands, fighting off the memory. 'He could have taken them! Dear God, he could have taken them!'

Max sat beside her, coaxing her hands into his and Luciana close into his protection. 'No—no, sweetheart! No, he couldn't.'

'But—'

'*Never*, Luciana. I wouldn't care how I stopped him!'

Luciana looked at him then, her whole being stilled. She should not ask him—anything could happen if she asked him—but she could not fight it.

'Max, why. . .*why* do you defend me so?'

She was melting into his kiss before he even touched her. Almost before she felt the tenderness of his mouth against hers she was suffused by this intensity that was the greater part of him and her body soaked through with need. With gratitude and joy and disbelief she knew, I can live! I can feel again! *I want him*.

For while he kissed her, he blotted out the world and her past receded. Max tasted her tears against his tongue, half understanding them. He lifted his broken hand to her hair and Luciana curled her neck into it. So far from repelled, she was fascinated by the warmth diffusing into every part of her as she curled her arms about his shoulders, shattered by the newness of it all, yet feeling she had known this all her life. Max threw back his head as the shock of her touch flared through him and he fought the hardest battle of his life.

He must not do this! He had to let her go. . .but he felt the giving innocence of her welcome resonate in the deepest heart of him and knew he needed her as he needed to be alive. And just for this moment, in her distress and her relief, he had her. It was the worst imaginable betrayal of her trust in him, but he could not have released her if he tried.

Max kissed her then as if he could scald her mind away, his own with it. He felt her gasp of shock against the sudden fever of his lips and knew he had always needed her like this.

But the Luciana who had kept him going through six years of war had been a dream only barely believed in, a starving hunger for something he could never have. This wasn't a dream, it was insanity, and it would destroy the only thing he really had of her, her friendship. Which mattered so much that he found the strength to let her go.

Max pulled back from her so abruptly Luciana thought that she had hurt him—that scar was so new, so raw at the edges of his mouth.

'Please say it doesn't hurt!' She was so dazed by him the words barely came out.

Max gazed down at her swollen mouth and raged at his stupidity—but whether in kissing her or letting her go, he was past knowing. She was so beautiful it hurt.

Philip's wife. The love of his best friend's life. How had he done this to her?

Max caught her hand urgently to his scarred cheek, showing her. 'No—no, it doesn't hurt! But, oh God, Luciana, I do!'

'Please . . .'

'I should *never* have kissed you!'

Luciana, her own doubts paralysed by his closeness, still somehow recognised the guilt in him. She had come a very long way from the child who fell in love with Philip.

'I don't know if *you* did. . .exactly!' Then her face flushed with uncertainty at her instinct for laughter; she looked away, praying for the reassurance of his.

It came. 'No, maybe I didn't!' Then, stunned by the truth of it, he smiled so very softly. 'In that case, my lady, be so good as to assert some restraint and try not to kiss me again!'

'I shouldn't dream of it!' returned Luciana soberly and knew that something very fundamental to her happiness had been saved.

Max was laughing as if he had made a most amazing discovery. 'But I should! I'm not to be trusted, Luciana!'

And instantly all laughter vanished. Reality blasted him like an exploding shell—he could not be trusted.

Luciana lifted her hand to his face again, knowing some terrible memory was hurting him. She had to stop it.

'*Tell me!*'

'No.'

'One day—'

'No. . .*never*, Luciana!'

So Luciana withdrew from his hold, sure of only one

thing in this bewildering new world of hers. We have something between us so strong it just saved our friendship; something so important it saved us from the destruction of embarrassment. She recognised at last a maturity in herself she had never been aware of before; she had been so long the grieving girl in everyone's eyes she had believed it. But not now.

Something so peaceful, so utterly invulnerable lay at the root of this friendship with Max Rivington and, God willing, one day it could be built on. Until that day, she would do anything to protect it, most of all from this past of his which was so brutal he would never confide it. She needed him to; if they were ever to be the friends they were meant to be, one day she must know.

But she would never get anything from him until he gave it willingly. Regretfully Max caught her hand into his and looked at it where it lay, so flawless against the ugliness of his own. 'So beautiful!' he murmured.

Yes, you are, she thought. Most beautiful of all was the way he just held her hand to his face again, as if just breathing in the scent of her he could unite them. Then he let her go and retrieved the sandalwood box. Rory's papers lay scattered and Luciana smiled.

Max saw it. 'Yes, that's largely how I found them in his quarters. He ever was a careless devil!'

'All the Standish are. Philip drove me to distraction when first we were married, nothing was ever where it ought to be. But I soon succumbed!' Then she stopped, because for the first time she realised he could not take the way she spoke so lovingly of Philip.

Luciana wondered again what had happened to Catalina's mother.

Max single-mindedly forced the subject back to Rory's papers.

'Here are the documents you need should Standish challenge you. I don't think he will.'

'No. . .' Lysander would never have the courage to challenge Max Rivington.

'But it does no harm to keep them safe. In fact, I'd prefer to keep them with me, if you're willing.'

'Oh, yes!' Lysander had frightened her enough for her to feel they would not be safe at Somerton.

'This one is Rory's will, dictated to the regimental chaplain and witnessed by Wellington himself. . .'

Rory had been taking no chances. Many a battlefield testament had been overturned on the grounds of unsuitable witnesses.

'This is a journal he was keeping.' Max handed her a much battered book of blue morocco. 'For Carlo and Freddie, all about what he saw and did. He was never much use at keeping up with it, but—'

'You've read it?'

Anyone would have thought she had accused him of a crime. 'Good God, no! What right is it of mine?'

'I meant. . .and you have every right! You're Rory's executor.' The will was simple and she had already gathered as much from a single glance at it. A glance that stretched her composure to snapping point because Rory's signature was so enfeebled, so unlike his usual flourishing scrawl. He had been dying when he touched this paper. . .

Max's fingers were stroking her tears away even before she realised she was crying. 'Don't think about it, sweetheart. Don't think!'

'I try! But, Max—'

'I know! But he wasn't in pain, I swear it, Luciana! The wound was clean through his chest, there was no infection. He just lost too much blood before we found him. It's not the worst way to die.'

No. Philip had known that. She had never forgotten the moment she first learned of the fires at Talavera.

So now another inescapable moment had come. It was the one thing she had never known, because she had not been able to be sure when Rory told her Philip hadn't suffered. Rory would have said anything to spare her. She wanted the truth and Max was the only one who knew it.

'Max...?'

'Are you asking me to tell you lies, Luciana?'

'No. No, I couldn't even if I tried! I've seen—'

'My hand? Yes, but it looks worse than it was, I promise you, it was my own stupidity saw my sleeve catch fire. I just had to be sure...'

'That Philip was dead before the fires took hold?' Luciana felt her hands lock into each other in dread at what he might say. But for both their sakes he had to tell it.

She could see that so clearly as he answered, 'Yes,' so distantly that she knew he was no longer with her but at Talavera. 'So many weren't, we could hear them. And we'd seen it coming, it had been so hot that day, blazing as only the Spanish sun can blaze. It was relentless. The grass was tinder dry—the fire from the cannon set it burning.'

'And... Philip?'

'Philip fell early, in some wild charge against the French line. The survivors got back to our lines— someone told us he was still alive.'

'Oh, God!'

'I'm sorry, Luciana. You asked for the truth.'

'I know!' She did not have to bear it.

'He can't have lived long, Luciana. I know that now. I just didn't know it then. Liam and I went straight out to find him, but we couldn't get to him. It was—the end of the world out there! Liam's leg took a hit from a canister shell, I had to get him back to safety. Then. . .it just wasn't possible to search for our injured until the fighting ended and by then the fires had taken hold. Philip was dead long before I got to him.'

'But he'd lain out there all day. . .'

'I would give my life to have got there sooner!'

Luciana closed her eyes, for what she could bear least of all was Max's pain. His guilt. Given his life—dear God, he so very nearly had done! He could never have done more. She could see it so clearly, God knew she had been seeing it for years, Philip, so young, so loved, lying in the blackened stubble. . .having time to know that he was dying. But this, her deepest nightmare, had been reality to Max Rivington, who was even now thinking only of her feelings.

'His last thought was for you, Luciana. *Yes*—' this as he sensed she could not trust it '—I *can* know! The last thing Philip saw was your face!'

'I. . .*please* don't say it if it isn't true!'

The most astonishing thing about Max was that he was not angry. He could have been. Just for the briefest moment he almost was. He had promised not to lie and yet she did not believe him. Then he looked down into that exquisite, exhausted little face and went on with a gentle conviction that could not be countered, 'He had your picture, right there in his hand. He always carried it. Remember, the miniature?'

'Oh!' She remembered. How tiresome it had been to sit still for the artist even for an afternoon, most of all because she had been so heavily with child. Carlo had kicked terribly. But she would have suffered any discomfort just to please her husband. Even now she could barely believe how much she had. . .she still did love him. '*Did* he?'

For a moment she wondered if Max would be able to continue. She had never seen a look so. . .it was desolate. . .on any man's face. But he was Max and she was beginning to see he was strong enough for anything.

'He was holding it. To me it seemed. . .it was almost as if he knew he did. I can't ever explain that, Luciana, but it was the reason I thought he was alive.'

Dear Heaven! The reason he had risked his life for a dead man and been so terribly injured.

'Oh, Max, I'm *so* sorry!'

'I would have done it, anyway.' And she knew he had taken almost as much as he could of remembering. 'I loved him. I suppose, like Rory, being so much older I felt responsible. We all did. He was so—so alive, Luciana! Game for anything. The whole regiment felt lifted just having him a part of us. No-one would have left him there. *No-one* could!'

Luciana felt her heart was breaking—for Max, as she watched him turn away, exhausted, and knew at last that he was hiding something.

Max had turned because if he looked at her one more second she would see that from the moment he had seen the picture in Philip's hand he would have done *anything*. He could no more have let it burn than he could have let Philip be turned to ashes in the fire. He could never explain.

Rory had come racing to find them, to force Max out of the flames and plunge his arm into water before flesh and cloth melted together inseverably; Max had said nothing, just looked at Philip's hand and watched Rory's face die. They both understood so well. Philip had never been the only one who loved her. Rory had taken a very long time to wrest the picture from Philip's grasp. It was Max's now and he could not give it back to her.

If he had to, it would be the only lie he'd ever tell her, that it had been destroyed. It had meant too much to him even before he met her. Now. . .

Now she was saying, 'Max, I. . . I would give anything not to have asked you to remember!'

And he turned back to her, strengthened by the magnitude of her losses.

'Angel, don't ever say it! I've told you, don't ever apologise for anything you want of me! You had every right in the world to ask and I hope you know now. He looked so very calm, Luciana. More at peace than anyone I've ever seen. It didn't frighten him to die, he'd had so much more in his life than most men ever know. He never stopped thanking God for that, I promise you, my lady. When you told him that you were to have a second child he was—I remember him bursting in on us like a schoolboy, he was so happy. He said he would never understand why he had been so singled out for fortune—'

'He deserved it! I only wish—'

'He could have known Freddie?'

'Yes, that he had another son. I wish he'd seen him. Freddie is the most like him, I think. . .' And had been born of a moment of perfect joy. She would never forget that, Philip home two days before she had expected him, racing down through the woods to find her where she had gone with Carlo to play in the stream. Watching his face as he first set eyes on Carlo. Then, a little later, sending Carlo back to the house with Nurse. . .

They had stayed all afternoon in the glade. Strange how all the most important moments of her life seemed fixed upon the woods of Somerton Rise.

Max had found her there, the most important thing of all now. As was turning this conversation for him. He was too tired and had not come home to be put through this. It was only to be expected that their first few days be strained, a draining complexity of sometimes shattering emotions, now it was time for a little peace.

She could never have expected it to come in the guise of Freddie.

He really was like Philip, as he stuck his tangled head round the door, so desperately trying to be tactful.

'What is it, Freddie?'

'We're all clean now, so can we come in?'

'Oh, I think we can survive that, don't you, my lord?' Please let him relax, please let the children calm him!

They always did. 'I can probably force myself to bear it for a. . .whole minute, maybe?'

'Don't be silly!' said Freddie, his whole scruffy self round the door now. 'You know you like us really!'

Max did like them. Luciana had every opportunity to watch them together over the next few days, for Max made no move to go on to Rivenal and seemed contented just to bring Catalina to Somerton each morning. The little girl was quite changed; it was impossible to be wary of anyone so naturally affectionate as Carlo and Freddie, of course, but she was relaxing with her father, too.

Luciana watched and wondered about it. At first it seemed simply that Catalina followed the boys' lead. Since they were not afraid of this tall, commanding stranger then she was not; Luciana saw her childhood self in Catalina's determination never to be less than ten times braver than mere boys.

Strange how it had not struck her until now that she and Catalina had so much in common, left alone and scared and miserable until some stranger came and brought them to a new home.

By the end of their first week Catalina was viewing her father as anything but a stranger. In fact, she took one hard look at the way Carlo and Freddie were all over him and made up her mind; Papa was hers.

Luciana would never forget the first time Catalina climbed possessively onto her father's knee. She was tired—they were all tired—after a long day out in the carriage. Max somehow had the instinct not to show his surprise. He simply drew her into his arms and smiled as she tucked her head into his shoulder, her thumb in her mouth.

'I wish she wouldn't do that.'

'She'll grow out of it. I did!' And Luciana's heart turned over as Max smiled at her and absently kissed his daughter's shining hair. So much darker than his own. Like her mother, perhaps?

Luciana was not ready to think about Catalina's mother. She wanted nothing in the world to shake her sense of security in this new, it already seemed age-old, friendship. It was all she had of him. Max had not touched her again, not so much as to help her over a stile or from the carriage, and she half knew why.

She didn't want him to. Because so badly she *did* want it and it frightened her. She had never felt anything like this for any man but Philip. She had never in her life imagined she ever could. Yet when she looked at Max she was as needful of the life-giving strength of him as of light and air. She wanted him that much. And, just a little, she knew that he would not touch her, would not come within ten yards of her, because he felt it too.

She saw it sometimes when he thought she was not looking. She could hear it in his breathing, so quickened then so ruthlessly controlled. They were so aware of one another they could have been deaf and blind and lost in space and still known the other's presence. Yet he held back from her and she held back from him. So all she had, for the moment, was her friend.

That at least she was sure of. He was as happy with the completeness of it as she was. So it came as the greatest shock when, as the second week merged into a third, he said at last that he must leave her.

They were alone together, the children worn out and in bed, Catalina so tired Luciana had insisted she stay at Somerton.

'Don't worry about her, she'll think it a huge treat!'

'I don't worry, Luciana. I've never worried from the moment she came here. You work miracles, I wonder if you know that.'

Luciana looked away, unwilling to take the credit and unable to cope with his intensity. 'The boys have done more. It has done her all the good in the world to have them follow her about like besotted spaniels. She'll be a heartless creature!'

'As if she's not smitten beyond recovering with Carlo and you know it!'

Luciana closed her eyes against the evening sun and smiled. 'Poor Carlo!'

'Yes, in my experience it is invariably the women who are ruthless!' laughed Max Rivington. Then he also turned away.

Too much was not being said that could be and they both knew it. Was it just too soon to say it? Or would it never be said at all?

They were recovering—the only word for it after another day of picnics and pirates and puppy training—on the terrace above the Elizabethan garden, now soft with late summer roses and the welling sweetness of stocks and thyme and rosemary. Beyond the lawns lay the road to Rivenal. Luciana saw Max recognise it and his face shut down.

So he meant to leave soon. Luciana could not believe how little she wanted this to be over.

He seemed not to want it to end any more than she did. At least, he did not yet mention Rivenal.

'Don't you sometimes feel isolated here, Luciana? From the company of your contemporaries, I mean?'

It had never entered her head until he came here. Maybe it had not been true until he came and she saw what it was she had been missing.

'I don't think I felt it,' she answered with habitual honesty. 'There has always been so much to do. You've seen for yourself just how much time children can take from a day and then there has been Somerton, ordering the house and seeing to the estate for Rory.'

'You've never been lonely? Most women would have sent for a companion years ago.'

'Do not you start to be starched up about it! You sound exactly like Lysander!'

He turned back to her then, shaking his head at her defiance of convention, but laughing. 'Don't you care what your neighbours say at all?'

'Not in the least—' Luciana lit up at his smile '—since that neighbour is the confounded Mr Standish!'

'Who has been mentioned quite enough for one day! But—no, I'm being serious, Luciana—is there no-one you visit? No particular friend?'

And at last Luciana realised he was building up to something. But she could not see what it was.

'I have friends, but we're all so busy with our own concerns. It's like that in the country, not at all like London. I can't imagine anything more dull than sitting about between routs and suppers having nothing to do but twitter about my jewels and muslins! I've never wanted to live in Town.'

'Lord, no! No more would I if I had a home like Somerton.' And she heard it again, deep tension, the coiling of a spring.

'I'm perfectly contented, Max, truly I am! I enjoy my life; it's all I ever wanted.' The best I can hope for now my husband is gone, she might have added, but she could never say it. 'Besides I have few friends my own age, I was always deemed a *most* peculiar child! Foreign, and one can't have that, you know!'

'What nonsense, that can only have made you a thousand times more fascinating!'

'Well, I confess a great many of the boys did think so. But Philip soon dealt with such pretensions!'

'Rolled up sleeves or swords and pistols?'

'Bloodied noses, anyway! As for the girls—'

'They must have loathed you, Luciana!' And suddenly
he realised she was just like Catalina. She could have
been a desperately lonely child, far too lovely to be
anything but envied. But it was not in her nature to be
unhappy, least of all here at Somerton.

'Well, if they did, I thought they were the deadest
bore so I was well served if they wouldn't play with me!
I could never be bothered with stitching and painting
and all those *female* things!'

'And yet you are more a woman than any I have ever
known.'

He could have kicked himself for saying it! They had
done so well to retrieve their friendship from the
damage done it by his kissing her. He had to be so, so
careful.

Luciana could have kicked herself for flushing. Did
she want him to guess how much she wanted such words
from him? She had to be so, so careful.

'I have one very good friend'—she changed the
subject urgently—'Lady Deverham. A neighbour of
yours and the greatest crony of Aunt Anne's. Carlo and
Freddie adore her.'

It was what he needed to know. Because Max knew
he must get away from Somerton; he had to think. He
knew what he wanted, but he could not trust his motives.

He could hear Rory now, as clearly as if he were back
in Toulouse. 'You know what I want! Someone must
look after her. I want you to marry her, you fool!'

After all, wasn't that what so very often happened?
Right through the ranks it was the thing a man did, he
took on his friend's dependants. Soldiers' widows, left

without a protector, had learned fast in the Peninsula to marry again before the corpse was cold. The first man who offered for them. It was not that they felt no loss, no anger at their untenable predicament, just that it was the only way to survive.

When Rory made him swear to come home and marry Luciana, it had seemed the most practical thing in the world. The army was finished with him, he had to go back to Rivenal. He was the Earl of Rivington, one day Marquess of Rivenal; he needed a wife, he needed heirs. To marry a woman he had barely seen was nothing out of the ordinary for men of his kind.

But he *had* seen her—he had heard all the worship that poured from Philip and from Rory. He had been out of his mind over Luciana Standish for years.

Knowing it had made him tell Rory; even though he could barely speak for his injured throat, he had told the truth about Antolina, the wife he had left so unprotected she had died. That was the moment he truly understood the meaning of friendship; Rory had not turned away, disappointed in him. Rory had gone on insisting. It was almost the last thing he said before he died—marry Luciana.

And when Max found that he had a daughter living it made final sense to him. Catalina was owed anything he could do for her. He owed her a mother—God knows, he had cost her her own. He had waited at Corunna for the ship to bring them home and thought about Philip's widow, alone with two small boys. He was already their guardian; to come to Somerton and offer their mother his protection had seemed, from the unreality of a distant shore, the only thing he could in conscience do.

But now he was here and Luciana was no longer an

icon but a living woman. He wanted her more than he ever dreamed a man could want a woman. He wanted her so badly to offer marriage was beyond the question.

It would be so wrong; to offer a girl as vibrant, as passionate as Luciana a marriage of convenience was— impossible! He could never do that to her. Never deprive her of her chance of happiness, maybe with another man. . .

His whole being rebelled. Most of all at the truth— she had no thought of other men, she had no thought of marrying at all. The truth about Luciana was that she had never been afraid to be alone. She had made a life for herself from what she had left to her and she was, within the limitations of her loss, contented.

She did not need him. He had to get away before he showed her how passionately he wanted her to need him. Before he broke with all honour and reason and told her the truth about what he had come here meaning to do.

But he would not feel happy leaving without knowing she had a friend to turn to.

'Does Lady Deverham know the truth about Lysander?'

'Yes.' Luciana was fighting to make sense of the look in his eyes, so hard, almost hurt, even angry about something. 'I. . .needed to tell somebody and she under- stands so well. I have known her ever since I came here. She was more of an aunt to me, really, until Philip died. Then she was the only one not to treat me as a helpless child.'

'Then I want you to promise me you'll go to her. At the first sign of threat from Mr Standish, I want you to take Carlo and Freddie and stay with her. Would that be possible?'

'Yes, I'm sure it would. But, Max, what are you telling me?'

He almost could not say it then, looking at her lovely eyes swept empty by desolation. The hardest thing he had ever had to face was knowing at last that she did not want him to leave her.

'I *have* to go to Rivenal.' It was almost as if he had been trying to argue himself out of it, or she had.

'I know, it's just that—'

'I know! I don't want to go, these past two weeks have meant the world to me, Luciana! I'll never be able to thank you for what you've done for Catalina. She's a different child.'

Was that all he meant? Luciana could not bear it if he had only been glad to stay for Catalina's sake.

'I told you it was nothing—'

'And I ignored you for the fool you are!' His smile was so soft his words lost any sting they might have had. 'I have to go, angel, I wrote to my father, he is expecting me.'

'With open arms?'

'With lowered portcullis, I imagine!' It was the first time ever he had been able to laugh at the sterility he was forced to call his home.

That bad? Luciana guessed, 'He doesn't know about Catalina?'

'No.' The laughter died out of him. 'No, but he will have to accept her. She is heir to everything, after all.'

Unless he marries. . . Luciana slammed her mind shut against this first tentative thought, shocked cold by just the idea she could be thinking it. She could never face

up to it. Or to the fact that from the very first moment
she had thought how good he was for her sons.

Her voice was just the barest whisper. 'I find it so hard
to understand. A family so at odds. . .'

'Of course you can't; of all people, you never could!
And the worst of it is that we're not at war, we are
indifferent. My parents kept me cossetted out of fear for
the succession—I was the only child of eleven to survive.
They kept me as isolated as an invalid, no friends, no
horses, no reckless games. I couldn't live like that. I
wanted what Carlo and Freddie have, somehow I knew
it existed. I left Rivenal at sixteen and I've never been
back. I lied about my name, my age, joined the army as
a private soldier and got as far across the world as it was
possible to be, so even my father could not find me.'

So the army had become the only family he had ever
known, Philip and Rory the first friends. It was an
appalling story.

'You can't take Catalina back to that!'

'I don't intend to. I'll let my father see her, but we
shan't stay.'

'What will you do?'

'I have property left me by my mother's brother. In
Yorkshire.'

Yorkshire! Luciana had to fight this. She could not
bear it, either for him or for herself.

'Max, I know you must do your duty by your father—'
she saw his bitter smile and understood it '—but don't
take Catalina to Rivenal just yet! I should be more glad
than anything to have her here at Somerton, please say
you will allow it!'

He had been telling himself for the past eleven days

that he must never ask it. He should have known
Luciana would offer anyway.

'I shan't say I must not put you to the trouble,
Luciana, I'm too grateful for that! She's so happy here.
It's done so much good to see how resilient she can be. I
would rather she stayed with you than anybody.'

Too intense again. Max looked away again across the
intricately patterned gardens and Luciana held her
breath, desperate to control her rioting feelings.

'Thank you, Max. I honestly didn't want to see her go
anyway, the boys are having such fun, showing off and
being all masculine and silly!' Then she asked what
really mattered. 'Will you be gone long?'

And when he came back, would he then go straight to
Yorkshire?

'A day, maybe two, no more. I have no reason to
stay.'

'So you will not quite desert us?'

And suddenly there was no point in the world in
pretending; he even wondered why he ever had. Max
came back to her then, so tall, so near, and said so very
simply, 'If I ever desert you, it won't be willingly,
Luciana. If I ever don't come back to you, it will be
because I have died.'

He did leave, of course, a few minutes later, because
there was no more to say. He had already said too much.
Only as he walked, then broke into a run across the
fields back to the Cat and the Moon he was no longer
sorry he had spoken. He could still see the shock in her
eyes, the pleasure. Max walked on, utterly at peace, and
never in his life more elated.

Luciana watched him go, curling herself into the

cushions she had brought out to the stone bench on the terrace. She watched until he was gone from her sight, then closed her eyes in gratitude. He would come back to her. To *her*. He wanted to.

She had the strangest feeling then, as the dying sun warmed through the lids of her eyes and all she could see was golden. Philip was close again. So close if she reached out her hand she could touch him. Philip had come to say goodbye.

They had never been able to in life and she had never been willing to in his death. Now the time was right. She was moving on.

Luciana burst into a flood of healing tears and heard herself sobbing, 'I love you utterly!'

She meant—without any conflict and without any doubt at all—both the husband she was parting from so finally and Max.

It was quite dark when she moved at last and made her way back into the house, no longer afraid of this nightly facing of an empty room. She had always expected to get used to it, with Philip away at war all but a few weeks of their four year marriage. But she never had and his death had made it impossible.

Tonight was different, so on her way she collected the box of Rory's papers from where she had left it, unable to face them, in the morning room. She could cope with them now.

She smiled at her maid but signalled her away. She would undress herself, she needed to be alone. She blew out all but the candles by the bed then opened the box. She knew what she was looking for.

Rory the ever irresponsible had surprised her by his

ruthless attention to what really mattered to him.
Looking after Somerton, his nephews. Looking after
her. She could never be surprised by him again. So she
knew that he would have left a letter for her, written
maybe years ago. He had faced up to the possibility of
his death when she had never been able to.

Here it was. Not very long and so wonderfully
illegible. Rory being Rory in his most appalling
scrawl...

I hope you never come to read this, Luciana; it will
mean that I am dead and I can bear anything but that
I will never come home to Somerton. Most of all as I
last saw it, with you and Carlo, and Freddie just a
baby. He is the most like Philip, but you will know
that by now. Carlo is a little like me, I think. They are
good boys, Luciana, and will always watch over you,
but I hope they never have to. God willing, it will be
Rivington who brings this letter to you. God willing,
he will stay and care for you. I want you to let him,
Luciana. He is the most honest, the most honourable
man I could ever wish for you. When he offers for
you, take him—for me, for the children, but most of
all for yourself. I would make it a command if I ever
thought you would obey me! I must end now—this
war has a barbarian's manners and must always be
intruding! We should reach Salamanca by morning. I
have said all I have to say, except be kind to the man
you marry, Luciana, for he will love you so. Don't be
angry with me—I only ever want you to be happy.
God keep you, beloved girl...

Had she read this even yesterday, Luciana would have
rebelled at it, wished her life away to have it unsaid.

Now it echoed so much the most healing dreams inside her, it became the most precious thing she owned.

He had written *when* Max offered for her, not *if*.

And *when* Max offered for her she would accept him. She was as sure of him as that.

He had been sure. They had needed no words; they never had, not really, not from the very start.

She loved him. Tonight she began to believe he loved her too.

Luciana fell asleep, her hand still holding Rory's letter. The first time she had slept so completely since she knew that Philip had died.

CHAPTER SIX

IT WAS surprisingly easy to communicate with Catalina
once Luciana had soothed her tears at finding her father
gone that first morning. Luciana had the inspired idea
that her own childhood Italian might just be close
enough to Catalina's Spanish to allow a degree of
understanding, at least marginally wider than that pur-
chased by Carlo and Freddie's pointing and repeating
everything very slowly, as if the little girl were deaf.

For three days Catalina bore the boys' superiority
with a Stoic's patience; she was holding in reserve a
vocabulary that utterly astounded them. It consisted
mainly of 'shan't!' and 'won't!' and 'imbecile!'; Catalina
enjoyed her revenge.

Luciana was watching them now from the shade of an
ancient cedar at Deverham where, since luncheon, the
boys had been practising, with passionate concentration,
a game so incomprehensible to Catalina she was mes-
merised. Cricket. Catalina stood at a prudent distance,
her nose wrinkling, as Freddie bowled a leather ball at
Carlo. Carlo took a mighty swipe and missed it. Carlo
flushed. He could not bear to fail in front of Catalina.

'So like you and Philip!' smiled his mother's companion, knowing Luciana could accept such comment
from her. 'Now—' the Dowager Lady Deverham dusted
her lap free of an importunate Poppy '—I have been
good and quiet and haven't demanded a thing, so stop
teasing me, child, and tell me all about Max Rivington!'

Luciana had grown so at peace with the thought of him over the past few days she could not mind interrogation.

'Am I so very obvious, ma'am?'

'Yes,' replied Lady Deverham seriously, 'and I'm glad that you are, Luciana, it has been such a very long time.' A very long time never to have shown the slightest inclination to remarry. The child did not even know, as Lady Deverham did, just how many men had longed to ask her. 'Why Rivington?'

Luciana had never even thought about it. Now, as for the first time she did, wondering if she could ever begin to explain how instinctively she was drawn to him, it became so obvious. 'Because he is kind.'

Lady Deverham was satisfied. It was the best of all possible reasons. Lady Deverham loved Luciana very much—mothered her just a little, as was her right at almost sixty. She wanted nothing more than to see her happy. 'How long does he remain at Rivenal?'

Max had already been longer than he planned; he had sent a message with his groom not to expect him back until the day after tomorrow.

'His father is unwell—no, Freddie, you may not play unless you're sensible!' Freddie had just launched a spinning ball at Carlo, who already had one black eye. 'He hopes to be with us shortly.'

'Not at Somerton, Luciana!' Lady Deverham was of an older school, a more rigid upbringing, than Luciana, and though she completely understood the girl's refusal to employ a companion, she would not like to see her break with convention so far as to invite a man beneath her roof until such time—God willing—they were married.

'No, he stays at the Cat and the Moon.'

Lady Deverham, much relieved, broke into the most delighted laughter. 'Oh, my dear, have you *seen* what Blackmore has done with his picture?'

'He *was* repainting it.'

'Ah, but that was weeks ago! Now he proclaims his whole life blighted, he *cannot* paint, he will *never* be able to paint, he as well might throw himself into the millpond! When I drove from church last evening he was *throwing* paint all over it—it truly was the most splendid thing imaginable!'

'Oh, but. . .are you roasting me? No, of course you're not! It explains the crowd when we came by this morning! Poor Jake, we mustn't tease, ma'am, he truly did mean to make a masterpiece! Oh, Lord, I have just thought it—does this mean he's so distracted all our hopes for the harvest match are blighted?'

She hardly dared utter such a heresy, for the pitched battle on the field behind St. Dunstan's was the highlight of the season as Somerton Parva took on the men of Upton Deverham at cricket. Jake Blackmore was Somerton's crack bowler.

'Well, he may take some persuading to discard his aspect of heroic suffering. . .but it looks that you may count instead on Freddie!'

Freddie, making loud swooping noises, had just bowled again. Carlo, smacked in the midriff, lost his now boiling temper and smacked Freddie, who let out a squeal of pain.

Luciana was barely on her feet to deal with them before Catalina slapped Carlo hard for bullying someone so much smaller.

'*So* like you and Philip!' repeated Lady Deverham.

And Luciana, no longer feeling pain at such a memory, for Max had healed her, headed laughing into the fray, pausing only to cast back over her shoulder, 'For that, ma'am, may Somerton trample Deverham into a thousand pieces!'

'They always do, my love, they always do! It is most dispiriting!'

Which was the last thing that could ever be said about Luciana's feelings as an hour later she rounded up the children to take them home. Having extracted a promise from Lady Deverham to visit them as soon as her grandson was recovered from his measles, she bundled the boys and Catalina into the Somerton landau with the promise that if they were good and quiet they could drive by the Cat and the Moon and investigate the next act of the drama.

The forecourt of the inn was not as crowded in this early evening sunshine as it had been at the height of Jake's despair, but a few hopeful patrons remained, who had nothing better to do than eye up Jess and her daughter, while Jake gazed into the millrace as if into the Slough of Despond. Jess was taking all in her stride as usual, dusting off the ancient trestles where supper would be served to those who wanted it, and dusting straying hands from her daughter's curves the while.

For the most part the evening drinkers were villagers well known to Luciana for men ever reluctant to go home to their wives. But in the shade of the sycamore sat a group she had never seen before, dusty and dishevelled; two make-shift crutches were propped against the taproom wall.

Soldiers, making their way home from the war. Luciana's throat tightened; any one of them could have fought alongside Philip and Rory. She must find out if they needed anything. Calling for the coachman to stop, she nodded to Jess who came across the yard all smiles at the change in Catalina.

'My, but she's a different child!' So changed and confident, Catalina was beaming at this old friend and holding up her puppy for inspection. 'And hasn't he grown, too!'

'*She*!' chorused Carlo, Freddie and Catalina.

Luciana smiled; no-one minded their high spirits here in Parva. The village, led by Jake and Jess and the Rector, had been wonderful through the worst of her bereavement, helping and encouraging and showing her that life could have purpose once again. Luciana felt quite at ease in teasing Jess, so very drily, 'No masterwork?'

To which the failed artist's wife replied succinctly, 'There will be, I'll paint the bless'd thing myself in the morning!' As women always do.

'Those men, Jess, the soldiers, are they looking for labour?' There was work to be had for the asking now harvest was approaching.

'Just passing—to the north, they say.'

Luciana knew it was a drop in the ocean of what the country owed these men, even so—'Give them supper, Jess. I'll pay for it.'

'That's kind, ma'am.' Not for her to tell Luciana these vagabonds were not worth the generosity.

That was what Liam was for. Liam had been the Count of Montefalco's closest henchman and followed his daughter to England when he died. It was for her sake alone he had followed Philip to war ten years later. Luciana knew she owed him more than she could ever

begin to repay so she always smiled and took it meekly
when he presented her with the reckoning.

'Rabble!' Liam was riding behind as the coachman
clipped the horses into motion. 'Scum! That's what old
Nosey called them and he had the right of it!'

'Oh, Liam!'

'Aye, you were always a soft one, *contessa*! Jailmeat,
the lot of 'em! The sooner they're roasting in the hell
they were born to, the better I'll like it!'

Until they were, he would keep an obsessive eye on
his *contessa*. He'd seen the way those bastards were
looking at her! Liam shuddered and crossed himself,
only just holding his balance as the carriage swung safely
in at the gates of Somerton Prior.

Luciana, for her part, thought little more about the
soldiers than to hope, as she bundled tired and fractious
children up the stairs to inflict the restraining of them on
Nurse, that they enjoyed their supper and didn't harrass
Jess too badly.

The next she heard of them was Liam's colourfully
expressed relief that they had moved on to Deverham
and Graveney.

It was on the morning of Max's promised return that
the north country soldiers were seen again at Somerton
and the children vanished.

The first Luciana knew of something wrong was when
the dogs burst out of the woods, scattering the deer and
barking so urgently her blood froze over.

She never would be able to say how she knew
something terrible had happened, but as she fell on her
knees to calm the hysterical Cass and Polly, she already
knew it was the worst day of her life.

Max! He was her first thought. It was a longing so desperate he must feel it. But he was not here and she did not know what time he was returning.

He was still not back a half hour later when, at the head of a party of stable hands, Luciana came over Somerton Rise and found Liam lying in the glade beside a whimpering Poppy.

'*Carlo*! *Freddie*!' She was shocked far beyond panicking as she called out. '*Catalina*!'

She knew they were gone. She had known it even before she reached the glade. God knew how, but some instinct had overwhelmed her. It was helping her now; the children needed her, she must not falter.

Luciana ran back across the grass to where a stable-boy was bending over Liam. She flung herself on her knees beside this oldest friend and took his hand; he had been left for dead, a wound to his head so brutal it would take a miracle to survive it.

'Don't you dare, Liam!' she urged him, the way she knew he needed if only he could hear her. 'Don't you go thinking you'll die and leave me, Liam Kennedy!'

He heard. At least Luciana took the twist of his mouth for a smile, almost for laughter, until the blood spilled out.

She'd lost him! The only one who knew what had happened to her children.

'*Liam*!'

She only knew Max was there when he caught her to her feet and thrust her out of the way. 'You, get her ladyship out of here!' he rapped at a gaping stableboy. 'Take my mare and get Lady Philip to the house immediately! Are you armed?'

The boy shook his head, overawed, as Max drew a pistol from his saddle. 'Use this if you have to!'

Which was when relief and rage hit Luciana like a storm tide and she turned on him. 'If you think—'

'I'm not thinking, Luciana, I'm telling you! Go back to the house and wait there!'

She had never known him like this, any man like this, so wild with anger, so ferociously controlled. She wanted to fight him—she needed to stay—but she actually did not dare to. Max had no thought at all but that she would obey him. No thought of her at all. . .

Then she understood how wickedly wrapped up in her own terror she had been. 'Catalina!'

Max heard the horror, the compassion in her voice and something snapped in him. He came to her, his arm so fierce about her waist, pulling her so close. . .

'Don't, Luciana! *Don't*! Not now! Just do as I ask. Get to the house and send for a surgeon—'

'A surgeon? But Liam's—'

'No, he's alive—barely, but he is alive! Now, show me what you are made of, Luciana!'

It was a kiss so shattering it was beyond imagining. It was elemental. Luciana clung to him for every atom of a second he allowed her and then turned, nodding for the stableboy to take her up behind him on the mare. Somehow Max's pistol had got into her hand. It was primed and loaded, but nothing in the world could scare her now.

It took an hour to get Liam safely down from the woods on a makeshift stretcher, it took an hour longer for the surgeon to reach Somerton. Max stayed in the woods, leaving Liam to Luciana, keeping back two stable hands to search for any clue to what had happened to the children.

The surgeon had just left when he came back. 'Liam?'

'In God's hands. I've left Nurse with him. The children?' They were all Luciana could think about.

'There were horses, three of them. Headed over the moor for Deverham.'

'*Deverham*?'

'Think what is north of Deverham, Luciana?'

'Graveney? But. . .' Luciana sprang up from the sofa, her stomach tight with horror. '*Lysander*!'

'It has to be. I've heard enough from the stableboys. They tell of some soldiers, deserters, probably—'

'Yes, I've seen them, too, and they *were* headed for Graveney. . . Oh, dear God!'

'If they were looking for work, I think they found it. Lysander has to have ordered this. Think, Luciana, scum they may be, but they wouldn't take the children for themselves. They'd have no means of asking for a ransom, no means of escaping unless someone gave them horses. And they had them this morning, one of your men saw them on the Rivenal road.'

'But—you can see the whole of Somerton from there!'

'They were watching to see when the children left the house—and they knew exactly where the children were headed. No villager would ever have told about the glade to rabble like that. Blackmore was barely happy telling me.'

So it had to be Lysander.

'Max, what can he mean by it? He. . .no, *surely* he could not *hurt* them?'

He had been roving about the room, tense and needing to be looking for his daughter, but he came

back to her then, reaching out to comfort her, and
Luciana pressed as close as she could to him, urgent for
his strength to reassure her. Beneath her breast his heart
was racing, but his voice was calm.

'No, no, that's not what he means. Trust me—' He
caught her face into his hands to make her look at him.
'*Trust me*, Luciana! He's a blackguard and a fool, but he
would never harm them!'

'Then I just don't understand!'

'He looked for a means to discredit me and found it.'

It was spoken so quietly Luciana's heart rebelled. He
was within an inch of blaming himself and he hadn't
even been here. If anyone was to blame she was, for
letting the children play beyond the deer park at all.

'Don't, Max!' It was Luciana's turn to shake him out
of it. Her fingers bit into his shoulders to make him
heed. '*Don't*!'

'If I'd just been here—'

'Stop this, Max, I'm not listening!' And the whole
world changed.

She had never felt violence in him before, least of all
generated by her. But it was there, raw and dangerous,
as he caught her hands away, hard behind her back and
held her, only just the safe side of his gentleness.

'It's the *truth*, Luciana, and you'll listen to me if I have
to—'

'*What*, Max?' She would not be afraid of him. How-
ever much he seemed to be warning her she should be.
She knew, if he did not, that if for one single second she
imagined he could harm her she would lose her friend.
'You *cannot* make me listen to you blame yourself!'
Then she stopped, knowing without question, This is all

about Catalina's mother. This nightmare had happened to him before.

Luciana stopped fighting. She would do anything to calm his anger now. Even accept the truth of what he was saying.

'It's obvious, Luciana. Lysander has no other means to take the boys than to prove me unfit to be their guardian. Just how much more unfit can I appear than allowing the Marquess of Standish to be abducted by the worst kind of—'

'You weren't even here!'

And she knew that she had calmed him when she felt the calculation in him, as he reassessed what damage had been done and saw a way to counter it. 'But Lysander doesn't know that, does he?'

'No. . .no, how could he?'

'Least of all when he sees they have taken Catalina, too.'

'Oh, Max—'

'*It is not your fault*!' He pulled her so hard against him then he drove the breath right out of both of them. Luciana clung to him, fighting for that breath, tortured by the pain she heard as he forced his damaged voice to comfort her. 'Lysander meant for the village to be set in uproar, to have the children 'found' at Graveney, so he could appear their rescuer. So you could not reach them. If we find them before they reach Graveney, he's defeated.'

'But if they went over the moor. . .' It was a hot, humid late August day and the clouds were smothering. They would blot out the moor in a mist so impenetrable no-one could find a safe way through it. Least of all these strangers.

'Max, please, we have to go now!'

'I've got men out on the moor already. I've sent to Parva and Deverham, everyone is out searching, Luciana.'

'But you don't understand! Dear God, I'd rather they were with Lysander than out there! Have you any idea what the moor can be—?'

'I'm not a fool, Luciana!'

'No...no, I'm sorry!' Then she drew herself up, strengthened by her urgency. 'We *have* to go now!'

'Not you.'

'Yes, I'm coming with you! Don't!' This as he made to draw her close again, knowing so well now that he could bleed all her willpower away. '*Don't touch me*, Max! I *have* to come; I'm probably the only one who really knows the moor. The village children were always kept away from it but Philip, Rory and I never listened—'

'No, you can't have attended to an order in your life, my lady!' And somehow, despite all that was happening, this overwhelming strain between them, he was smiling, that laugh she so loved back in his voice just when she needed it most.

'*Please*, Max!'

'I wonder if I shall ever be able to deny you, Luciana.'

Thunder roamed above them as if trapped behind a ceiling of cloud as the mare picked her way carefully towards the moor from the safety of Somerton. All about, distorted by mist, voices called out, asking urgent questions—who had checked which places and where had no-one yet been. Max and Luciana left the other searchers on the edge of the moor and stepped out of the familiar into the unknown.

It truly was another world out there, dank and cold,
yet the day had been stifling and still seemed hot up
where the lightning pricked the clouds but could not
penetrate. Already their faces were damp and their
clothes clinging with the insidious vapour, and from
beneath the mare's hooves came the shifting, sucking
sounds of ground that was not quite stable.

'Oh, *please* hurry, Max!'

And she felt his arms tighten about her as he touched
his lips to her ear. 'Not in this. Never over this ground,
Luciana! Are there any places you know to be particu-
larly dangerous?'

'There's the mire, between Rivenal and Graveney.'
Shock raced through her as she thought, He ought to
know! He lived sixteen years at Rivanal yet doesn't
know what's just beyond its walls. Everyone knew about
the Rivenal mire except the man who would one day
own it.

'You'll have to show me. Guide me as best you can.'

She heard nothing in his voice to suggest he guessed
what she was thinking, just the same Luciana caught her
hand against his where it held her so softly against her
womb, pleading him closer, as if there was any comfort
for him anywhere. 'I know what landmarks there are.
There's a track across the moor the drovers use, it
breaks off just before the mire.' Then she heard what
she was saying.

So did he. Max forgot all caution and kicked the mare
into a racing canter towards the drover's track, which
was nothing but a hardening of the ground between the
wild gorse and the heather. Strangers would follow any
track they could find; the soldiers would ride the
children right into the mire.

Luciana was never sure if she was crying or if it was the rain that began to beat down on them as the ground rose higher and met the weighted clouds; as if they were deep inside the clouds where everything was numbed to silence and no living thing could breathe. All Luciana was certain of anymore was that Max was holding her, holding on to her sanity as she fought to keep her fear under control. The only sensation at all now was the mare's pounding hooves. They might have ridden off the edge of the world.

Luciana found some comfort. 'Carlo knows!' She almost had to shout against a sudden roar of thunder. 'Carlo knows about the drover's track, he'll stop them in time!'

If he wasn't too frightened. If he wasn't harmed. It was asking the unimaginable of a boy only seven years old.

Max read her mind as if it were his own thinking. She felt the words, urgent against her neck where her cloak had fallen from her shoulders. 'Remember whose son he is!'

Philip!

It was as if he was right inside her. 'Yours, my perfect Luciana!'

Luciana cried in earnest then. So wrong a moment, so right, for him to say so finally that he cared.

She needed to know it. She needed every support she could cling to as an hour passed and still nothing; then another hour. It was late afternoon but the day had died long ago. The sky was so black it might just as well have been night on Somerton Moor.

Max stopped the mare where the track ended and

leapt down. His landing was muffled by the proximity of mud as insubstantial as water. They had found the mire.

Luciana held her breath, not knowing what to do, trusting to Max, who had survived a lifetime of war, to have the instinct and the experience to know for them. She just watched him and wondered how she ever imagined she had loved before.

It had never been like this and she could not bear it. Philip had been her life, her joy, the axis of her being. She had loved him beyond imagining but it had never even begun to be like this.

Luciana flung her head back in the face of the torrenting rain and wondered what more could possibly happen to punish her. To betray Philip so completely. Their sons were in danger of their lives and she was kept sane only by her love for Max Rivington.

She tried to tell Philip. 'It's because he's helping them, he loves them too, I know he does! His daughter's out there with them'. But Philip was gone. She had said goodbye all too effectively. He couldn't hear that she was sorry.

Luciana jumped down from the mare, too over-whelmed to stay alone. This was her punishment and she would never find her children! She *had* to, she must, they needed her. . .

Max felt her move towards him in the ground's shaking and roared at her. 'Go back, Luciana!' Then he saw the absolute desolation in her eyes and could not allow another second of it.

'Don't, God in Heaven, *don't*, my lady!' Then all restraint was over. 'My *love*!'

'Oh, God, Max! Oh, help me, *please*!' She was sobbing, out of anyone's control, and he understood it.

'Don't—we'll find them! They're coming home! Don't cry, angel. No need in the world to cry!' He stroked the rain from her face as if he could hold the world at bay. 'I love you, Luciana!' It was unforgivably wrong but it was all that mattered.

'I. . . I need you so much! Max, I'm so *frightened*!'

And so was he. For the reason he knew and could never tell her. Only Rory ever knew it. Max had been here before—in a situation just like this—with a woman who needed him even more. Antolina had had none of Luciana's strength when it came down to it and he had failed her.

Not this time. Somehow, worthless though he knew himself to be, a craven coward, not this time!

'Don't ever be—there's nothing to be afraid of, Luciana!' And he held her to him as he would comfort a weeping child.

She felt she was. There was not one atom of desire in how he held her now or in how she clung to him. It was love, beyond all need but for knowing that love existed.

Luciana pressed her cheek against his aching heart and calmed herself.

'But where are they, Max, *where are they*?'

Then she heard a child screaming. Catalina.

Max raced out into the mire without any thought but to reach his daughter. Luciana could only hold the mare, the animal's breathing the only sound left in the world.

Until she heard Carlo—felt someone running as the mire trembled and a shadow began to grow, darker and darker, gathering substance. Two of them. Carlo desperately tugging Freddie.

'*Mamma*!'

'I *knew* you'd come, I *knew* you'd come!' Freddie was repeating it over and over as if it had been a prayer. Luciana fell to her knees and wrenched her sons against her, clinging to them, not caring that they saw she was crying so long as they saw that they were loved. Luciana kissed them, Carlo and Freddie clung, sobbing with relief and anger.

'Oh, thank *God*!' she whispered. And she meant it.

It was a full minute before she realised Max was not back with Catalina.

Carlo was trying to tell her. 'I told them not to go near the mud but they wouldn't listen! They hit me!'

'They hit me, too!'

Luciana's entire body froze. 'Where are they?' She wanted to face the men who took her children. They would suffer for all eternity for this.

'They ran away.' Freddie wiped his face on his sleeve, then started to cry again, deeply ashamed of his tears, although he was only four. 'The mud shook and scared them and they left us!'

'Catalina?'

'She hurt her leg when they put us down from the horses. We. . .we were coming to find you.' Carlo meant help of any kind, but to him that would always mean his mother. 'I gave Catalina my coat. . .' Luciana had just noticed he was in his shirtsleeves. Thank God he'd ever been in a coat at all, Liam had suspected rain.

'They killed Liam!' Freddie stated baldly. He loved Liam and he was hot with anger.

'No, they didn't, angel!' Luciana heard herself use Max's word. 'They *didn't*! Liam has a head like a cannon-ball and he's going to get well again!'

'Catalina's all alone!'

'No, Carlo, Max is with her.'

It meant more to her than anything in the world when she saw what this simple statement meant for them. Their new guardian was here, so everything was going to be all right.

Only it wasn't. For a whole dragging quarter hour it wasn't until Max, unfamiliar with the safe parts of the mire and moving so carefully, appeared out of the mist, his daughter in his arms. Mercifully the child had fainted.

Luciana went to him, never taking her arms from around her boys, and wondered as she saw the look in his eyes, what was this going to do to Catalina? The child had been so happy, felt so safe. Now all she had ever been afraid of had happened to her, soldiers had come and they had hurt her. God alone knew what that would do to a barely healing mind.

Max was exhausted but somehow still greeted the boys with the nearest to a grin a man that tired could manage.

'I told you I'll never see you clean and tidy!'

It was the most wonderful sound they had ever head.

'Urrgh!' scathed Freddie.

There was no way in the world Max would leave for the Cat and the Moon that night; it was all Luciana could do to get him away from his daughter to bathe and change into some of Rory's clothes. He was in far worse case than the children, who were washed and into bed, making the most of being treated to extra apple cake and strawberries. Except for Catalina.

The child was so silent. If she had cried it would have been so much better. But her face closed down, as locked and as hard as any adult's, and she looked out of stony eyes on a world she would not trust again in a very long while.

Max did his best, but she would not let him near her. She went quietly with Nurse, who soothed and wrapped her swollen ankle, and just as quietly to bed. When Max went in to see her she did not respond. Not even to turn away which at least would have meant a healthy rage.

Max eventually came away at Luciana's insistence. 'She thinks I let it happen.'

And Luciana found the strength he needed. '*You* let nothing happen.' But I did. She knew if she had been more careful, Max would not have lost his daughter now.

She took a long time over bathing herself clean of the mire, bathing herself warm, though she wondered if anything could wash away the chill of guilt and misery. It seemed to have soaked right into her bones. She loved him and, in the worst imaginable way, she had failed him.

But when she joined him in the dining-room an hour later she forgot her feelings. Max was shattered. There was so much more to this than what had happened today. Quietly Luciana sat and used the only weapon she had against this intense remoteness; his manners were too good for him to ignore her questioning.

'Please eat, Max; you can't have had anything all day.'

'It's not food I need!' Then, 'I'm sorry, Luciana.' His anger was so close to slipping his control she could have cried.

She did not like what she learned about herself as she watched Max suffering now. She had leaned on him like a child; he had seemed as omnipotent to her as he had to

Catalina. He was so strong, too strong, and she had clung to the relief it gave her and never thought he was simply a man. More resilient than any she had ever known, so much more powerful, but just a man.

She had spent her life with heroes. Papa, Marquess Charles, Philip, Rory, whom she had looked up to and believed in and unquestioningly adored. Who had never let her down until they died and left her.

And when they died, their faults, all those maddening human habits, died with them and they had ceased in her memory to be the men they really were at all. To judge a living man against such idols was the instinct of a fool. Max was real and here, and if she was ever to deserve the love he offered so generously, she must be the woman she should have been long ago and not a worshipping child.

Woman enough not to hide behind her own instinct for avoidance. 'What happened to the men who took the children?'

Max sensed the effort it cost her to talk of it. He had been avoiding it too, treating her like a baby. He just wanted her to forget—as if any mother could forget such wickedness against her child!

'Blackmore came from Parva while you were dressing—they never made it out of the mire, they would have been seen if they had. They got what they deserved, Luciana.' And so would the man who had hired them when Max got near him. There was no doubt at all now. 'One of the horses got safely back to Graveney.'

'So it was Lysander.'

Max took one look at her face and took control.

'Leave Standish to me. You don't go near him, do you understand me, Luciana!'

Luciana had come a long way these past few minutes watching him. 'Yes. Yes, I promise I won't.'

It went so much deeper than that he needed to see she trusted him. It went to the heart of how she must feel about him if ever their love was to survive.

She had made gods of the Standish men and they had made a spoilt little goddess out of her. They had indulged her, allowed her anything, taken laughing pride in all her wilfulness. They would have done anything in the world for her and had let her know it. Her sons were just like their father; she could no more do wrong in their eyes than she could leap the moon.

Luciana looked at Max and knew she must change for him. For both their sakes she had to learn—as she had learned about him—that she was mortal. That he was right and this time she must obey him.

He always had been able to read her mind. And miraculously he was laughing at it.

'Have a care, Luciana, you will have me think you biddable!'

The newly mortal Luciana knew to mock herself. 'You don't think meekness sits well on me?'

'If ever I did I would know I had lost my reason! I will never understand how you can look so like an angel!' And then his whole mood changed.

Luciana felt the softness of his eyes pierce through her even before he rose from Rory's old place at the table head and came to her, taking her chin in his hand to lift her face to his, as if ever she could have looked away. The kiss was so gentle it hurt.

'Yes, I can! You are the most perfect woman I have

ever known. You are so. . .' He laughed, his words swept away in a flood of tenderness. 'I love you utterly, Luciana. Will you marry me?'

He meant it. He meant it so much, he would never understand her hesitation.

Luciana wanted it so desperately she had no words to say. Yet she felt so worthless after what she had cost him today. So she found the only answer she could give him. 'Why?'

Max was so stunned he could not believe she said it.

'I *love* you! I love you so much I nearly walked away!'

'I. . . I don't understand.'

And he kissed away her bewilderment. 'No, of course you don't, and if I ever were to tell you'd despise me.'

'*No!*'

'Oh, yes you would, my sweetest angel. Don't you see? From the first second I looked at you and you looked at me we *belonged*. But that was an enchantment, Luciana; it made us friends. It hasn't changed the fact that we are strangers.'

'Max, I just don't—'

'Know what I mean? How can you, my perfect girl, when you don't really know me at all?'

'It doesn't matter!' She had a sudden terror that she could lose him. But, of course, she couldn't. They could never break free of each other. Even if they wanted to.

There was so much pain in his eyes when he whispered, 'No, it doesn't matter. We have no choice at all. I may be the worst thing ever to happen to you, but it's too late now. I can't live, not *live*, without you, and you can't live without me, but we may spend the rest of our lives wishing to God that we could!'

'*Never*!' He was right—they were strangers, but...'I can't *breathe* without you!' She never could.

'Then marry me, Luciana. It's far too late to matter what I've done!'

Done? What had he ever done, but tried his best? Whatever crime he believed he had committed, he had not meant any living person harm.

'*I don't care*!' Suddenly she felt so very calm. 'I just don't care, whatever you have been or thought or done!'

It was almost enough to make him believe he could be good for her. Max rested his brow against hers and began to build the future. There was so much stacked against them if only she would see it. He took a deep, hurt breath and laid the strongest foundation they had.

'Rory wanted this.'

Luciana helped him. 'I know.'

'For Carlo and Freddie—I think I could be good for them, Luciana.'

'Yes...you *are* and I hope I—'

'Catalina needs a mother.'

It was a very strange thing to be in each other's arms, physically shaking with love, and telling each other it was a marriage of convenience...it being true.

Luciana wrenched her mind from the battle ahead of her, getting Max to trust that she could never be disappointed in him. Locking away the honesty that knew, if it was something bad enough, maybe she could. It was almost frightening to be so committed to a man she did not know.

Until he bent his head, just the softest penetration of a kiss, and she knew she would walk the world across shattered glass to keep him—to know and be known by him, to turn their friendship into a marriage that could survive.

Luciana curled her arms about his neck and swore that if she had ever deserved all she had taken so unquestioningly from Philip and from Rory, she would be the woman they had believed her to be, and she would return it, a thousandfold, to this man who was her future now.

'People marry with so much less to hope for than we have, Luciana.'

Some people married without any hope at all.

CHAPTER SEVEN

LONG after Max had left her to return to Catalina's
bedside, Luciana remained restless. Thinking. Trapped
by her own doubts and, for the first time ever, by
Somerton. She needed so much to be free from the
shades of her past, yet the hardest thing she would ever
have to do was make this decision alone.

There still was a decision to be made, for all she knew
it to be true what Max had said, they could never really
live without each other. Not *live*. Breathe in and out, go
on, take pleasure and pride in their children, but live—
no. She would never know the meaning of living again if
she changed her mind about marrying Max Rivington.

Almost she wanted to, though why she did she didn't
know, except that suddenly her whole life had changed
and it had once been so easy. Pain filled, defiant, but
something she was familiar with, something she understood. She had been glad of those years of emotional
extinction, beyond mere numbness; they had been
almost peaceful, so long as she never allowed herself to
think of what should have been.

Now she would never be at peace again, not if she
turned her back on this marriage. Her only chance of
being happy lay in accepting Max and working till she
bled to make it right, for both of them.

It was not as if she was the only one taking a step into
the dark. No, not dark—she could never feel that about
a future with Max Rivington—but the unknown it

certainly was. Things had been so simple, just herself and the boys and her efforts to give them the love and the confidence they needed. Now—how in the world were the boys going to take a change so absolute? Freddie might be pleased, but Carlo. . .

Carlo was her protector, her little marquess, looking after her for his father and his Uncle Rory. How he would feel, once over the novelty of Max Rivington's arrival, she was not sure, other than that he would not like his demotion. He would hate the advent of a new authority, caring for his mother as he believed he alone should care. Carlo was going to be a problem.

And Catalina? Lord, but if ever she and Max had tried to strew their path with obstacles they could not have done better than to come to each other each the parent of such independent children.

Catalina had a mind of her own and at the moment it was hurt and frightened. How would Catalina take to yet another change forced on her already bewildering existence? How would she take to staying at Somerton?

And that was when it hit her—Somerton! It struck Luciana so physically she could not bear the confinement of bricks and stone a second longer. She needed air and cold and privacy to cool her raging heart. Out in the real world the storm had cleared and the night was fresh and shining.

Luciana fled down the terrace steps and across the Elizabethan garden, running for the haven of the deer park where moonlit shadows moved like whispers as the sleek herd recognised her and settled again, as used to her as she was used to Somerton. And she was going to have to leave it!

She, Carlo, Freddie, they all were. How could they

stay when this was not Max's home? He had his own,
the estate he had mentioned, so far away Luciana barely
knew where Yorkshire was. She could not leave here!

But live where she had lived with Philip, the wife of
another man? She could not do that either.

Luciana found shelter from the moonlight on a
tumbled bench beneath a chestnut tree and closed her
eyes against her thoughts. Her guilt. It was guilt. It
shouldn't be; she knew Philip would never have asked it
of her, would have died all over again to prevent her
from feeling one atom of what she was feeling now, but
it could not be reasoned away. This afternoon she really
had believed she would lose her boys because she had
betrayed her husband by loving Max Rivington.

It was no good in the world to remember, and truly
accept now, that her husband was dead. That his own
brother, who loved him, had sent this man here in the
hope that she would marry. No good to know Rory had
seen Somerton not just as Carlo and Freddie's home but
hers—it was, it always had been. It was all her children
knew, it was their heritage. She could no more take
them away from here than she could be wife to Max if
she stayed.

For the second time she never heard him coming,
until his shadow fell across the moonlight and she heard
the seriousness behind his gentle teasing.

'You looked like a ghost, flitting across the park, all
white and fragile.'

Then he stopped. She looked in such pain he had to
reach out to help her, but for the first time he realised he
could not. He, of all people, could not, yet he had done
nothing to hurt her that he knew of, nothing to make her
feel this way.

Except tell her that he loved her and ask her to be his wife.

God knew he had had doubts as he left her to check on Catalina. So punishing were those doubts he had come right back down from the nursery again, needing to see Luciana, needing to know she was as calm, as accepting as when he left her. She was so far from calm Max took her chin in his hand and lifted her face, so pale and lonely in the moonlight.

'Have I done this to you, Luciana?'

She did not pretend she didn't understand him. 'No.' Then she turned her face from his touch, so miserable at hurting him. 'Somerton.'

He had not even thought about it! No more than she had—there had been no time. Everything had moved so fast; too fast. Dear God, he should have thought about it! She could never live with him here. No more could he ever ask her to leave.

Max could not believe this was happening to him. No—to them. She was as stunned with misery as he was. Worse for her—God in Heaven, how much worse for her! She was thinking about Philip so tangibly, Philip might as well have been there.

The worst was, Max did not know what Philip would say if he could be. Better than even Luciana, Max knew how possessively Philip had loved her, so jealously his own brother had had to fight every second he was in his company to hide the fact he loved her, too. Philip had never doubted Luciana, but never had it once occurred to him that one day, in dying, he must let her go, and she might give her love to someone else.

She had not done that yet. She had poured out her loneliness, her relief, her desperate need for friendship, with all the hope of the brave woman she was, and believed it to be affection. It would need to grow a great deal more at peace with itself to survive.

Philip was the one who still had the love of the real Luciana, the serene, happy-natured girl Max so passionately believed in. The hardest battle he would ever fight was the moment she began to know it.

She mattered to him so much he almost did not fight it. Almost it would be the greater act of love to leave her. At least, to withdraw into the frustration of being only her friend. But he did not. Somehow, like a guiding light inextinguishable inside him, he believed he could turn the love they had now into the love she really needed. So he said, so very gently, 'I'd never ask you to leave, Luciana. Never! I came to do well by you and the boys, I would never want you to leave Somerton.'

He was standing over her so closely Luciana could barely breathe for needing him. It frightened her how imperative it was she reach out to him, to touch him and be held by him. It took all the strength she had not to fling herself into his arms as she whispered, 'But... Max, I don't know how to stay!'

She had so much not dared to look at him she felt rather than saw him turn away. He understood so well. She hated herself for ever speaking.

Most of all when he showed exactly how well he knew her, this stranger of hers. 'Philip. I do understand, Luciana, believe me, I understand it! The hardest part of all is I understand so well I know I cannot help you. I can't choose for you. I can't decide.'

He couldn't — and yet he just had. If for one second he had failed to understand, failed in the compassion she had grown to believe was the very heart of him, he might have lost her. But not now.

'Max, if you think *you* can bear it. . .to be here. . .in Philip's house.'

He lied to her for the very first time then. 'I can bear it.' For you I can bear anything!

But he could not say it. To know how much he loved her was the last thing she needed now. Luciana needed only reassurance. To be allowed to believe in this myth they had conjured into reality between them, that this was a marriage of convenience alone.

Luciana almost knew him well enough to disbelieve him. Enough to try to explain. 'It isn't just selfishness on my part to say I must stay.' God knows, I don't know if I can bear it either! She thought. 'It's what I must do for Carlo and for Freddie. They've had so much disorder in their lives and so has Catalina. I would face any. . . anything just to keep them in the security of what they know.'

Max heard her fighting not to say out loud how powerfully her guilt was growing and suddenly he saw a way. The last way in the world he ever wanted, but he was going to make it work.

'Luciana, don't think about it any more. It isn't so insoluble a problem.'

'It isn't?' Could there ever be an answer to loving Max and feeling so much that it cheated Philip?

Max could not help touching her then, because he had just accepted he might never touch her again. At the least, not for a very long time.

'Sweetheart, I didn't come to change your life, to make you so unhappy and uncomfortable!' He felt her head shake in denial beneath his hand so tenderly stroking her golden hair. 'Listen to me—and trust me. At least always do that, Luciana!'

'I do!' Luciana could hardly bear this touching of his skin against hers, so comforting, so desperately needed.

And he was denying it! 'Angel, I have to marry you. God knows, after today you have to marry me! We have to keep your children safe. Standish attempted something so desperate, so reckless of Carlo and Freddie's safety—any man who can risk trusting scum like that is stupid enough to risk again. As your husband I can better protect you, in law as well as in fact. He knows it. I don't know what Lysander thinks he can achieve, other than to get his hands on the Standish fortune by ousting me as guardian and trustee. He has to learn once and for all that that will never happen. No, angel, *don't*!'

He had felt the fear. 'The boys are safe now, we're all safe here at Somerton, Catalina will come to love it, too. I believe that. Luciana, we need all we can do for one another and for them. We need to live here, husband and wife, and make them happy. But you don't have to accept any more of me than that. I don't ask any more than to have you here beside me, helping me be a father to my child. Friends—I ask nothing more, Luciana!'

Luciana was so stunned by what he was saying she almost did not understand him. And when she did she could not take it in. Because this man, who wanted her so burningly she could feel it in his barest touch, was saying that he would never touch her again. If she could not live as his wife in her husband's house. . .

But Max would be her husband now.

It was her moment of finally growing into the Luciana she should be.

'No, Max.' And she turned her face into his tortured

skin, just needing the scent of it to keep her sane. To fight his madness of generosity. 'No. If we are to marry, then. . .it must be a marriage.'

This was so difficult. *So* hard to speak of feelings she had only ever known were felt, not decided upon so cold-bloodedly, part of a contract, as she seemed to be signing her name to now. 'You came to me, to help me and look after me, and all for Rory's sake. No, Max, in the beginning, at least, it was so! You offer marriage to me, no thought that maybe you could do better —'

'For the love of heaven, Luciana!'

'No.' She caught his hand to her heart without any hesitation. 'I believe you. . .you care for me! How could I ever doubt you when you would do this? Max, I can't ask you to live as you have offered! Do I owe you nothing —'

'*Owe me*!' And Luciana knew instantly that she had angered him so deeply she might have lost her friend. He was barely in control of it.

Luciana fought to save it. 'No — I don't mean it that way! Dear God, you cannot ever believe I would think such things of you that you would demand a dutiful little wife just because you were kind to me! But you have a right to expect it. You *do*! Is this marriage to be only for my sake? Don't you think anything of your future?' She meant as Marquess of Rivenal. He needed heirs.

Of course he did. But he was lying to her again, because to make her mother to his children was the last thing on his mind when he looked at her and wanted her so badly.

'Yes. But the future is the future, Luciana, as well think of such things when we are used to one another. It need not be now.'

No, it need not. And Luciana, her whole adult life given already to motherhood, even knew it might lead them to disaster. God knew they had so much to do to come to know each other, to ease the children they already had into a new family. Another child. . .she had never once let herself think about it since Philip died. It had never been going to happen to her. If she married Max, it could. Maybe it shouldn't happen now. Not too soon. Yet Luciana knew if she was ever to leave her old love, her old life, behind her she must give herself completely to the new from the very start.

She said it so very simply. 'If you don't want me, I would understand.'

The most miraculous moment of her life was when Max just started laughing. He was laughing so much she could never have begun to make him stop. Luciana just watched him, as eventually he sobered and looked at her with such derision she blushed so hotly it was visible even in the moonlight.

'I should hope so, Luciana!' Then he came to her, half lifted her into his arms. 'If I thought even for a moment you believed one word you said! Luciana, this—*this* is the most precious thing we have!'

This instant, unquestioning melding of his body into hers, the rightness of it as separation dissolved in his kiss. When he held her like this, nothing in the whole world mattered. This absolute need to be part of each other was the most honest, the most hopeful thing they had. It was the binding force that would keep them together in the face of anything. No fear existed at all. Not when he held her, laughing, in a moment so rich with promise as this.

He had taken all doubt away. She could not leave

Somerton, she could never let him go. If there was to be a battle with her past—her conscience—then she would face it. She would not be alone.

It was late into the morning when the time chose itself quite naturally for telling Carlo and Freddie what was happening.

The boys had left Catalina in the nursery, still sleeping off her fear and injury, and come running down to find their mother and Lord Rivington in the gardens. Freddie was still clutching the larger part of his breakfast—cold beef wedged between indecent hunks of toast—and Cass and Polly came bouncing in his wake trying to snatch it from his flailing hand. Carlo was trying to control them. They were back on form so quickly, Luciana's spirits soared. Their ordeal of yesterday might never have happened. They were boiling over with noise and silliness and his lordship was the major reason why.

Freddie pelted right at Max and hugged him. 'You and Mamma are really brave!' He punctuated this accolade with a bite of toast and a 'Get *down*, Cassie!'

Carlo was the steadier of the two, the graver, the more grown-up, but his eyes were vivid with relief and admiration. The nearest to hero-worship the self-sufficient Marquess of Standish would ever come. Luciana, after a long healing night of sleep so filled with Max he might already have been lying there beside her, could only thank God for making her task so easy.

'Aren't we! Indeed his lordship is even braver than you suppose. . .'

'Oh?'

'He's going to marry me. Now what do you think about that?'

Her heart was shaking as their assimiliating silence stretched towards a whole minute, she would even have given her eyes for an 'urrgh' from Freddie. But that was not what happened.

'I'm very glad, sir.' It was Carlo, holding out his hand to Max for all the world as if he were father of the bride just consenting to the marriage. As, in his way, he was.

'Thank you.' Max took his hand with simple courtesy and added, 'So am I.'

Carlo withdrew then, beginning to think about it all, but still quite liking the idea. Lord Rivington was something exciting and something safe and he had never seen his mother really happy. Except that once, when Papa came home. Carlo didn't see that this had anything to do with Papa. . .not right now he didn't, anyway. Carlo expanded his role as head of the family and dealt a reeling blow to Freddie's ears.

'Haven't you any graces, you little runt, say something!'

Freddie threw his breakfast at him.

'*Urrgh*!' raged Carlo.

Freddie smirked and turned to Max. 'Aren't you going to tell him it's a horrid noise?'

Freddie had completely accepted Lord Rivington's authority from the start. He liked him so much he wanted to hug him again, but was so sticky there was little chance it would be allowed. Besides, he was four now and four year olds don't hug their fathers. It struck Freddie what he was thinking. 'Are you my father *now*?'

Luciana saw the memory of Freddie's first greeting sting across Max's face so painfully that she reached for

Freddie to draw him closer; anything not to reach out
for Max. She had no fears that Max would not say the
right thing. He had always got things right with her
children.

He didn't fail her. 'It seems I am—and you're still a
disgusting specimen!'

'But you do *want* to be?' Freddie remembered Max's
first words to him with astonishing accuracy.

Max understood his role as father to these boys so
well it agonised Luciana that he could not manage with
his daughter. 'Oh, I think I might. If you stop shedding
bits of—what *is* that, Freddie?—all over your poor
mamma!'

Freddie did hug him then, shedding bits of beef all
over Max instead, and Carlo just could not stand to be
out of it any longer. He was not sure about this father
business—he had a father, he remembered him—but he
envied Freddie's certainty about it. Luciana was not at
all surprised when Carlo came up and slipped his arm
about her shoulder, pretending he was merely propping
himself, not cuddling her.

She smiled at him, teasing away his act of being too
big for this, and kissed him as he wanted her to do. Carlo
threw away all inhibition, flung his arms about her neck
and kissed her, too. It was nice to feel everything was so
safe, and it wasn't really fun feeling *so* responsible for
her all by himself. . .

Max would do.

Plainly Cass and Polly, who now jumped all over him,
thought so, too. So now there was only Catalina.

Luciana allowed Max time alone to try to get his child to
speak to him. She left him telling Catalina she must do

as Nurse told her and get out of bed to eat her breakfast.
Somehow he had the courage not to smother her.
Somehow he understood that quiet discipline would cut
through her terrible disillusionment and bring her back
to him.

Luciana hurried from the nursery to Liam's room—
rather, the very best of the guest rooms at Somerton
where Liam had been taken the better to be quiet and
recover from his injury. He had recovered. Even to the
point of trying to sit up and being ordered very smartly
to lie down again.

Luciana had had such a scare she was furious with
him. 'Liam, I thought you were killed!'

'Aye.' Liam felt so bad about what had happened he
did not know how to begin to say that he was sorry. So
he clung to the old, teasing ways of her childhood. 'Bit
me tongue, so I did, when they belaboured the lights
right out o'me! But Mary and Joseph, *contessa*, only you
would have thought—'

'And only you would have lain there like a corpse a
whole month buried! Never do that to me again!'

Liam looked so stricken then, because he understood
that she was not blaming him. It had never entered her
head at all. She only cared that he was better.

'Oh, *contessa*—I'm sorry!'

'You're an idiot, is what you are, Liam Kennedy!'
Strange, Luciana thought, how she was always just a
little bit Irish still with Liam, just a little the last
Fitzgerald of Montelfalco. She spoke with him in a way
she had almost forgotten she ever had. Only with Liam
did she remember herself as that little foreign orphan.
Poor Catalina! She hoped Max was getting through to
her. Meanwhile it was time to relieve Liam of his

lifelong responsibility. 'Liam, I'm going to marry Lord Rivington.'

Liam had been expecting he was about to let it go; he couldn't pass the protection of her to a better man. 'Thought you might find the sense you were born with, *contessina mia*! He's—ah, he's not so bad as Englishmen go!' Colonel Max was about the best that men ever came. 'Saved me life, so he did, and your old Da would have liked him.'

Luciana knew Liam so very well. He was the one constant in her life and much of her sense of stability was owed to him.

'You're not so bad as mad Irishmen go!' Then she held the hand he gave her very tightly. 'Go to sleep, get well for me in time for my wedding!'

'Oh, that's it, is it, haul a sick man from his bed so soon!'

Yes, it would be soon. Luciana and Max had not discussed it but she knew it must be now. There was no reason in the world to wait, unless he had failed with Catalina.

Luciana went back to the nursery filled with hope but prepared for the need for patience. There she found Max with Catalina up and dressed and handing him a little wooden pony. The first present Carlo had given her, commandeered from Freddie.

'*Pony*,' repeated Max, plainly having repeated it several times before yet optimistic just to have her responding to something. Not him, but a lump of wood was better than nothing. And so was Luciana.

Catalina turned as Luciana entered and seemed for a moment stranded in her nervousness, close to Max yet in a desert of her own making. Her eyes were huge and her face pinched with the pain of her swollen ankle, but she was making the best of things in the way she had long ago learned to do. . .deal with each new thing as it came and shut every other thing ruthlessly out of her mind. Catalina shut out Max and came to Luciana.

'Penny?' she tried out.

Luciana bent and inspected the pony as curiously as if she had not seen it a thousand times before. 'Pony, sweetheart. Liam made it for Freddie, he's very skilled, isn't he?'

Catalina had no idea what skilled meant but she knew gentleness when she felt it. She came so close to Luciana she almost touched and Luciana knew what to do. She picked her up without hesitation and stood up with her, carrying her back to Max. 'Papa wants to tell you something. . .something fun for all of us, angel, I think you will like it very much.'

She saw Max's eyes as she so easily used his pet name for Catalina. A little jealous, but pleased. It was why he was marrying her, after all. This was what Catalina needed.

Max had never seen Catalina with her own mother. It racked him through with guilt to see now, right in front of him, all that his selfishness had cost his child. He would never thank God enough for this chance to give something back to her. He rose to his feet from where he had been kneeling and took Luciana very gently into his arms. Catalina clung closer to Luciana, but Max fought off the pain and explained in Spanish so simple even Luciana followed it.

'You like to be here, don't you, angel? You like Carlo and Freddie and the puppies and Luciana.' She knew who he meant and tucked her head into Luciana's neck, listening very carefully. 'I thought it would be fun for you to live here, too. For both of us. Luciana is going to marry me, do you understand, Catalina? Yes? Good girl! You're going to be very happy, I promise it!' If the child even knew what happiness felt like! 'Luciana would like it so very much if you would let her be your mother now.'

It was the most dangerous moment. No-one had ever been able to tell him if Catalina had even known her mother, let alone remembered her. It had been such hell up in those high Galician mountains when the French raided though the villages in the wake of the Corunna retreat, punishing the Spanish for their humanity towards the exhausted British soldiers.

Antolina had saved his life on that mountain pass where he had been close to freezing to death from the injuries he sustained, part of the cavalry rearguard fighting off their French pursuers. He had been grateful to her, he had liked her; she had liked him and in a world so uncertain they had grabbed what life was left to them and were lovers.

They had only two months. Antolina conceived his child; he married her. What happened when he left to walk his lone way back to the stronghold of the British army at Lisbon he never knew. He meant to go back to her. He could at least tell himself that, he had meant to go back.

But it was too late from the moment he left her. . . convincing both of them that it was his duty. . .knowing in his heart the war could do without him and he should have stayed where he was truly needed. In one wild, vicious night Antolina and her whole village were annihilated. No-one could tell him exactly when. He only knew that a passing priest had heard a child crying from beneath its mother's body, had rescued her and taken her to the safety of the San Bernarda convent. How old Catalina had been...what her mother had meant to her he could never know.

Maybe Catalina would never know either. She watched him, taking in what he was telling her and sensing some tension in him so fierce, it set her shaking. Luciana felt it and reached out to Max's face, softly running her finger down his scar, showing him she needed calm from him. Getting it. Catalina sensed it and relaxed.

She thought for a very long time about what her father had just told her. Then she pressed her cheek against Luciana's and smiled.

Luciana had never seen a man cry, or even come close to it. Max was very close and the greater part of it was guilt and envy. His daughter had accepted her new mother. It was her father left resolutely outside.

But it did not last, for Catalina was living each day as it came as any other child. Besides, she could not stay long in the doldrums in the company of Carlo and Freddie.

Luciana had taken them all next morning to see Lady Deverham. Max, too. She needed to know that her old friend supported her, was happy at what she planned to do.

Lady Deverham was delighted but Luciana sensed in her voice a very real reservation. It couldn't be about Max; the Dowanger had taken one summing look at him and liked him. No question at all. She had nodded her head as if he was only as she had expected and pronounced, 'You'll do!'

Max had been delighted with her. 'You speak your mind, ma'am, no wonder you are so valued a friend of Luciana's!' So much so, he had no need for the formality of calling Luciana Lady Philip. He hoped to God he never had to do it again. The rage of jealousy he felt every time he spoke those words appalled him.

'I do, my lord—and now must speak it again. Luciana, child, I could not be happier, *truly* I could not, I have never seen the boys so. . .so *well* with the world and as for little Catalina—what a lovely name that is!—she is fond of you, Luciana. I can see that.' She could see enough to know it was her father the child would not attend to. Difficult, very difficult for Luciana, but that was not Lady Deverham's worry now. 'But to wed so soon after Rory's death—oh, I know he wanted it, you don't have to tell me, I very much believe he planned this! He loved you so much, I think you must know that now. Rory would not have cared a straw for gossip but you, my dear, you must. Not four months since Toulouse, not even six months in mourning for the head of the Standish. . .to marry so soon, it will make acceptance so difficult for you both.'

Acceptance. Luciana looked at Max then and wondered. Acceptance by whom? His family? He had made not the smallest move to take her to Rivenal. He had not even told his father of his plans. Max owed Lord Rivenal nothing. As for everyone else—these people who would gossip so unkindly—where had they been when Luciana needed companionship and support, a little more than ineffectual pity?

'I do understand, ma'am, truly I do, and I'm not being tiresome just for the sake of it, so please don't look at me like that! It is just that—well, the people who matter to me are contented. You and the children and Liam. The servants are happy for us, the village, too. . .'

No doubt of that at all as they collected Max from his socially acceptable exile at the Cat and the Moon that morning and half of Somerton Parva just happened to be on the forecourt to inspect him.

The village had only ever wanted to see her happy — as much for Philip's sake as her own and the children's. He had been greatly loved, simply because he had been so loving. He had been a joyous personality and had left her a legacy of good-will and affection she cherished.

'There is no other world, not for me, not really. The friends I do visit may be a little stiff with me. . .'

It was Max who concluded so very drily, 'Oh, never with the Countess of Rivington, Luciana!'

A whole lifetime of contempt and disillusion went into that condemnation; Lord Rivenal was one of the richest men in England, for all the good it had ever done his only child. Lady Deverham heard it and knew it was time to change the subject.

'I was a fool to mention it, forgive me!' She kissed Luciana's cheek. 'Now, to more important matters. You would marry by the end of the week you say and yet — Lord at his most merciful, Luciana, however in the world will you tidy up Carlo and Freddie!'

It was managed, although Freddie was decanted from the Somerton landau at St Dunstan's that last August morning with just the suspicion of dust upon his knees. He was not in the slightest pleased to be in velvet coat and satin breeches, but Carlo had taken one look at Catalina, so graceful in her fresh new muslin and mantilla Luciana had made from a white lace veil, and

decided to make the most of looking a match for her, all
elegance and very much the Marquess of Standish.
Carlo blushed hotly as he helped Catalina down from
the carriage, earning a gusty sigh from the host of
spectators, but that was the only mistake he made.

Luciana watched them as they waited in the sunlight
for her to descend to Max and thought, Nobody ever
tells you that you can love your children so much it
hurts. She was luckier than anyone she ever knew, she
not only loved them, she liked them. All three of them.

She had been shaking with the enormity of what she
was about to do but Carlo, Freddie and Catalina had
made it right for her. Everything was right. She and Max
had as much chance as anybody. The sun was soft with
the marriage of summer to the birth of autumn, the tiles
of St Dunstan's twisted old tower shone like silver
fishscales and the bells rang out their famously tuneless
peel. Everyone was happy. . .so she was too.

Luciana had looked at herself in her bedroom glass
that morning and known, This is the last time I shall
ever come in here. She had turned from her own
immaculate reflection to look on this room of hers and
Philip's. She might enter it again one day, when she felt
less guilty. When she felt more at peace with what she
had chosen to do. For now, this truly was the end of the
life she had known with him. All they had ever shared.
Such children really—barely seventeen and only just
nineteen. It was frightening, looking back, how much
confidence they'd had. Frightening, but it made her so
proud.

She had one so precious legacy from her happiness,
her complete lack of doubt about her marriage to Philip;
it had left her the courage to fight for such certainty

again. She had been so lost in this room over the last four years, unable to run and desert it and yet made so lonely by its emptiness. Now she smiled and leaving it did not hurt her any more. Philip had been as good a husband as that.

She owed it to all he had ever given her to be the best wife she could be to Max.

She had looked at herself again and barely remembered the bride she had been when Aunt Anne and Uncle Charles had come and made presents to her of the Standish diamonds. She wore none of them now, only the simple collar of pearls given to the Fitzgerald of Montefalco by the Medici of Florence. No girlish confection of golden lace and honey this time, only her simplest white silk and her veil of lace. Her widow's veil. She would not wear it again once she was Countess of Rivington.

Married to this man watching her so unreadably now. Max looked—more wonderful than she had ever imagined him! For as he came forward and took her hand to help her from the carriage she saw he had finally given in to the boys' insistence that he be married in his regimentals. Against his sun-gold skin the dramatic red heightened the gold of his eyes and somehow his scarring was diminished. He had such authority, seemed so at ease, was so much as he had used to be, she smiled.

He understood it. 'I had to—you heard them, Luciana! There would have been just cause indeed why I could not marry you if I turned out in a plain blue coat and breeches! We would never hear the end of it!'

Luciana said what mattered to him most. 'Catalina loves it too, it doesn't frighten her, having her Papa a soldier. She's so very proud of you!'

As Catalina seemed to be; she came limping over, evidence of former jealousy in her haste. She wanted this exciting being's attention, too. Max caught her up into his arms before she could be nervous again and a murmur went round the villagers now sitting, standing, and jostling about the churchyard walls.

Luciana turned and smiled at them. He was doing so well. They wished not just herself but Max good fortune. It mattered. If he was to run Somerton beside her until Carlo came of age it mattered terribly.

She came so close to tears in that moment she was glad for the Rector, Josiah Lawton, coming forward to greet her at last. She nodded and smiled to him, then looked up at Max, just to see if he was ready—and the whole world stood still.

It was going to be easy, after all—she really believed it now. The most natural thing in the world to walk beside him into the dusty coolness of St Dunstan's and speak those vows she never thought to speak again. And mean them.

So it was quietly, so very simply, Luciana and Max Rivington were married, in the age-old silence scented with candles and end of summer roses. Luciana closed her eyes for a moment, listening intently to what it was this man was promising. Believing him. If she opened them she would see the memorial she had set in the wall for Rory, who had given her all this hope.

'*I will not leave you comfortless: I will come to you.*'

If there was any time in her life she thanked God for everything he ever did for her, it was now as she opened her eyes again to her new husband's smile and felt his ring slip so finally onto her hand.

The most natural thing in the world. For both of them.

As it was to walk back into the sunlight to the cheering good wishes of the villagers, her hand still held by Max, lost in a dream that could not be broken. She was surrounded by all she had ever loved and yet the only thing in her world at this moment was her husband. His hand tightened on hers and she knew even more—she was the only thing in his.

They felt it absolutely as they greeted and thanked and laughed with everyone and held back Carlo when the blacksmith's boy rushed forward with a handful of pretty weeds hastily ripped up from the verge for Catalina. Lady Deverham was here, to witness their marriage and to take the children back to Deverham. Luciana had fought the idea at first, but knew it to be right now. And only fair, she and Max needed time alone together, for everyone's sake. The children seemed aware of it, quite contented to go because they knew they were coming back again. Even Catalina seemed at ease. She had found another easy victim in Lady Deverham's grandson Anthony.

So it was that Max and Luciana did what they had planned to do—they had asked for no fuss and no wedding breakfast, they were still in mourning, the village would understand. They simply slipped away and walked together back across the fields to Somerton, the village celebrations already an ebb and flow of sound in the distance. Jake Blackmore was playing a tin whistle very badly as they walked towards the glade where first Max had found her. Where they hesitated, lost in each other but, just for a moment, unsure.

Enough for Max to draw her into his arms and just hold her. Until he found the voice to whisper, 'Whatever you want, Luciana. Only what you want of me. Always!'

And somehow she found her own. 'I want only you.'

It was true. They were as separated from the world as that.

It was so quiet here. Luciana had always loved it, knowing no-one ever came here but herself and her children.

Max, too. It was his place now. So much so that just being with him healed the terrible desecration of what had happened to the children here. Luciana rested her head against the braiding of his coat and time stood still again. He could always do this for her.

She could always do it for him. Just as he shared her mind.

'Come.' And holding her close Max turned her away from the glade towards Somerton Rise. They needed—with all the calm of complete commitment—to be home.

So much were they caught up in this need to be alone together Max broke into a run and Luciana ran with him, half laughing as she caught up her skirts, at last—as she had never thought to be again—the wild Irish *contessa* of the Tuscan hills. The Luciana she really was. The deer lifted their heads but nothing else moved in the shimmering summer haze. Home for both of them, Somerton truly could be.

They reached the terrace, Max laughing as joyously as she was, bending to her feet where she had shed her shoes.

'Are you hurt, Luciana?'

'No.' Nothing could hurt her now, nor ever again. Not now Max was here. The most promising thing they had was that she said so. 'No, not now, Max, never with you!'

And for the first time her headlong faith raised no bad

memories in him. 'I'll keep you safe—until you know just how much I love you! I don't think you do. I don't believe you ever could!'

And Luciana kissed him to silence, needing him to see she would trust in anything he told her. Max caught her against him, almost into him, both shaking so much they could hardly stand.

It was right that Somerton was deserted, the servants at their own celebrations. It was right that it be empty of all presence now but his and hers. They went side by side up the stairs, the only focus for her his urgent breathing, the only reality for him the helplessness of hers. Max holding her hand, leading the way without hesitation to the wing not used since Marquess Charles had died. Luciana so much belonged to him it was as if she had already forgotten where she had existed since Philip died.

She shouldn't have thought of Philip!

Just as Max pushed open the door of their chamber, so new to her, so sweetly scented with lavender and roses, Luciana hesitated. It was impossible, it could not be happening—but she held back.

Max knew, of course. Closing the door behind them he stood in front of her, not quite touching, and only his eyes spoke now. I'll leave if you want me to, Luciana.

Luciana gazed into them, pleading for help, but he could not take this last step for her.

It terrified her that she couldn't. She felt so safe, so needed with Max. He was her husband now.

But not the only man she had ever known.

She had never thought there would be anyone but Philip. She knew only Philip. She barely knew herself, they had had so little time together, so in love, so

instinctive, so passionately young. She wanted more
than anything in the world that it could be like that now.
As it had been while she ran with Max across the deer
park, so sure of each other they had been laughing out
loud in their need.

She was not a child, she ached for him; she knew how
that aching could be assuaged. She wanted more than
anything in her life to be able to give herself now as she
had given herself then. But her past intruded and she
found she did not know how.

She might never have known if Max had not had the
strength to face it, understanding all that was inside her,
finding he could make himself accept it. She need not
take this step alone after all. He took it for her.

He knew by every instinct they had ever shared how
to bring her back into his arms and kiss the fear right out
of her. How to hold her until the shaking stopped and
they could breathe and think and she stirred against
him, crying just a little but needing him so very badly.

He knew to kiss her then as if she was the most
precious being in the world, and coax, with that teasing
breath of pleasure she so loved, until at last, she kissed
him too and began to search for what would please him
as profoundly as he pleased her now.

And suddenly she knew just how to touch him, just
what it was about his need for her that tore the breath
from his damaged throat as she moved against his hips;
just what it was that made him lift her into his arms,
because he had waited his whole life for this, as she had,
too.

Max lay with her, pushed her deep into their bed and
Luciana reached for him. The most natural thing in the
world. Most of all when she curled her legs about him,

knowing it must be now—it had to be now—and heard
her own voice so helplessly pleading.

Just his name. 'Max!'

Just hers. 'Luciana!' And he moved into her and
kissed her silent, held her absolutely still, just feeling,
and waiting, and healed beyond any healing she had
ever known.

'Oh God, my perfect Luciana!'

And he moved at last, so deep, so giving, Luciana lost
all thought, all self, all pain and cried out for him, over
and over until she lay sobbing like a child in his arms,
shocked, reborn, and irrevocably at peace.

Such peace! Such perfect, unbreakable connection.
Max held her so close, so she would know this was just
the beginning and if it killed him there would never be
an end. No life was long enough to share all he had to
give her. No words would ever be enough to tell what
she had done with just that crying of his name.

Max held her, soothed her, stroking away tears he
could barely understand because she could never find
the words to say what he had done for her.

She tried. 'I . . .'

He kissed her with such passionate tenderness to
silence. Stroked her hair where it had escaped from the
pins that held it—the first time ever he had seen it loose
like this, this exquisite river of gold. Drowning his face
in it, the words wrenched out of him. 'I would die for
you, Luciana!'

Overwhelming her. She buried her face into his
scarred neck and begged him,

'Never, Max. *Never*! Just *live*!'

* * *

Luciana opened her eyes a minute, maybe an hour, later and found that he held her, inside her still, as if they had never drawn apart. Luciana stole her hands into his hair, needing this chance to hold him, to watch over him as he would always watch over her. Wondering if he would ever know just what his loving her so unselfishly had meant. Needing him to open his eyes and see. . .

Would he always read her mind? She knew he had the moment she felt his smile curve against her breast and he began to kiss her as there had been no time for kissing before. They had needed each other too desperately.

So desperately he was laughing at it, his eyes blazing with discovery. 'Why did I never know it could be like this?'

Luciana simply shook her head, mute with shock and happiness and the final truth—it had never been like this with Philip.

He knew. Luciana felt a shudder of exultation run through him—through him into the deepest part of her. She had never realised it mattered. Mattered to Max that there be something no other man could ever have of her, that was his alone.

It was because it mattered so much this truth could not hurt her now. It would. She would grieve terribly for this final loss. And yet she had been given, at last, her truest self.

By Max, no-one else, and it mattered more than anything in the world that he believe it. 'I don't know either!'

'I didn't ask for that—dear God, I wasn't asking for that!' Meaning he was, though he hated himself. . .and he did not quite believe her.

Luciana took his injured face between her hands and tried to tell him, knowing it was beyond her, praying to God he would see.

'Trust *me*, Max—please trust me! You have given me. . .oh, I cannot say! It's too much—I don't know!'

'Don't try! Ssh, don't cry, not now. . .not now, Luciana!' And he drank her tears away in a kiss so elemental it was absolution.

This could *never* be wrong, never a betrayal of anyone. . .this trembling need to be so close not one breath of air could come between them as he kissed her again, just the most intimate of smiles against lips so bruised, so hungry for him he never would believe it. Or the beauty of her, so long imagined, as at last he unlaced her gown, twisting away from her restless hands, warning her. . .not yet, too much, too soon.

Luciana was stilled by just his laughter as he teased her urgency, her breathless need to see him, too. And when at last she did she could not believe any living thing so perfect. So beautiful and he did not know it! Luciana followed his eyes as they took in his ruined hand against skin so pure and white it seemed a desecration. She saw his pity for her and covered it with her own, holding it so tight against her breast the breath ripped out of him. She wanted even this shattered part of him. . .

He wanted every inch of her.

'I will never have enough of you, Luciana!'

'No. . .don't ever!' Never have enough. Never want an end to this loving that was given so instinctively. 'Just, please—oh, God, Max swear it you will never leave me!'

It was the most sacred vow either of them had ever

taken. Max knew it was true. Whatever else happened between them. Whatever went wrong.

'No, my perfect Luciana. I won't ever leave you.'

They both believed in that moment that he never could.

CHAPTER EIGHT

LUCIANA stirred in her husband's arms and realised something terrible. They had had three days alone together and it was not enough. The children would be home tomorrow and she did not want them here. Luciana buried her face against Max's shoulder, closing her eyes, her senses, to everything but him, unwilling even to face that she had thought a thing so shocking. Unforgivable.

Ever since she had met him Max had been like this, understanding without being told, feeling the tension in her and kissing away her instinct to hide. Luciana felt that smiling touch against her hair and looked up at him; saw the regret in his golden eyes and knew what he would say.

'We've had three days, Luciana, how could it ever be enough! You don't want Carlo and Freddie home, well, I don't want Catalina! Sweetheart, if we didn't think it then... God, knows, these days would not have been what I've believed them to be! How often must I say it before you hear me, I shall *never* have enough of you!'

'Yes, *yes* it's the same for me!'

'You're not only a mother now, you're my wife. I'm not just Catalina's father, we need time for ourselves. Whatever can be wrong in that? And you'll be as pleased as anything when Carlo and Freddie come spilling mud and puppies all over you, you know you will! You don't love them less just because you have enjoyed this first ever rest you've had from them. Don't make more problems than we have already—and stop trying to be perfect. I thought you had decided you were only mortal, after all!'

At which Luciana squirmed away, laughing yet burning with embarrassment. They had lived these three days so free from inhibition it was impossible she should feel awkward with him and yet she did. Most of all at being reminded she had found such release in his arms she had even told him that.

And Max was no help at all, bursting into that teasing laughter she loved so much and yet sometimes it filled her with rage. It made her feel so young and foolish, most of all when he seemed so at ease with feelings that overwhelmed her. Of course he was right but. . .

'Oh, dishonourable! How *can* you repeat—?'

'The things we say in bed, my lady?' Just the words ran her through with need. 'Because we mean them. . . however idiotic!'

'It was not idiotic! Oh, I hate you, Max! Truly I hate you! And don't laugh at me; it isn't the slightest bit amusing. *Don't*, Max! *Don't touch me like that*; *don't take my mind away*! It. . .no, *please*, Max, please listen! It's just that I am not used to. . . I'm used only to living with my children, I don't know anything else. I have never. . . I never had time to really live as a wife to Philip.'

It was the first time she had mentioned Philip since she married Max, since they had become lovers such as she and Philip had never been. Almost the first time she had thought about him because she had been so lost in Max, so passionately absorbed in her new self. She was terrified at the damage it could do.

Max hated it, she felt it just in the tension of his arm

about her waist, but he accepted she had had to say it.
He had accepted so much when he married her and he
was not such a fool as to imagine even the burning
intimacy they shared could banish Philip. Philip never
would be gone completely; he was there in every stone
of Somerton, every expression and gesture of his children. Here in this glade, too. . . .

Luciana felt her fingers tensing into Max's sun-
warmed shirt, frightened by his silence, knowing she had
made him angry.

It took everything Max had to pretend that she had
not. 'I know that. Just as I know you've lived only for
the things Philip gave you, with no thought for anything
else at all. Out of the schoolroom, straight into motherhood—but it was right for you. It has made you as happy
as ever you had hope to be but, Luciana, there always
was more to life, even yours, angel. Don't you think
Philip would say so, too?'

That was the most frightening thing of all. 'I don't
know. I don't know what he would have expected of
me.' For one destructive moment she thought, I didn't
really know Philip at all! Only the boy, not the man he
became. Which could never be true and yet, 'I don't
know how he would feel about this. . .us.'

It was the most dangerous risk Max had ever had to
take. 'Sweetheart, he can't feel anything.' And in the
shudder that ran through her he knew he had somehow
got it right. 'Don't ask me to say he would want me for
you, I can't know that. He never thought of anything but
growing old with you. How Philip would feel about us is
something we can't ever know—no, sweetheart, *never*!
But I do know he loved you so much he only ever
wanted what was best for you.'

'*You.*'

'I want to be—I will be if you don't fight me! Angel, your life would have been as altered if Philip had come home to you as it has been in marrying me. You and Carlo and Freddie would have had to get used to him too, and until you did, however much he knew you loved him, he would have felt just as much an interloper as I—'

'You're not!'

'I *am*. And when you and the boys try to settle to your old ways you'll see I'm right. I'll try and you'll try, but nobody said it was going to be easy. Don't make it harder by denying such natural feelings as—'

'Natural! Wishing my boys anywhere but here with me!'

Max caught her face between his hands so she would read every intention in his eyes. 'Yes, natural, Luciana, or we would have no hope for this marriage at all! Just now—damn it, I can't even *think*! I don't want to think, I don't want to do anything but lie with you, I don't want to be anywhere but so deep inside you—'

'Oh, God, Max!' How was it possible to feel like this—to feel flooded just by his words, to need anything so badly? If ever he let her go it would terrify her that she could be so governed by her senses.

But Max held her, kissing all awareness away, until she no longer knew where she was, or cared, except that she was with him and everything was still secure.

'Oh, God!' she whispered. He was changing every-thing about her, the whole balance of her existence, and she had no power to fight him at all.

* * *

The moon was high and clear, piercing the room with brightness as Luciana rose from the bed and drew a crumpled sheet about her, needing to be alone with emotions only she could ever feel. Hugging the still warm linen about her, she crossed to the windows, shivering in the dead-hour cold, and looked down on Somerton, so long loved and yet so altered.

Yet she knew as she gazed out over the silvered gardens, following the stable cat as he rippled ghost-like through the shadows of the herb walks, that it was she who was so completely changed, not one familiar thing would ever be the same.

She was used to that; she had coped with unalterable changes before and they had been terrible things, not like this. This was something clean and inspiring and good. He was.

Luciana looked back to where Max lay sleeping, so protective, so strong, even fathoms deep in sleep still so aware of her. Max stirred, Luciana saw that broken hand move against the bed as if it were her body and her whole being contracted in need. Every time she looked at him she wanted him more. She wanted him so much she could barely breathe.

Even as she made her way back to him, transfixed by the barest movement of those caressing fingers, Max woke, aware at last that she had left him, and Luciana stilled in awe at his frustration—until he turned and saw she was not so far away, and smiled to set her heart hurting, as he rose and came to her with such purpose Luciana almost fainted.

She was so dazed she caught her hands to his shoulders just to stand. Scars. There were so many scars. Even with her eyes closed against the intensity of wanting him Luciana could feel them, fragile tracings across his sun-gold skin. Old, old scars. Not Toulouse. Not even Talavera. Luciana opened her eyes, looked up to ask him. Then stopped, her hands falling away, because in the drugging darkness of his eyes she saw the warning—Don't ask; bad memories.

She knew it for sure when Max caught her hands behind her, as if to punish her for standing so alluring in the moonlight, and bent to kiss her throat as the sheet fell from her helpless fingers. Distracting her from all thought again, for the first time not for her sake but for his, shutting her out from all his secrets.

When Luciana started shaking then it was not just from the touch of his hands, nor from his kiss. It was from a distress so acute she could barely comprehend it. That he could shut her out still! After they had lain together, laughed, talked, loved together so instinctively she believed they would never hide from one another again.

She knew he sensed it, this sharp pain that invaded her because the impossible was happening and couldn't be. The pain of knowing that they still were strangers. It was the first time she ever wished he did not always know what she was thinking. Luciana caught her hands into his hair, desperate, because for the first time she knew, as he knelt and took her, with just the most teasing enticements of his tongue, that he was seeking not just what they had come to mean to one another, he was reaching for oblivion.

Luciana was angry and scared, but not for herself... not only for herself, not completely. She was angry that a man such as Max could ever have suffered so greatly that even his overwhelming sensuality could be driven

by the need to hide. Luciana felt her tears against her
cheeks and could not stop them. But no more could she
ever let him guess them. God knew, he felt bad
enough. . .he must never know she could see every fear
inside him too.

'Max!' Her fingers convulsed into his hair and her
head fell back. 'Oh, Max!' She loved him so much she
would give him anything. Even the mindlessness he was
seeking.

But her whole life at Somerton had taught her to love
herself, too. He must not get away with this. So even as
she gave herself so helplessly into the restless heat of his
mouth she knew. . .not like this. Not only like this! And
she knelt with him, her eyes blazing, almost in rage,
thinking, 'Don't ever think you control me! Us. You
may seek all sensation you please but I'm here too!'

'Oh, God, Luciana!'

He almost fought her then—fought as she took
control of both of them, but she was too much for any
man when she was like this. The sheer instinct of her
was too much. There was a wildness in her tonight and
he had to have it. Just when she needed it most, Luciana
sensed that what he wanted more than anything was her.

He could have anything he wanted. She loved him so
much she gave him everything but what he lusted after
most of all. That she say she loved him.

They woke the next morning so late Luciana's maid was
hovering outside the door wondering whether or not to
remind her mistress the boys were due back from
Deverham by noon. Not daring to go in, least of all
when she heard the new master's laughter.

Max was deriding Luciana's complaint of aching exhaustion, anything but sympathy in his tones.

'Now you know how it feels to be campaigning so relentlessly—'

'It is *not* amusing, Max! Oh. . .how shall I ever move at all! Go *away*! I—you *couldn't*!'

And he fell back against the pillows, cradling her against him, his eyes flaring at the truth of it. 'No, my angel, I couldn't!' He felt the heat of her blush against his neck and teased it with his fingers until she shook herself free in protest. Whereupon Max compounded all the crimes he had ever committed against her. 'Don't be shy of me, Luciana!'

'Oh. . .you. . .you. . .! Besides it isn't you, it. . .it's. . . I feel shy of myself!' And she sat up, shaking that hair he so loved down her back and thought, It's still all right. Somehow, in loving him with such abandon last night she had saved something. Her own self-esteem. Her belief in his helpless greed for her. She needed it so badly. Just for a moment last night she could have lost him. . .but she wasn't going to think of that again.

She had learned long ago never to think about the unbearable once it was gone. Instead she smiled at him with such light in her eyes, Max stilled where he was twining her hair about his fingers and said so very softly, 'You looked like a. . .like the most self-satisfied little cat, Luciana mia!'

And she found that despite his keeping secrets, she had lost all need to keep her own. She could tell him anything.

'No—satisfied by you.' She had won herself so much confidence. The confidence to lean forward and kiss him so gratefully. 'Thank you.'

They had grown just enough from what had nearly destroyed them last night for him to smile and just stay silent. Believing that she would say anything, do anything just at the moment to take away the pain she had sensed in him. The terrible self-loathing. She had done things last night. . .

That were not to be thought of if ever they were to get out of bed in time to greet the children. Max urgently distracted himself. 'Lord, but I'm starving!'

'Do I look as. . . ? Oh, Max, you wretch; I must look as if I am washed up from a shipwreck!'

'You look. . .*you*, my perfect Luciana! Now, in the name of all sanity, go to your maid and put some clothes on.'

'You just said you couldn't. . .'

'I lied!'

And they laughed, so much in harmony that Luciana thought, This is special, this is perfect, and she needed to know, 'Will it always be like this for us?'

She was overwhelmed by the seriousness in him as he replied, 'If we want it to be.'

Which made it so much easier to face the real world when only this bedroom intimacy was real to her. Luciana made her way down to the morning-room, the first time she had gone back into the part of Somerton where she had lived as Luciana Standish. Luciana Rivington now.

If she felt disorientated it was because she was happy. . .of course it was because she was happy. Moving on, growing up from who she used to be. It was only because she was so lost in change she could not look at Philip's portrait as she passed it. Of course it was.

Philip would be happy for her. He would not be angry
that she dared not think about him yet. She had so many
other things to occupy her. Practical, day to day things,
to distract her and protect this optimistic beginning to
her marriage. It would be wrong to linger in the past
with Philip. . .she knew it would.

There was so much to be attended to before she and
Max could let the outside world encroach upon their
privacy. The Standish papers to be put in order for the
family attorney; all the testaments and contracts attendant on her change of circumstances, Max's guardianship
of her children. Their children. She must remember
that. They were a family now and so much had to be
decided.

So much she had not even begun to think about, but
had to now as, deeply restless, she went out into the
gentle sunshine of the gardens wondering at last, 'What
is my role from now onwards? What will Max expect of
me, what is it I expect—want—for myself?' Facing the
first change she could not readily adjust to.

She had managed Somerton alone, controlled everything, trusted by the Standish men to do so. A million
times she had felt she did not want the burden, that it
would be such a relief to have Rory home to share it
with her. But she had always thought in terms of sharing,
never his taking over, as presumably her new husband
now expected to. It was Max's right, he was Rory's
choice, but. . .

Luciana faced for the first time her feeling that Max
already controlled too much. He controlled her as she
had never thought she could be. She could not give him
everything. And not only because she could not bear the
retreat into tedious wifely duties; from crop yields to

unaired linen was far too great a stand-down. She had never been, she had never wanted to be, mere mistress of a house concerned only with domestic trivialties.

She had achieved so much, gained even more, in managing Somerton, she could not give up all authority to any husband. She saw so clearly how easily she could begin to resent Max taking it, to see him as the interloper he said he was, a truth she had so passionately denied. The fact that she had not the smallest idea what Max was thinking on the subject reminded her, insidiously, that they were strangers.

They were half lying, close together, on the terrace where Max had come to join her and from where they would see the children returning. The Somerton ledgers were scattered around them and Luciana knew she was avoiding this most destructive issue.

So did Max. 'Luciana?'

And because she did not know where to start, she tucked her feet childishly between his and gazed as if absorbed at the solitary peacock, now doing his best to display a tail so wilted with age it would barely fan at all.

Max dealt far too swiftly with her cowardice for her liking. Catching her chin in his hand, he said, 'Look at me, Luciana. What is it?' Then he guessed. 'Ah, you are wondering just when I am going to banish you to your rightful place, my Lady Rivington, three paces in my splendid wake, all downcast-eyed obedience!'

'Must you be such a fool!'

'Only when you are.'

'*Am* I?' Could such a serious matter be teased to insignificance?'

'If you think I'm going to take up the reins of an estate as vast as Somerton without experience I should say you are, my doubting Luciana! Good God, you idiotic girl, the most I have ever had to manage was a collection of ham-fisted Irishmen putting up a tent!'

'But—'

'Are you planning to gamble away the Standish fortune on three-legged horses? No? Shower it upon pedlars of dubious doctrines, invest in quack remedies for—'

'Max—oh, for heaven's sake, are you *never* serious?'

For the first time Luciana knew that this flippancy of his annoyed her. It had annoyed her in the Standish men, too. They were not playing devil-may-care in the Peninsula now. Most of all it annoyed her when he made her complaint seem snappish.

'I am being serious. I cannot for the life of me see why you should suddenly turn liability, run mad and fling the inheritance away. You want me to be serious, then allow that I feel so ignorant of land husbandry I *must* laugh at it. I no more like running to my wife for advice than any other man, but I will do it, because it is best for Somerton. And Rivenal. Luciana, I don't think you realise what we have done. We have all but joined the richest holdings in the country. I need everything you can ever teach me.'

He had distracted her. Even as he succeeded Luciana wondered if it was on purpose. Max had a practised way of making sure only the things he wanted talked about were said. She took the bait, anyway, as he must have known she would.

'Rivenal—Max, don't you think you should at the very least write to your father to let him know you are married?'

'No more than any other man do I like a wife who

nags me!' And she knew this time he was not entirely teasing. He could never be accused of laughing when they spoke of Rivenal.

Luciana was setting the pattern for many battles to come when she fought back, refusing to be teased into submission. 'Lord Rivenal has a right to know.'

'It wouldn't interest him.' Max was tense enough to get to his feet and move away from her. Luciana hated this reminder of how shuttered he could be, it brought back memories of last night already uniquely disturbing to her. But she was learning, feeling her way towards how to deal with him.

'No, I don't suppose it would. But it would still be courteous—oh, don't look at me like that!'

'You would have me play the dutiful son, after all these years?'

'Yes. For your sake, Max, not his. Just to know you did everything you ought to.'

'As he always did for me?'

He was so tense, so close to unleashed anger now, yet he was letting things through, maybe not knowing he did, and Luciana fought to win a little more from him.

'No. I still cannot think about what you told me of your childhood withot feeling the profoundest rage.'

She had won. . .just. Max came back to her, reached for her; no more than the softest stroking of her cheek, but he was smiling, if only in recognition of her tactics.

'You once asked me why I defend you so, Luciana. Why is it you have always felt so angry for me?'

It was only because she did not realise she had never said it that she did not tell him now. It seemed almost foolish to state a truth so obvious—I love you. So she said, 'I should feel the same about any child so wickedly ill-used.'

Max's hand fell away, angry again, but with himself this time for asking too much of her, too soon, and getting only what he deserved. . .feeling he damned well deserved more and yet not able to punish this stranger-wife of his whose compassion had meant so much from the very start. So he said, very quietly, 'I didn't say I was ill-treated, Luciana.'

'Well, I do say it! Just because you were not beaten and starved, though for all I know you were—'

'No. Just lonely.'

And Luciana felt her heart wrenched out of her. It exactly felt like that. She felt eviscerated. She could barely find her voice. 'How did you ever escape, Max? I don't understand. How in the name of God did you know there even existed anything better to escape to?'

'I had a tutor, the youngest of a military family too impoverished to buy him his commission. He was as frustrated and as confined as I was, condemned to a life of brattish infants when all he ever wanted was to soldier. He talked of it incessantly. I was only Carlo's age when he came to Rivenal and he created a whole new world for me with his stories. He showed me there was something beyond my prison at Rivenal. He was worse than useless as a tutor, but I owe him everything. He gave me hope.'

And a life of ritual, regulations and danger. Was that really better than what Max could have known as the cossetted heir to Rivenal? Luciana looked up at her husband and knew, no, he could never have been a Lysander, never have wasted his energies, his entire self on the fatuity of Society living. Even as a boy no older than Carlo he had been too much his own man for that.

'*Are* you glad, Max—glad that you found the army?'

'I needed it. I needed to learn I was not the centre of the universe—yes, I too, Luciana! All my life everything had revolved round me, within the limits of my father's anxiety. Out there in India, the Americas, I couldn't tell anyone who I was. I'd lied to enlist, I had to live the lie, the ordinary man, living on the meanest soldier's pay. I hated every second of every day at first. Dear God, I must have been the most obnoxious brat imaginable! But it was soon kicked out of me.'

Literally kicked, Luciana knew. By men so hardened the greatest proof she would ever have of Max's strength was that he had come through it anything but hardened himself.

'When I reached my majority, free of the fear my father could demand me back, I owned up to who I was. I wasn't such a fool I wanted to moulder in the ranks, but I'm glad I started there. I had been taught the best way how to govern, how to lead men under my command.'

Why would he never see, this husband of hers with such authority and such self-doubt? 'You always knew that, Max. It was always in you.'

'You're defending me again, Luciana!'

'No, telling truth. Is that not what we promised one another, always?' What she needed so much for him to do.

It did not work. He would not free his deeper secrets. Maybe could not. But Max pulled her to her feet and into his arms, glad she had the courage, despite all warning, to want to know him. One day she must or they had nothing. But not yet. Dear God, not yet! Maybe not for years.

'Anything I *do* say will be the truth, I promise at least that, Luciana.'

It was the best that he could do for her and she accepted it gratefully. It was a calm September morning with only the barest breath of autumn in its softness. They had come so far so quickly, just now it did not matter that they had such a long way to go.

Luciana melted serenely into his kiss, so in love with him she ached, both so wrapped up in each other they were aware of nothing beyond the warmth of the arms that held them now.

Until they heard a clip round an ear and 'I wasn't going to say *anything*!' from Freddie.

Max was right—Luciana was overjoyed to see her boys again, as full of hectic questions as they were boiling over with inaccurate information.

'Lady Deverham cannot possibly have said Anthony may have *three* puppies!' Luciana objected, smoothing over any awkwardness the children might feel at finding her in Max's arms, even as she tried to judge if they did, how much they did.

Freddie was perfectly at ease with it, as was Catalina, save for a stern and jealous glare towards her father. Carlo... Carlo his mother was not so sure about. But she had successfully distracted her eldest for the present.

'Yes, she did!' he said, defending this wildest of his statements.

'*Didn't*!' Freddie's ear was smarting horribly.

'*Did*!'

Catalina had plainly put her time with Lady

Deverham to good purpose. 'No,' she corrected firmly. 'Two. Puppies,' she added, in case the grown-ups proved as dim as Carlo.

'Even that sounds a *bit* unlikely. I've never known Lady Deverham to be so reckless.'

But Catalina was adamant. '*Two.*' She counted out this incredible sum on elegant fingers. Carlo and Freddie defiantly held up three.

It was all so much as before that to Luciana, so altered, it seemed miraculous.

Much of it thanks to Max as usual. 'Well, I'd make the most of her ladyship's insanity, my Lady Rivington. Which of the gluttonous little monsters do we most want rid of? Which two are the loudest, smelliest and scruffiest of the brood?'

Everything was wonderfully back to how it had been. Better than anyone dared dream.

'Carlo and Freddie!' denounced Catalina, with the innocent air of one who might in mitigation claim not to understand a single word anyone was saying. Then she tugged her father's sleeve and asked imperatively, 'Papa, aren't you going to kiss me, too?'

Luciana just looked away, her husband's shocked pleasure almost too unbearable, and encountered a wrinkling nose and a *sotto voce* 'Urrgh!' from Freddie.

Even while she laughed and feinted to chastise him, she noticed that Carlo stood a little apart from them. Watching Max, watching Catalina, his dark Standish eyes narrowed with jealousy, which he hid the moment he felt his mother looking at him. Retreating into his quietness, Carlo looked so lonely.

Luciana had always known any trouble would begin with Carlo. She would have done anything to protect

him from the confusion of the half-grown feelings he
was suffering. So she picked up a squirming Freddie and
called out to her eldest.

'Don't just stand there, Carlo! Come and save me
from your odious little brother!'

Luciana felt it, the split second before it happened;
Max moving towards her to relieve her of her laughing
burden. Realising just too late that he had blundered
into Carlo's territory.

The two stood looking at each other, the head of the
Standish and this first masculine authority he had
known; both summing up the opposition. Luciana's
heart tightened. They were smiling, joining together to
tease the now squealing Freddie, but wary, Carlo somehow distanced even from the noise that he was making.

They were being so careful of each other even
Catalina felt it, her thumb creeping towards her mouth
as it always did when she was nervous. The hard realities
of fusing this new family together leapt dauntingly to
meet Luciana as she looked on and knew that the
honeymoon was over. This was where the painful
testing, the forging of new loyalties began.

Shaking off her disappointment—their old ease could
never have lasted—Luciana went laughing to the rescue
of her youngest who was giggling, yelping and otherwise
pleading for his reprieve.

Of course there was no getting the children to bed, not
quietly and sensibly, before their parents were worn to
the barest thread. Had she not been so overwhelmed
with exhaustion, Luciana would have laughed to see
Max introduced so ruthlessly to these delights hitherto
unknown to him, family bedtime in full spate.

An afternoon of squabbling and chasing, shouting, hiding, throwing things and generally showing off had reduced the children to that state all mothers recognise with failing heart—wide awake, silly, and determined their perfect day must never end.

It took all Luciana's experience and Max's imaginatively Gothic warnings to finally see the three of them tucked as far beneath their sheets as they would go, yawning just enough for Nurse to have the smallest hope of settling them before morning. Max stood in the doorway, surveying the field of a battle he was far from convinced was won, and could only shake his head in sympathy for Nurse as at last he wrested Luciana from the nursery.

'If I had not seen it for myself, I'd believe none of it. The Peninsula was never like this!'

And Luciana recognised that behind the teasing that was so ingrained in him was real strain. Carlo had been very quiet, but he had given Max the most relentless trouble. There was something about a Standish being so courteously uncooperative. . .something disastrously like Max himself.

For the first time Luciana saw the problem went deeper than she had feared. They were too alike, Max and her unsettled son, and Max, knowing it, recognised the first shots in a long and dirty war when he encountered them.

Luciana nearly made a serious mistake then. She almost said, 'I'm sorry.' Meaning that she understood how he was feeling. But something stalled her. Some passing shadow in his eyes, warning her that this was forbidden territory again. Whatever problems he had, he would work out by himself. Luciana could only laugh

with him, and the added burden of pretending drained
her.

She did her best. 'But you have seen nothing, I
promise you! Do you really think this is the best that
they can do to plague. . .us?'

Another mistake; she so nearly said plague you.
Because that was the worst of this; Carlo was not angry
with her. He did not blame her. If his life was changed
and he did not like it, only Max would ever be held
responsible.

Why did it have to be so hard? Luciana pressed a tired
hand to her cheek. Why, when it was so much to
everyone's benefit, for everyone's security and happiness, could this marriage not be accepted from the start?

Carlo did not dislike Max; in fact, he liked him as
much as Luciana ever could have hoped. He respected
him. Perhaps that was the root of her son's resentment
and confusion? It would be so much easier to rage at
someone he despised. Carlo was angry with someone he
knew he could love and was feeling guilty.

Luciana knew all about guilt and ached for her
bewildered child. He was such a little boy to be facing
such adult uncertainties; he understood just too much
for his own good, but not enough to make it all come
right. If only there was a way, a word, a conversation
they could have that would help him see Max was only
here to care for him.

And for her, as Max showed her so instinctively now
by taking her hand, looking down at it as he always
seemed to, as if he still did not believe a thing so perfect
could bear the touch of his.

Luciana felt a twist of pain for him and acknowledged
her helplessness. She could not make things right for

him either. She could help neither husband nor son, just watch and support and hope to contain the conflict until the time came when they could help themselves.

Max had never seen her so exhausted. He knew he was the reason, his handling of Carlo's resentment the heart of the problem. But she should not look like this, all warming of colour faded from her face, the smallest speech an effort.

He should have managed his new role better than this. They should be going downstairs now, relieved to be alone, amused, anticipating the privacy they so badly needed. Not this, as Max looked into her half closed eyes. She wanted sleep—it was written all over her—so she needed to be alone.

The anger he felt at Carlo then appalled him, but he could not pretend it away. Because this withdrawal of hers was so utterly wrong, would be wrong whatever he had done, however many years had passed, when they were old, old people. He wanted her, she wanted him. . . their discovery of just what this could mean to them so new. Nothing could be more wrong than the fact she was so weary with disappointment that she could not want him.

Luciana looked at Max and wondered just what it was had burned such fury into his eyes. It felt like a hot, sore brand against her skin and she wanted him to stop it; to comfort her. She just wanted to be alone with him. . .not talk, they didn't have to talk if he didn't want to. . .just be together, have a small part of this new world that was for themselves alone.

And he was shutting her out; she felt it even before he said, 'Go to bed, Luciana; you can barely stand.'

Go, not come, and spoken with such tight restraint of anger, it felt like a door slammed in her face.

Did he feel so bad about Carlo he could not even come near her for fear she would blame him? She could never be so stupid! Had she not promised to expect no miracles? And yet she knew, in a moment of unwelcome honesty, that she had. He had got so much right so far, she had let herself believe he always would; that ordinary, human uncertainty was outside his nature. Thinking him a god again. And he knew she had, she saw it.

She was wrong. All Max knew, as he saw and misunderstood her misery, was that somehow he had done, said, something wrong, too late to take it back. He could only go on in the same gentle, excluding tone, wearing his natural born tact as a shield.

'I'll have your maid bring supper to you—don't look at me like that, Luciana! No...please, angel, do as you're told! Set a precedent, an example for the children!'

And Luciana's sense of being shut out overwhelmed her, so much she could not fight him. He had made it true; she wanted to sleep and sleep and sleep—alone.

But not *be* alone. Her confusion was absolute when she heard her shaken voice say, 'But I want to stay with you!'

Max believed her. There was enough of a plea, almost fear in her voice to make even a man as uncertain as he was trust to his instinct and reach out to her, marvelling at just how moved he could be by so small a gesture, as she turned her face into his palm and admitted, 'I *am* tired, Max, it's true I can barely stand, I cannot think, I *do* want to sleep. But I don't want to go to bed... without you.'

If only she was saying what he wanted to hear. And then he realised that she was; something much more important than that she needed his physical greed for her, she needed *him*. Just the knowledge he was near.

Luciana never would understand the relief in his eyes as he took her by the waist to lead her to their chamber. Or the hard, harsh break in his voice as he denied himself to give her the privacy she needed. 'I won't be far away. There are papers I have to see to but—'

'You can sit with me. . .read by the fire, I won't mind the light. I shall sleep anyway, *truly* you won't be disturbing me!'

He would not. But the raw, frightened edge to her feelings most certainly did. She was demanding his presence like a pleading child and it scared her. She was too new to this marriage—to any marriage—to recognise that this intensity of contrary feelings was only to be expected at the start.

With Philip she had been too young, too confident of unstinting happiness to be afraid. She didn't know even the beginnings of what loss had taught her now. She had entered into that marriage with no ambivalence at all.

This. . .this was so different. It was the marriage she was born for and it was utterly confusing her. There was so much at stake, so much she could not live without, so much to lose. She was happier than she had ever known, and yet. . .

She was too young, still, in many ways, to know that so close on grief such joy can be a burden, too.

If he understood, Max said nothing more. If he had a right to love her at all he must care for her now as never before, she was at her most vulnerable. That he did understand. Living so long with loss, she was afraid of

happiness, of trusting it. Somewhere unacknowledged
inside coiled the feeling, 'I don't want to care and lose
again. If I believe too much in magic it might go away.'
It was a fear that went against her whole optimistic
nature, but not his. It lay heavily in him, too.

'I'll call your maid. No. . . I'll come and be near you,
angel, I said I would, but I really do have to attend to
those papers and if I'm to have a hope of finding—you
know what Rory was. . .'

'The most vital papers are the last things you will ever
find!'

He was going to find out very quickly that it was a
Standish habit. The boys were impossibly disorganised.

'If I start excavating the library now I might be back
by morning!'

Luciana understood his tact in leaving her to gain
control of her uncertainties, but could not joke about it.
Her hand caught at his arm before she could be angry at
her neediness and restrain it. 'Not long, Max, don't be
too long!'

And she wondered if she had said something terrible,
his face was so shuttered, his voice so raw.

'I won't be. I told you before, Luciana. I can't be
where I can't see you for long!'

Luciana was left watching the empty doorway
through which he vanished, listening to his already so
familiar footsteps ringing through the house on the way
to Rory's library. His now, she supposed. . . Carlo's.
Dear God—she sat bonelessly on the bed—it was like
gasping for breath after the tidal wave, knowing she had
yet to face the storm.

How selfish could she be? Expecting so much, when
he had given her more already than any human being

deserved. He is just a man, she *had* to keep telling
herself—just because he arrived like magic at the very
moment I began to realise I needed him, he's not a
magician.

He was better than most, and he had done the best he
could, getting more right than most men ever will, she
knew. It was wicked to feel disappointed, unsettled by
one small mistake. Not small to Carlo, but for that it was
unspeakable to lay the blame on Max.

Her maid came and went, puzzled by the silence as
her mistress undressed for bed and refused even her
favourite dish of eggs for supper. Luciana barely knew
the maid was there. She was lost in thought and, because
she was honest with herself, becoming calm at last. It
was only natural that she should feel so uncertain, not
always sure of what Max might do and say; she did not
know him.

Luciana sat before her glass brushing out her hair in
the old comforting rhythm she had learned from her
nurse as a girl. I have married a stranger, she repeated
silently, face it, accept it, until she began at last to realise
just what it must mean.

It was so unsettling a truth, she had been clinging to
every last indication that they were not, every smallest
proof that they had a rapport and had had it from the
very start. Which was looking at things the wrong way
round, forgetting, because it had been so long since
Philip left her, that no-one ever can know anybody so
well that they know everything they hope, will think or
do. . .

Philip she had known most of her life and yet she
never would understand why he went away to war and
died there.

Luciana laid down her brush and accepted something still more difficult. . .that Philip was the key to helping Max. Philip was all she knew of any adult relationship. She could no longer run away from memories, however much they hurt her. Her marriage to Max was too important to risk it through such cowardice.

She had to remember; *all* of it, not just the things that had made her happy but the things that had hurt and angered her. The things one sets aside when someone dies, as if they never even happened. If she let herself remember those things. . .that she had often fought with Philip, argued, been irritated and upset by him, as he had been by her, yet they got over it.

If she let herself remember that *that* was marriage, that was friendship. Not perfect harmony every living moment, but not giving in, not giving up when things felt bad.

She barely heard Max come into the room she was so exhausted, so drugged with her calm and determination. Just live in the minute, and don't make too much of little pricking pains. She had survived much worse than childish disappointment. Luciana smiled, at last aware he watched her every last expression in the glass, and Max came to her, his hands safe and familiar against her shoulders.

'Refusing your supper, ma'am?' He nodded to her untouched tray.

'Don't bully me, I wasn't hungry!' Except for you, she thought, and gently touched his broken fingers.

'Tired?'

'Very.' And one healing step closer to real understanding.

'I won't leave, I'll work by the fire. . .'

'I know.' Then, 'Max, *thank you*!'

'I'll hold you to that, my lady! Do you think you can sleep now?'

Oh, yes, she thought. For the first time in years, sleep without effort and hard dreams.

Almost she felt like a baby again, lying in the soft, safe shadows beyond the firelight, watching him as the languor of sleep crept over her. Loving him, wanting him and yet, even more, not wanting to reach out to him. There was something new, something quite particular and special about now and how she felt as she looked at him, fascinated by the strength of him in repose, as if even in stillness his strength was absolute.

A memory stirred in Luciana then. A memory years old and a lifetime away. Far away, in Italy, her father sitting with her in the long summer nights, watching over her. Luciana closed her eyes against a sting of tears. To feel *that* safe, that protected! A woman grown, as comforted as a child.

She loved Max, her body ached for him, but this was precious beyond anything they had so far shared. This moment of knowing *this* was home, this was what their future was, this subtle subsiding into sleep, aware of him, conscious even while all consciousness relaxed. Free from all fear or urgency. Max was here.

She knew—even while she slept she knew—when he came and stood over her, looking so lovingly down at her. Max watched her for so long, so silent and still, the room grew cold and he knew he must not disturb her. He wanted her—his body screamed with the pain of wanting her, but this was special, new. It *mattered*.

Because in sleeping so like a trusting child she showed a faith in him he would deserve if he had to struggle every day of the rest of his life to earn it. Max reached out a hand to her golden hair—even so lost in sleep she was aware of him! He had to leave her.

Just as he reached the door Luciana woke. It was not enough—she stirred in need for him. She felt unfinished, incomplete, without this man inside her.

'Please—please, Max, don't go. Come here.'

Quietly Max closed the door and came.

Luciana woke to the first chill of autumn rain against her windows, so secure in her husband's love it was as if rain and cold and winter were a world away. Yet Max was not there when she opened her eyes to a sun much brighter than she expected, a day so far advanced that she laughed, remembering the night that had preceded it.

She had never felt such contentment as she knew now, such confidence, knowing he would come back soon. He always came when she needed him. Someone was coming now. . .

Luciana was so lost in her thoughts of Max that for a moment she did not register it was her maid who entered, always a little diffident since Max had come here, always a little late. Mary crossed the room to open the curtains and Luciana smiled at her, wondering for the first time how the servants were feeling about all these sudden changes. Then she sat up to accept her silk-lace dressing gown and her morning chocolate. Beside her cup on the Meissen tray lay a plate of sugared biscuits and Luciana felt soaked through with guilt.

To have forgotten Carlo and their morning ritual! Even as she fought back her rage at herself, Luciana could hear him coming, feet skidding and scuffing as he took the corner at the bottom of the nursery stairs just a fraction too quickly as he always did and tripped himself up on a turned up edge of carpet. Carlo, so excited to be back to normal, and she had forgotten all about it! Luciana hugged herself into her robe, chilled at her selfishness; it was the only mistake she would make that morning, if it killed her.

So she was already laughing at him when Carlo spilled across the room to greet her, damp from his morning wash and hugging the breath right out of her. Thank God that Max was not here! Luciana caught her son close against her and understood that Max had known; somehow he had found out about Carlo's morning visits and made sure that he would find his mother alone.

Aching with love for both husband and son Luciana made room for Carlo on the bed beside her and complained, as she had done all the years they had played this game, 'One day I suppose I shall be blessed with better fortune and actually have you pounce upon me *quietly*!'

'If you think *that* was noisy. . .' Then Carlo spotted the biscuits were his favourites. 'Are those for me? They've got those lovely nut things on them.'

'Almonds, my idiot offspring, and try, if you can possibly contrive it, to keep them *in* your mouth. . .and your mouth *closed* —'

'Sorry!' Carlo wolfed his second biscuit, liking it even better than the first. Liking all of this, too, because he had his mother to himself again. It felt as if nothing much were changed. Except little things. . .and perhaps one big one, for his mother was different this morning. Not trying so hard to be funny, not tired, not sad. Carlo knew she was the most beautiful mother in the world, but somehow she was even prettier today as she sipped her spiced chocolate and pretended to take the most almondy biscuit for herself.

Luciana felt her son relax against her side and was warmed right through with her relief. He was a thoughtful child, a child who cared about other people's feelings. She had to talk to him about his behaviour with Max last afternoon, but it might not be so difficult as she feared.

She started where they always did. 'Has Freddie been good so far this morning?'

'Well, we only just got out of bed so even Freddie hasn't had time to do anything too. . .well, *Freddie*!'

And Luciana knew it was safe to be serious.

'Well, I shouldn't blame him for behaving quite horridly just for a while. After all, he's such a little boy and it cannot be easy having a new sister. A new father.'

It had to be said. Avoidance, however much the easier option, could only make family life more difficult. Luciana almost lost her nerve as she felt the tension in her son's body then, resisting against the softness of her own.

But he had to face this. It would help him if he accepted the truth of it from the very start.

'Freddie never knew Papa, not as you did, so maybe it is a little muddling for him. After all, he's used to having only you and me and Liam to plague him. And Catalina—it must be very strange for her to be with so many people she did not know before, and she can barely understand a word we're saying. I'm glad you're looking after her, she must feel so much safer now you're her special friend.'

If it had not been true, Carlo would have been no easy

target for such flattery. But it was, and no-one knew better than Luciana just how true it must be that Catalina needed her first real champion.

'Remember I told you how it was when I first came here? I was frightened too, but Papa was my friend, he looked after me. He looked after me all his life. It made me happier than I have ever been, until now.'

This was the dangerous part, these were the words that might lose the trust she could feel building as Carlo listened and believed her.

'Will you listen very carefully, sweetheart, because I want you to know something I've never told anybody else? I'm telling you because you'll understand. I've felt like Catalina all over again since Papa was killed—so *very* lonely. Yes, of *course* I had you and Freddie to look after me but. . .well, grown-up people need grown-up friends, too. I needed a friend my own age more than I ever realised, and now I have one. . .can you see that?'

If only Carlo were not so still—a nod, even a head shaken in denial would have been better than this resisting silence.

'I needed someone to talk to about all those grown-up things that bore you to a thousand pieces—oh, yes, they do! I needed. . . I haven't been very happy sometimes and—'

'*I can make you happy!*'

'I know, my darling, and you do, you always have, because I'm prouder of you than anything in the world and I always will be! But there will be a day when you have someone else you want to care for more than me—'

'*No!*' For the first time her too strong son was tearful. 'No, no, I *never* will!'

And Luciana buried her face in his curls, so like his father's and fought her own tears from her voice. It was a terrible thing she had to do, but it was time to teach Carlo just a little about letting go.

'You will, and because you love me and I love you, you'll feel quite horrid about wanting to be with someone else, unless you know there is someone good and kind watching over me. And you know there is, there always will be now—'

'You mean Lord Rivington?' Carlo's voice was sore with jealousy, and anger too, because he was beginning to like what he was hearing, but he did not want to.

'Lord Rivington, yes.'

Strange that she had not thought about what her children should call her husband or his child call her. Did she want her sons to call anyone but Philip their father? She wanted to be Catalina's mother, but Max had revealed so little, she could not truly know how he felt. Catalina's mother was the wife he never talked about. He must have loved her. . .why else this terrible punishment for her death that he inflicted on himself so relentlessly? It was unbearable just to think of it, and impossible to know what he was feeling now.

About Carlo she knew a little better. He was thinking, and thinking very hard, and the tension that had been building in him was dissipating; slowly, but he was relenting. He was an honest child and was accepting the truth of what she told him now. As far as he could bear to, as far as anyone only seven could understand all the grief and fear and loss that lay behind the words she whispered so softly now.

'Please let him love me too, Carlo. It's so much better now, isn't it, truly? He is my husband, one day you'll know what that means, one day you will understand just what it is he has done for me, for all of us, in coming here. Will you do that for me, Carlo, even if it feels strange at first and makes you cross sometimes? Will you be happy he has come to us? It's been so much fun, you know it has, you do so many things with him you didn't do with me. Not even your appallingly improper mother will climb trees with you, and Lord Rivington will take you hunting, and shooting, and do all those things Papa planned to do. You'll have such fun, you and Freddie and Catalina, I promise you that, angel. More fun than anyone ever had in the whole wide world!'

Luciana stopped then, because she knew she could not say much more without dissolving into tears and utterly confusing him. How to explain to a child that it is possible to cry tears of happiness and loss at the same time? She had explained all she could, pray God it was enough, not to change Carlo's feelings, but to help him see that change was possible. That he had lost only the responsibilities he should never have been burdened with and gained a normal childhood world.

The silence had reached the unendurable before Carlo at last sat up, needing to see his mother's face. He didn't really understand what was behind her words but he knew that it was very important she had said them. Grown-up things, expecting him to be grown-up too. Well, he was seven and a quarter after all, not a baby; he wasn't Freddie. And Lord Rivington. . .it was true he was fun and said scandalous things and played games grown-ups usually won't let you.

'Well, I suppose he *is* a cracking sport. . .would he

really take me hunting? *Really* let me do things Liam says I oughtn't?'

'Liam is quite right to say you oughtn't if you mean that little matter of Cousin Lysander's gamebirds last season!'

'Um. . .yes. . .but if I wanted to do *sensible* things?'

'Max would like that.' Luciana treacherously sold her husband into hours of slavery, knowing it was true. Max was like a boy himself running about with their children. He had a lost childhood to make up for and no care in the world who saw him do it. 'And you could help him keep Freddie and Catalina in order.'

'Yes.' Carlo got up from the bed, suddenly all small boy who had had an idea about how the day should be spent and was just about to bully his guardian into condoning it. 'I suppose I could.' Then the gravity of the old Carlo broke through for the briefest moment. 'I didn't mean to be bad to him yesterday, Mamma. Not really I didn't! Please don't be unhappy any more!'

'Unhappy with you, Carletto?' She teased him with his baby name, knowing he would rage at it.

'*Urrgh*! I'm too big for that! I'm not *Freddie*!'

And with that he headed for the door, leaving his mother with all the hope in the world that his good behaviour would last just as long as he needed Max to indulge some wild scheme. . .just a small boy for whom the grown-up world was light years away, where it should be.

Luciana set down her chocolate, now too cold and full of almond crumbs to be remotely pleasing, and swung her feet out of bed, hopeful and excited. Because somewhere in the not far distance she heard a loud

collision. Carlo had intercepted his quarry on the way
back to her.

'I've been looking for you *everywhere*! Sir!' added
Carlo, in the interests of getting what he wanted.

'What in the world have I done to deserve that fate, I
wonder?' countered his victim.

Luciana called for her maid and smiled.

She was still smiling several hours later when Catalina
gave her father his first black eye.

CHAPTER NINE

'You can't do that!'

'Why. . .not?' Catalina struggled with guilt and English while Max wiped his streaming eye.

'Well, it's just not. . .it's just not—' Freddie blurted.

'*Cricket*, that's what!' And Carlo wrested the rock hard leather ball from Catalina. Over-arm bowling—he could barely take in the enormity of her crime. *Over-arm bowling*! It would never catch on.

'Not. . .cricket?' Catalina hid the ball behind her back. Carlo grew even sterner, Luciana tried to hide her smile and failed. So like Philip. . .so like Max. For the first time she looked at her husband and sons and realised, there was a real likeness. Astonishing she had never seen it before. Luciana handed Max a second handkerchief and wondered aloud.

'How extraordinary. . .' No, not extraordinary, just another reminder of how little about him she knew. 'Are you related to us. . .? No, don't look at me like that, you idiot, I know you're related to us *now*, but—'

'I'll have you know, my unsympathetic spouse, that I am having trouble looking at anything just now!' His eye really was very red and bleeding. 'That daughter of mine is a monstrous shot—and, yes, we are related.'

It was Carlo who astonished Luciana then. 'Yes, I looked it up in the Standish bible. Lord Rivington's grandmama was Grandpapa's sister. . .'

Luciana fought hard to hide her excitement—that was

a great deal of interest to show in a man he would not
accept.

'What's related?' asked Freddie, climbing over Cass
and Polly to reach the tray of tea supposedly safe beside
his mother. It tipped over.

'You greedy oaf!' Carlo pulled rank on Freddie. 'And
you know perfectly well what related is, it's. . .well, it's
like Lysander!'

'Why, you evil brat!' Max choked with laughter
despite being in very real pain. 'Luciana, I swear it, I'll
drown that child! Like Lysander. . .*Lysander*! Dear
God—'

And Luciana's heart froze. For the first time she did
not know how her son was going to react. How was he
going to take being teased so personally by someone he
regarded as an interloper?

Carlo did not know either. For a full half minute he
puzzled, as if fearing Max had meant it. He had been *so*
bad, so naughty yesterday. Then Carlo knew. In his lazy,
tactful way Max was forgiving him. No, not even that;
wiping the slate clean as if Carlo's jealous and resentful
behaviour had never been. Finding he almost wanted to,
Carlo smiled. Then, not so surprised after all that he
liked the feeling, he laughed.

Luciana looked on, fascinated by the interaction of
two strangers accepting a new intimacy; with her other
hand she rescued what was left of the damson cake from
Freddie.

'Catalina, angel, come here. . .'

Not for the first time Luciana smiled at how it was
with mothers, seeing sixty things at once and handling
seventy of them.

'You didn't mean to hurt Papa, sweetheart, but I'm

afraid he needs another handkerchief. What a mess he's making—Max, for heaven's sake, not with your cravat! Catalina, will you fetch Nurse for me, to bring some vinegar? Understand? Good—and yes, you will, Max, don't be such a baby! Freddie! Oh, *no*! Oh, *Polly*!'

Then she stopped, shocked through with the look Max gave her, understanding it. This was how he had seen her the very first time, up to her elegant elbows in mud-spattered children, dogs cavorting. *This* was what he wanted, what he would stay for, come what may, however many days like yesterday were sent to trouble them. Max remembered.

She even knew what he would whisper when he leaned so close and kissed her, regardless of the nudging children. 'Imagine that, my Lady Rivington—so besotted I wanted even this chaos!'

Chaos now took the familiar shape of loud yells from Freddie, Cass and Polly as Liam came limping across the lawns towards them, and the whole day died.

Luciana felt the chill of what he had to say even before he was close enough to show it. She just could not think what it might be. . .

The last thing they could have expected. 'A messenger, from Rivenal, Colonel Max, sir! It's your Da. . .your Da's taken himself bad. . .'

And Liam, never on ceremony with his much loved commander, subsided onto a relinquished chair, still shaky from his injuries. His bandaged brow was promptly mopped by Catalina.

'There's me darlin'!' Liam approved gratefully. Then, 'You best hurry, Colonel Max, sir.'

'So bad?'

And Luciana realised at once that Max had not the

first idea what to do. What he should do, let alone wanted to do. He only knew that they were not the same thing. Luciana took control.

'Liam, take the children indoors when you have caught your breath. Carlo, make certain poor Liam is not obliged to run after you all, he is much too tired for trouble. It's almost time for lunheon. . .'

Max was so wrapped up in his thoughts he did not even notice the results of her tact until the two of them were quite alone. The garden suddenly looked bleak and tired to Luciana, dying. Autumn and hard reality intruded.

'Hurry, Max, I'll have a valise sent over for you—

'You seem very sure I'm going.'

It would never cease to shock Luciana, how he could change so abruptly from openness and laughter to such inaccessibility. As if just the thought of Rivenal could wipe out any hope and pleasure. The memories were so repugnant to him, maybe all the more now he had begun to enjoy a family, know what a family could be all about. His very love of Somerton made him stubborn about going to Rivenal now.

Max saw her protest coming. Guilt made sure of that. He knew it was behaving unjustly, but he stalled her just the same. 'We've said all we have to say, my father and I.'

And Luciana grew stubborn too, because she knew what Liam had been warning and knew even better how terrible Max would feel if his father died with this resentment still sore and cold between them. 'You can't have done, or you would be hurrying to him now!'

She was so right she might just as well have said what she thought of him—Be a man, can't you! You cannot always run away from trouble. Max so much hated the fact that he always did, he turned on her.

'Because he is my father, that is supposed to be enough? Because an old man I do not know and cannot like, who never liked or cared for me, is dying, I am meant to. . .what, Luciana? What holiness do you expect to overtake me? Or him? Has he *asked* to see me—?'

And Luciana, suffering his pain, raged back.

'Go and see! For God's sake, Max, just go and see. Do you really want it to turn out that he *had* asked, that he did want to say that he was sorry, and you did not go? You said it yourself—he's an old man. Can't you allow him a chance to die in peace?'

It was a terrible thing to say, so cruel she was in tears before she finished it. So shocked at herself because never in her life had she let slip her temper. It felt like letting slip her whole being, it felt dangerous. How to get back?

Luciana, sensing the familiar numbing of shock seep into her, looked at Max, his face so white with hurt his scars, his bruises, stood out quite painfully, and she thought, I *had* to say it. I have shattered all we had, all we have built, right back to the foundations, but I have done the right thing.

She knew it even as he turned on his heel and strode away, breaking into a run as he neared the stables, not from urgency to get to Rivenal, but the urgency of rage. She knew even before she saw him coaxing his mare into a reckless gallop across the deer park that he was so angry with her she had lost all sympathy. But she had grown from the risk she had just taken. She knew his anger was because he had no pity for himself.

Luciana turned back towards the house, all at once

dreading the children. Too tired for noise, too raw to the elements, as if just a childish laugh would blow her right away. She felt. . . Dear God, she felt so strange suddenly. Giddy with anger and shock, of course. . .

Feeling. . .*strange*. Yet not so strange. Tense. Yet not just tense with rage. Something else was happening to her, she knew it instantly, yet she was too miserable, too weighed down with what she had just done to give mind to it.

Steadying herself, Luciana shook her head wearily at the fallen tea tray. Damn Freddie for being such a careless boy! It had been Aunt Anne's favourite service, now all shattered on the ground. Max was gone, for days, perhaps. She had been married not five whole days. . .and it felt as if a lifetime would be needed if she was to make that marriage right.

The children helped, although she was more distracted much of the time than she liked, let alone understood. Luciana had had four years of ruthless practice in controlling her feelings, putting the children's welfare first, and yet it was not working now. Almost as if this was the worst thing that had ever happened.

It was not. . .remember that, it never could be. The worst had been losing Philip. . .

Then she wondered again if she had just lost Max.

No! Not if it took her the rest of her life on her knees begging his forgiveness. And yet she had not done wrong. She had done something she had had to do, and he knew she had. He had known she was right. She understood enough to know that was why he was so angry with her. Stupid, stupid fool, not to tell her why he felt so bad! Not to believe her when she told him all he could ever be was good!

What in the world was the matter with her? Max had been gone not quite a week, his father was recovering. Why was she so intent on anticipating trouble? So *tired*. Luciana sat up in bed this sixth morning after he had left her, her head swimming with sleeplessness. She felt so awful.

So awful that Carlo took one look at her when he came for his morning conference and called out for Mary. Which was when Luciana knew she must control herself. Carlo was frightened. He had been worried since Max had gone away, suddenly in charge again, and his mother so quiet, so tearful. What was the matter with her? She was never one to weep at nothing. Today Luciana felt so aching, so sick with it all, it was as if her skin had pulled to stretching point, and hurt.

Familiar in some way, but Luciana would not think about it anymore. She was going to get out of bed and behave sensibly for her children. If it killed her. When she first struggled to her feet she felt it would.

So she spent the rest of the day ordered strictly to stay in bed, pinned there by Freddie, Carlo and Catalina, who murmured stories in soothing Spanish while Luciana closed her eyes to snoring puppies.

Which was how Max found her, and there was something so explicit in his mood that Carlo cleared the room of other visitors at once, and earned a nod from Max that made him feel appreciated. Grown-up. They were both looking after Mamma.

'Mamma's not very well.' Carlo hesitated in the doorway.

Max nodded again, knowing it was all his fault. He

could hardly bear to wake her she was so pale, so dark about the eyes. What had he done to her? Except be angry when she had only meant to help him. *Had* helped him, which is what he had come racing back to say, simply, his father was better—everything was better. Not good, but as good as it ever would be. Max had not even taken the time to breakfast, he needed to come home.

To a wife who had every right to be as cold with him as his weak and selfish temper deserved. Max sat carefully on the bed beside her and stroked her cheek to wake her, not wanting to jolt her from the sleep she so plainly needed, dreading the moment he saw the rejection in her eyes. . .

He had come to apologise, to salvage what he could. To swear, and mean it, never to be so stupid again. If she could forgive him. . .

Luciana woke to this gentlest of touches and the tears spilled down her cheeks before she could begin to fight them. Not that she could—she was crying like a baby for no reason at all these past few days. It wasn't him— please don't let him think it all his fault!

He did. Max dragged her into his arms, so hard against him neither he nor she could breathe. Breathing mattered nowhere near as much as saying he was sorry.

'Oh, God. . .my *love*, did I do this? No, Luciana—no, angel, don't cry! Just hold me. Let me hold you. *Don't cry*! Don't let me frighten you again! Don't you know I would never mean to? I'm so *sorry*—'

And Luciana found that she was sobbing into his neck, just sobbing. It wasn't pain, it wasn't misery, it wasn't even relief. Just love. Just being back in his arms, soldered together by this overwhelming need.

'I'm sorry too, Max; I didn't—'

'*Sorry*! Darling, you have nothing in the world to be sorry for. And you know it! You know I'm the world's most despicable fool! You were right—'

'It. . .*did* it go well, Max? Oh, how is your father, not too sick? Is he—?'

'As well as can be expected for a man his age whose blood is weak. He has been ill for a very long time, though he told no-one of it. I'm sorry for it.'

'Truly?'

'Yes, angel, truly. Oh, I cannot like him, I cannot care for him except as for another human creature suffering, who knows his end is coming. We're not friends, Luciana, no miracles'—except that he was able to tease her optimistic nature—'but we. . . I suppose we have reached some understanding of each other. I know better now why he did what he did, he knows—I think he always knew—why I had to get away. His motives were not cruel, his actions only thoughtless. Yes, mine, too—I saw that look!'

A look Luciana buried gratefully against his shoulder.

'I suppose. . .no. . .well, maybe, almost I regret, and he does, that things had not happened differently, that we had not resolved this earlier, but. . .we are who we are. At least we can accept that now and let it be.'

Better than Luciana had hoped or imaginged. She knew her stubborn husband and suspected his father of being the same. 'He is. . .what about Catalina?'

She felt his smile against her cheek. 'Apparently at least I did not "disgrace the Rivenal name"! He accepts I had to marry Antolina. . .'

Her name at last. So beautiful. *Had* to marry? Whatever could that mean? Unimportant now. . .but one day the most important thing she had to know.

'He will see her child?'

'Oh, yes, he wants to see you all. Yes, you too, my lady! He seems pleased about our marriage. A "nice-behaved girl", I believe he said. Can't think who he has been speaking to!'

And at last it was all over. The tension of days, the fear, dissolved in a jest. They had taken only the slightest step backwards, after all. 'Wretch! I'll have you know I am the most—'

'Demure of women, Luciana mia!' Teasing more intimate still and hot with memories.

Luciana curled closer into an embrace, altered now, soft and coaxing. Where she wanted to be. She had missed this so terribly. 'Is he well enough, Max? I don't want to overwhelm the poor man with a host of squabbling children.'

Max was no more thinking of Rivenal any more than she was. 'Not for a few days, perhaps. Next week, after the cricket match, we are invited. Carlo is sensible enough to keep the baby ones in order!'

That was not even said to please her, she knew, Max thought it the truth. It was, now Carlo understood this role was his and no-one else's. 'Yes, after the cricket match. We cannot miss that, the boys would never forgive it. Nor the village either. Somerton always win, you know. . .'

And she felt a shudder run through him which she found impossible to understand, until he murmured, his voice quite raw, 'Somerton. Do you know, Luciana, all the time I was riding back, every mile I was thinking, Almost home? Rivenal is where I was born, Rivenal should be home, and yet Somerton *is*. . .it just *is*! I have never felt so. . .' Inarticulate, lost for words, only really able to feel the depth of what he meant, not say it. 'It's you. . .how you make me feel. I'll never forget it, never be able to begin to repay it—'

'*Repay* me?'

Suddenly it was Luciana holding him, urgent with love and disbelief, and almost anger that he, who had done so much for her, should be so grateful. Only to be grateful in her turn because for the first time he had shown his vulnerability for what it was. He was not fighting her, but letting her see and feel, and help. Not hiding from her. This was a turning point come before she ever had expected it.

'Oh Max, do you really. . .*are* we really home to you?'

'You, *you* are home!' So much so, it was Luciana comforting him for his losses, his private grief, and he did not mind it. He was seeking it, needing it. It no longer felt a weakness. He had given so much away, because he trusted her.

Luciana knew it. Knew it and felt soaked through with a tenderness she had never known. This was something truly new. Never before, not with Philip, not in her most intimate imaginings, had she thought to comfort the man she loved as if he were her child. Feeling it absolutely, and at the very same time, feeling loved, protected and calm.

We have quarrelled, she thought. We had our first quarrel and this, *this* is the result of it! No need to fear her temper any more, fear her feelings. No need to fear being so exposed.

She wondered if Max knew that she was learning what he had learned now, that it was enough just to trust.

Love like this cast out fear. She smiled. It was a love she only barely understood. Now, very quietly, alone with him in their room, it was hers.

The day of the cricket match it was as if all the towns and villages, the great houses for miles around, had emptied onto the meadow behind St Dunstan's church for the last great outing of the summer. Harvest was come and so was the battle of Deverham and Parva.

Instigated by Marquess Charles and Lady Deverham's late husband, the cricket match was the highlight of the Season. And to suggest it was other than all out war would have been to insult the depth of enmity between Jess Blackmore of the Cat and the Moon and the Deverham Arms's Mrs Mortlake.

To the devil with Jake and his hefty team of blacksmiths, labourers and the Rector! Jess was baking for Parva and everyone within scenting distance of her wonderous pies would know it. The village was *en fête* and Luciana had never been so elated.

She knew all eyes were on her as the Somerton carriage drew up beside the meadow gates and the Rector came to greet her. The villagers may all have inspected Max before, but her own circle, if they could be called such, had not yet had the opportunity. More of them would be here today then ever before. Even Mr Snazeby who said the meadow always made him sneeze would not miss quizzing Max for anything.

After all, Max was the Marquess of Rivenal's heir, who ran away, never to be seen or heard of, only to be speculated about in ever expanding tales quite as gothic as any in a library. Some said Max had made his fortune in India, others were convinced that he had died.

Helvetica Barrymore said he would certainly have married a native girl, but then Helvetica—Lord, what a hat had alighted on her head!—would say anything, the sillier, the more unkind, the better.

Luciana looked across at her husband as the horde descended and saw her war hero blench.

'Lord!' He tugged at the glove on his broken hand as if wishing himself anywhere but here.

'For shame!' teased Luciana. 'It is only Lady Dalby and the Sneezing Snazebys! And, Freddie, if you repeat that—'

'I wasn't going to say *anything*! Look, something dead's on Miss Barrymore's head!'

'I'll have you know that is the height of fashion, young man!'

'Now you sound just like Sneezy Snaze—'

'*Carlo*!'

'What's sneeze?' asked Catalina.

Luciana knew just what kind of day she was in for when her appalling offspring showed her.

One would have thought a man from Mars or at least the Moon had come to St Dunstan's Mead from the way the Somerton party was surrounded the second they descended from their carriage. There was a surge of 'ah's as Carlo, wielding much more Marquess-like hauteur than he had managed at the wedding, helped his mother and Catalina from the landau, neatly sidestepping the oncoming Freddie, who leapt out, not looking where he was going. Carlo managed not to smack him and encountered a grin of solidarity from Lord Rivington.

Carlo grinned back. This was *fun*. This felt good. Today it did, at any rate. The mid-September sun shone down upon grass scythed to the sheen of velvet, and somewhere not too far away, a halfpenny a piece, were Mrs Blackmore's pies.

Then the social riot began.

'My *dear*!' craked the impingingly loud voice of Mrs Snazeby. 'But. . .oh, for heaven, Asquith, do not you have your handkerchief? *Must* you be sneezing all — ?'

'I have it somewhere, my love — ahh. . .ahh.'

'Oh, Asquith!'

Luciana read Max's soaring eyebrows. Marriage!

'But we have not seen you in an age, you wicked girl,' continued Mrs Snazeby, who had barely, if Luciana had anything to say it, seen her in her life. 'And then what is it we hear but you have married Lord Rivington! Oh, *Asquith*!'

'Sorry, my sweet. Ahh. . .'

'Freddie!' warned Luciana. Then she controlled her urge to laugh out loud at Max's growing horror — he would face the French cavalry sooner — and managed, 'You have not the acquaintance of my husband, ma'am. My lord, may I present you to Mrs Snazeby?'

Oh, but she would strangle him soon — he would wish it were Napoleon he was encountering! Max might be bowing with the most impeccable charm, but Luciana knew, felt it in every vein, every fragment of bone, that he was laughing.

Today she felt everything about him, as if they were still joined, as they had been not so long since, in the warmth of their bed. She felt a part of him, felt him deep in her, more than just memory, and knew he felt the same. They were here in Dunstan's Mead and yet separate from the world, and just the way they walked, and smiled, the light in their eyes, their synchronicity of movement said so.

Luciana watched Max getting to know his neighbours and saw the looks those neighbours exchanged; people felt it. They knew. Soon they would be saying, a love-match, after all. There is a visible connection between two lovers satisfied.

For the briefest moment, Luciana felt exposed by it. More exposed than ever before, and not because for the first time she went in public without her widow's veil. She was still in white, for Rory—besides it being all she had, new gowns had mattered so little until Max came here. Elegant and simple it stood out almost shockingly among the latest garish fashions and the sober Sunday clothes of the villagers. Luciana felt herself draw closer to Max, had no thought of stopping herself. She felt too much was encroaching into their privacy. . .

And yet she loved the festive atmosphere. She always had, since she had first come here as a child and witnessed this strange and infinitely pointless game, while Philip tried to make her understand it. She loved the banter and the crowds and the partisan roars of disapproval as the teams jogged by, in a hint to the spectators that places must soon be taken. The match was soon to start.

Luciana came round, suddenly aware she was one child short. Catalina. Even as she began to worry, she spotted her. What a marvellous sight! Catalina had sought Jess out and was showing her first friend in England just how much more Poppy had grown since Jess last saw her.

Poppy! Oh, *Lord*! 'Max, in the name of heaven, the

dogs!' Visions of Cass and Polly absconding with the ball assailed her.

'Home.' And he invested the word with such depth she felt the Snazeby's fascinated glances. 'Locked up; only Poppy made a successful break for freedom and I'll keep an eye on her.'

Luciana almost laughed out loud as he leapt at this chance to escape a grilling by the Snazebys.

The traitor! For she never had a hope of fleeing in the same way. Least of all when Lady Dalby and Mrs Caterham, ill-matched friends, captured her.

'My *dear*!' They pounced together as they always did, then looked cross with one another. They always did that, too. Thank the Lord for Lady Deverham approaching!

'So *good* to see you, my love. You look so happy.' Lady Deverham took her hands and Luciana hung on gratefully.

'But what a sly little thing you are!' Mrs Caterham's tones scraped everyone's nerves worse than Mrs Snazeby's. 'Not a word to anybody, and *so* handsome a gentleman!'

'So good with those boys of yours,' sniffed Lady Dalby. 'Looks like 'em, too, have ye noticed? Related, of course, Sarah Standish wed old Rivenals' father—'

'Never been a Sarah Standish, Ernestine! It was an Eleanor,' corrected Mrs Caterham. 'That's his own little gel, I take it?'

Luciana gritted her teeth on her laughter and Carlo dutifully stamped on Freddie.

'Indeed, ma'am. Lady Catalina is a joy.'

'Hmn! Foreign, eh. . .the mother?' Lady Dalby managed to make birth sound like an international incident.

'A Spanish lady,' replied Luciana carefully.

A hat with violets so deeply empurpled they looked
years gone in decay poked in, as the nose beneath it
always had to. It was an extraordinary thing about the
Honourable Helvetica Barrymore that her mouth could
be in one place and her mind in quite another, at present
sourly engaged with the fact Luciana had yet again
married the only eligible *parti* in the district.

Miss Barrymore winced beneath her sprawling hat in
a manner vaguely related to a smile. 'Foreign, did not I
tell you all and you would not listen—'

'And shall not listen now, Helvetica, if you cannot
mind that I was speaking!'

'But, Mama—'

And then it happened. So much a part of the usual
pointlessness of Helvetica's observations that at first no-
one really heard it. Max had caught up Catalina and
Poppy and was carrying them back to the rest of his
family. Miss Barrymore saw his face for the very first
time.

'Oh. . .oh, but his *face*! Oh, Lady Philip, how can. . .
how *can* you bear it?'

Luciana froze. She saw Max freeze and knew the most
passionate anger because he might not be a vain man
but he cared. He had always cared, always felt somehow
too damaged, too ugly for a wife he thought so beautiful.
Hardest most of all for a man so handsome to feel so
damaged now. Yet he was beautiful! Had not Mrs
Caterham just said so? Never ugly. Luciana could have
taken Miss Barrymore's craning neck and wrung it. But
she was not given the time.

For a voice spoke behind her, the voice she had hated

all her life. The one person she had forgotten, who of course would be here. Lysander Standish.

'Oh, but you are forgetting, Miss Barrymore. Not Lady Philip any longer. My Lady Rivington.' And he effected a bow so carefully insulting Luciana felt it as a blow.

Max had told her nothing about what he had said to Lysander for so endangering the children. That he had gone over to Graveney one morning, she knew, but she had not asked. Max had said to leave Lysander to him, and she had so badly wanted to. She never wanted to think of the creature again.

She had so much dismissed Lysander from her mind it came as a real shock to see him now, see the familiar cold light in his eyes, the light of threat. As if he had been listening so intently to the gossip of their neighbours and. . .what?

What could he hear that he did not know already? And yet he had. It was as plain to Luciana as his enmity when he bowed in turn to Max and she knew Max saw it too. Lysander had thought of a way to get back at them for all his failures. But what it could be. . .

And suddenly, thankfully, there was no time to think of it, for the scratch band of the Cat and the Moon's more hardened drinkers stopped playing their cidery tunes and the Rector was calling order. . .the game was starting. The children were hot and tugging with excitement and Luciana forgot Lysander.

She loved this place so much, this yearly festival, as she took her place on the makeshift dais decked out in harvest bales and twists of corn and fading poppies. Carlo, for the first time, was to present the prizes; the flitch of bacon to the winning team. He was Marquess of

Standish now and so aware of it as he perched beside his
mother, and ordered Freddie not to kick the Rector's
furniture. Catalina was hauled onto her father's knee,
the better he could keep control of Poppy. And battle
began.

Almost at once there was the most terrible disaster.
For Somerton had gone in to bat and Mrs Mortlake's
husband was bowling for Deverham. He had heard what
Jess had said about his Sally's pies. He bowled in a
manner worthy of Catalina—and Jake lay sprawling on
the wicket.

'Oh, I . . . I *say*, that's not—ahhhchoo!'

'*Cricket*!' chorused Carlo and Freddie. Then the
enormity of what had happened struck home. 'Oh, *no*!
our best bat. . .what are we going to do! They'll *beat* us!'
Since this had never happened in Carlo's lifetime he
could barely believe the shocking thing that he was
saying.

Asquith Snazeby was agreeing with him between
sneezes. 'Quite right, young man! This won't pass at all!
Not one of them a candle to Blackmore, though the
Rector's—'

'*Hopeless*!' wailed Carlo, who was fanatically for
Somerton. 'What are we going to *do*?' And then he
knew. As Jake was carefully wheeled off the pitch in
Gaffer Bradshaw's barrow, Carlo turned to Max, his
eyes blazing, and Luciana's heart stood still. What best
for Max to do?

Play, was the answer. But could he? His hand was so
badly damaged, besides his eye was so swollen no
amount of witch hazel applied to it that morning had
redressed the damage. If he went in to bat and *failed*—
but if he did not go, he still had failed in Carlo's eyes.

Jake's accident was the most impossible disaster. Max and Carlo had been doing so well since she had her talk with her son. Carlo was much happier. Max had been so careful to involve him in grown-up decisions.

'Oh, *please*, sir!' Freddie scrambled to his feet and tugged Max onto his, dislodging Catalina. But it was Carlo who Max was watching so intently.

He knew the risk, but he was going to take it. His hand was bad, it could not grip too well, but he had managed a bat in Lisbon well enough when the regiment had been holed up there, bored out of their minds and with nothing else to do but boggle the local fishermen playing cricket. He *could* do it.

And he couldn't not. Simply, he had no choice. So he made it look as if he had not even had to make one, and Luciana screwed up her hands in nerves and pride.

'Papa play.' Catalina commandeered his vacated seat, clutching her squirming puppy. It was not a question, just a statement of the only thing she could imagine her father doing. Luciana smiled and nodded. To Catalina her god-like parent was never going to fail at anything.

'Oh, but. . .well, is it *wise*, sir?'

'*Asquith*!'

'Only askin', m'dear, no point mincin' round the matter—*ahhchoo*!'

'I can manage, sir—I hope!' Max accepted this well-meant if tactless concern with grace. 'It is the damage my daughter did me will wreck the plan, not Bonaparte's efforts to dispatch me!'

And with that he walked out onto the field, much to the Rector and Liam's relief. The thought of losing was. . .unimaginable. They would win now Max was here.

Luciana saw the whole team think so and wondered if Max would ever understand. If his appalling childhood could do so much harm he really never would see how much faith he instilled in others, quite instinctively. They had no need to know him, just believe.

Lady Dalby was saying as much. 'I like that man of yours, Luciana. I like him very much indeed!'

Luciana caught the pride in Lady Deverham's eyes and smiled. That Lysander, standing a little behind them with Lord Dalby, was narrow-eyed with anger was suddenly quite meaningless, no threat at all. Luciana cast him a look to chill the marrow and turned back to watch her husband win for Somerton. She knew he would, only she would ever know how much he had to.

'Oh, well struck, sir! Did you see that, Dalby— *ahhchoo*! Dem'me! Oh, my pardon, ladies—'

'*Asquith*!'

'Oh, fine shot! Does he hunt, have you asked him, Snazeby?'

Luciana felt as if she were quite literally soaring, dizzy with pride. Her children were roaring uninhibited support for Max, Catalina was clapping, Poppy barking. . .

Quite dizzy. Very. . *so* dizzy! Really, she felt. . .

'*Luciana*!' The voice came from a long way away. 'Luciana, my child, are you unwell? Need you to go home?' Lady Deverham waved away the vinaigrette Mrs Caterham was wafting beneath her nose and Luciana came round to the realisation she had fainted.

She never fainted! She was never ill. It was not as if the day was airless. . .

'*Luciana*!' It was Max, who had seen her fall and run to her. Catalina was clinging to Lady Deverham's hand, Carlo and Freddie looked frightened.

Luciana herself felt. . .what? Ridiculous. And shaking. . .it seemed familiar in so many ways. She felt hot, and cold, and as if she were trapped too tightly in her clothes, as if she were swollen and sore and could not breathe. Reminding her of. . .what? But enough of this! She had to think of Max and the children. She must not worry them so she pulled herself together.

'Forgive me. . .no, Max, please, I'm quite well! I cannot think. . .'

Only at last she could. So *soon*? Impossible. . .and yet she *had* felt like this when—

'Come, sit here! Gently, sweetheart! Carlo, run and fetch Mrs Blackmore, ask her to bring some wine for your mother.'

'Mamma?' Freddie, not asked to do anything useful, felt helpless.

Impossible! Luciana kept telling herself. And yet it was not. She had known within a matter of days about Freddie. . .

Impossible, no, but it was too much. She had to be wrong because it was too soon, too overwhelming to cope with. Most of all, because she wanted it so badly to be true.

It would explain so much. Why she had been feeling so tense and tearful. She really had been just the same within a day or so of conceiving Freddie.

She was so pale with shock Max could not take his eyes off her. Impossible to know what was in her mind but something was. She looked ill, and yet—no question that what flashed in her eyes was near elation. Something he had never seen in anyone before. Something private, not shared, that went to the very heart of her.

Luciana looked back at her husband and no-one else

existed. She had no doubts at all as she looked at him,
she knew that it was true. It was not as if she had not
been like this before. With child.

Max's child! She knew, as if she could already feel it
taking strength from her. Just as she knew that she
would be better now she understood, she would thrive.
She always did. . .she had always been so lucky.

It felt so strange, so precious a secret, that he had
given her this baby and he did not know yet.

She would tell him—choose when to tell him. Wait
until he thought he could feel no happier and then show
him that he could. He would be. She was certain of that.

'I'm all right, Max, don't fuss!' She hugged her secret,
utterly at peace with it. There was nothing in the world
now that anyone, even Lysander, could do to harm her.
'Were you winning? Or losing so disgracefully everyone
will say I fainted to rescue you from disaster?'

'We were winning, you little traitor!'

'Then you had better go back and make sure of the
victory. Go *on*, Max!'

And, having to take her word for it that she was well,
Max went back to answer the anxious questions of his
team-mates as best he could.

'The air is so stuffy today,' lied Lady Deverham,
clearing the spectators all about them. 'Ah, Mrs
Blackmore, wine and most welcome! Don't look so
anxious, children; all is well now.'

More than well, and sooner than ever she could have
hoped for them. Lady Deverham looked contentedly at
this expanding family, and wondered how long it would
be before Max knew.

* * *

The only thing Max did know was that Somerton
smashed their way to resounding victory. He would
never know how. Luciana had fainted and it was all he
could think about. Was she so tired out by the children?
He must take them aside and come to terms with them;
a lot less noise and disruption around their mother for a
while. He would pay the price, fishing, and looting
Lysander's coverts, whatever it was they demanded him
to do.

Max listened to the congratulation all about him and
heard none of it. What was wrong with her? He was sure
she was happy. He *knew* it, looking at her as he pushed
his way back through the throng to where she was sitting
with the children, as breathless with excitement and
pride as they were. She *must* be happy. It was all that
mattered to him.

'Luciana?'

'Max, don't *fuss*!' And she smiled, knowing just how
often she was going to be saying this over the next few
months, puzzling him with that smile and much amusing
Lady Deverham.

Carlo was so obsessed with cricket he had quite
forgotten about his fainting mother. 'You won!' He was
almost beside himself with delight. His first time as
Marquess, just like Grandpapa and Uncle Rory, and he
was going to give Somerton the prize. Carlo stopped
jumping about. Who did he give the prize to? Jake was
captain, but Jake was lying, heels in the air, in the vestry
with the Rector's wife standing over him. *Could* one
present a prize to one's own Papa?

Carlo stilled completely, appalled. Appalled most of
all that he repeated this traitorous word to himself, half

out loud and still it did not seem too horrible. Not too
wrong. But it wasn't true, and it wasn't *quite* right either.

Carlo hurried to avoid the idea that he was beginning
to accept the changes. 'Mr Snazeby?'

'Yes, young man—*ahh*—'

'Oh—'

'Oh, *Asquith*! Yes, my love, I do know! Now, young
Carlo,' smiled Mr Snazeby. 'What is it you want to
know?'

'It's the prize, sir. Who do I give it to now Mr
Blackmore is—?'

'Winded badly, poor fellow! Out like a light, eh,
Dalby?'

'Indeed, Snazeby, indeed. Now, what was that about
the prize? I think it most appropriate it be presented to
Rivington, don't you?'

'Oh.' Carlo really did not want to. Luciana
understood.

'It would look even stranger if you didn't, Carlo, since
he saved the day for Somerton so bravely.'

'But. . .well, he can't possibly *want* a lump of
bacon—'

'Flitch, darling! And no, I should very well imagine he
does not, I don't want it either! Imagine taking it back
to the house in the carriage!' Luciana started laughing.
It was too wonderful a notion. It was too wonderful a
day. 'Present it to Lord Rivington, congratulate the
whole team and then he can send the bacon over to the
Cat and the Moon in Farmer Bradshaw's barrow. Jess
will know what to do with it for the team's supper.'

'Won't Pap. . .um. . . Lord Rivington want supper,
too?' asked Freddie, uncannily reminding Carlo of his
dilemma.

'I should think so, Freddie, I know I should be starving hungry after such a game!'

'I'm starving hungry now!' Freddie always was. . .and Jess Blackmore's pies were beckoning.

'Very well, run along and ask Jess *nicely*! *When* Carlo has presented Lord Rivington with the prize.'

It was a very solemn moment for all concerned—or at any rate Luciana made certain that it looked as if it was—as Max came forward at the head of the victorious Somerton team and accepted the flitch on behalf of all his comrades. A cheer went up and Freddie shot off in the direction of the pie stall.

'Congratulations.' Carlo held out his hand to Max who took it courteously. 'Um. . .well played!'

Luciana was not the only one who noticed that for some reason the Marquess of Standish was a little tearful.

He was saved from the shame of everyone knowing it by Catalina, tugging at her father's sleeve so happily. 'Papa?'

Max picked her up, recognising for the first time this jealousy in her that would allow no-one else to take his attention for long. Max hugged her closer than he had meant and wondered again at the vividness of Luciana's eyes.

For the second time the whole world vanished for Luciana, as if all her senses, all her being were channelled only into him; only Max, holding his beaming daughter, was real. Only Max mattered. Carlo had performed his first duty as Marquess with a dignity that made her ache with pride, Freddie was off somewhere demolishing pies in a manner just asking for him to be aching for a much less happy reason.

Home. A real family. She could see it in everyone's face, even the dismal Miss Barrymore's. Max had got it right. He was accepted. Even the Deverham supporters were delighted with him—though Deverham's crack bowler remarked Boney could usefully have done for Lord Rivington's legs instead.

Everything in the world was right, and comfortable. Only to get better.

It was at that very moment that everything went wrong.

It happened quietly. Just Max's groom Gabe weaving his way through the crowd, his face expressionless. So expressionless the moment Luciana saw it she knew. Lord Rivenal had died.

She saw the groom touch her husband's arm, saw him murmur, and saw Max's world stand still. Luciana forgot where she was, forgot everything in her need to reach him in this last moment before he really took it in. His father was dead, just as he was beginning to know him. And it mattered.

Max could not believe it. Any of it, but least of all that he cared. It was irrational. It was Luciana. She had made him care; made him believe even his family was worth repairing. He had not said so, had not even thought so consciously, but he knew now—he had hoped it.

Max felt his stomach clench in the old familiar defence against bereavement and thought, I have hated this man for the whole of my life. . . I thought I did. I was wrong. I pitied him. And now he's gone.

Luciana reached him, no more able to believe than he was. 'I'm so sorry, Max!'

All around him people were saying they were sorry.

They had believed the fairy tales as much as she had. Prodigal son come home, to marry a widowed mother and find peace with his family at last. It was impossible it should be snatched from him so brutally. Max had not wanted to believe that fairy tale, but he knew he had.

'Max, I'll take Catalina and the boys home at once. You go to Rivenal. Don't think about us.'

And the most astounding thing to Max was that he was not. His thoughts were all for Rivenal, the home he should have had but never did. His inheritance. He had never wanted it. How much less he wanted it now.

Absurdly he thought, Luciana, Lady Rivington not fourteen days, now Marchioness of Rivenal.

It was not right. Gabe had to be wrong. And he was going to Rivenal to find out.

Luciana watched him leave for the second time in no more than a week and thought, at least this time he has something secure to come home to. Poor Max. Most of all because she could not feel with him any of what he was feeling now. Grief, she knew better than most, was something that can only be felt alone.

It can be supported, but the death of a hope is a private thing and she knew that Max had been hoping. Looking forward to taking his daughter and showing her off to her grandfather. Looking forward to taking Luciana and her boys there too, knowing they would be made welcome in Lord Rivenal's cool, unemotional way. The old man would have liked them at least, if he had never in his life loved anyone but himself.

Poor Max! He looked so alone as he rode off ahead of Gabe, who had paused to explain to Liam just what happened.

'Seizure,' Liam came to tell her. 'And just when the

just when old Rivenal was looking so recovered.'

Too much was happening at once, Luciana felt stunned by it. Two impossible things had happened today. A new life—and a death. She smiled gently at Lady Deverham's offer to take the children but declined it.

'No. No, most important of all now, I think, is to have all of us at home. He needs that. . .so much.'

It was an indication of just how shocked Luciana was, that she disclosed so much even to her oldest friend.

'I know, my love, I know.'

And, because she knew, Lady Deverham somehow achieved an almost painless escape for Luciana and her children, for they were soon safely in their carriage and heading for Somerton, Freddie still clutching the remnants of his kidney pie, wide-eyed and asking, 'Has something awful happened?'

Luciana had never lied to her children about such things. And of all things these boys would understand this.

'Yes, Freddie, something very sad has happened and we all have to be good and kind and helpful when Max comes home. His Papa has died, you see, and he. . .you know how he is feeling.'

It was the moment she knew Carlo would always, whatever battles were ahead, be fundamentally on Max's side.

'His Papa,' he repeated very quietly. Then, 'I'm very sorry.'

Catalina, who could not understand the words, understood the emotion, the tension all about her as Freddie suddenly found his pie was tasteless and argued, 'I'm *tired* of sad things! I want nice things to happen!'

And Luciana suddenly realised. . .a nice thing was. Inside, safe, and taking life and strength from her was Max's child. And she could not tell him. Not yet. He had taken too much—she knew what it felt like to be bludgeoned from all sides by events, uncheckable emotions. To need a little respite.

And—selfishly, she knew—just a little she wanted not to tell him now because she wanted it to be the best, the most exultant moment in his life. Not tempered with loss. Perfect, theirs alone. A joyful thing. No, she could not tell him now.

All she could do was bide her time quietly, keeping the children happy, keeping everything calm for when he came home again, herself most calm of all, as he would need it.

Max had had enough. God knew, she had!

But it was not all she was going to get. Because as they rounded the corner onto the carriage sweep and puppies spilled through the open doors to greet them, a second carriage drew by.

Impossible! Would she spend all day thinking, *impossible*? Cousin Lysander was here.

CHAPTER TEN

'YOU have been told never to come here, Cousin. Can
you have failed to understand just what the word never
might mean?'

The children had been safely dispatched indoors and
Luciana faced her enemy across the sunlit carriage
sweep; Lysander would not set foot inside Somerton
again. She could barely stand it that she must look at
him now, over-dressed, over-confident, yet physically
and morally so shabby. Plunged into shock after shock
in one afternoon, Luciana was close to real loss of
temper, too angry and preoccupied for caution.

She was too wrapped up in Max, in her family's real
problems to sense the danger, or even hear it when
Lysander contradicted so suavely, 'But I have decided
that such exclusion does not suit me, Cousin.'

He spat the word so bitterly; cold, excited, and at last
the threat of him got through to Luciana. Even in the
teeth of Max, faced with inevitable humiliation,
Lysander could not help himself. He could not break the
habit of a lifetime and leave her and the children alone.

Luciana had had enough. That he must plague her
now, at time like this. Fragile with exhausted emotions,
her patience snapped.

'Well, that is just too bad, Lysander, if you cannot like
it. It is how it is to be! You are not welcome at the very
best of times, which this could never be. As well you
know, for everyone at the cricket match has heard it,

Lord Rivenal has died. Even in the light of your past
insensitivity, your intrusion quite astounds me. Have the
courtesy to behave like a civilized being on just this one
occasion, and leave a house in mourning in peace!'

'Mourning. . .mourning! Oh, yes, I *do* like that! How
very quaint a notion after all.'

'Lysander, there is *nothing* you can say to shock me or
offend me, I have found you an offence beyond all
measure from the start!'

'Now is that the way, I must ask myself, to speak to a
man who has come only to render you a service?'

And in his soft, unnaturally controlled voice, Luciana
heard a malice that quite repelled her. He meant it to.
He meant for her to start to be afraid.

'Of course I heard of Lord Rivenal's most unfortunate. . .not to say, well, *opportune* demise, and I am
enough of a Standish, if you are not, Cousin, to have a
care for what people will soon be saying of the subject.'

'*Saying*? What in the world can people possibly say
but their condolences, Lysander?'

'You cannot mean to say you have not thought it for
yourself, my *dearest* Luciana?' Each word was the
sharpest stab to her quickening heart, as at last Luciana
really saw the danger. On guard.

For he went on so smoothly then, almost as if he were
discussing the changes in the autumn weather. 'But then
again, quite possibly you have. Quite possibly you do
not mind that is quite the most remarkable coincidence
that a man of so robust health as Lord Rivenal should
sicken so dramatically, should *die*, just at the moment
his long lost son returns. Quite possibly it has struck
you, too, how many deaths there have been.'

Luciana almost laughed then; she was alarmed, she

saw the way Lysander's evil mind was travelling. But this—this was gothic beyond the imaginings of the most lurid mind! It was so much an absurdity. . .not even Lysander could be so stupid.

Then her heart stilled. Lysander was not stupid. But she was, if she did not listen to what he was saying now. Listen, think—think how to deal with him! Anticipate. . .

Mr Standish saw her sudden pallor and his cold heart triumphed. It was ludicrous—all that he was saying was beyond all credibility, and yet it could be used against Max Rivington and Luciana knew it.

No smoke without fire. That most useful of all blackmailer's assistants. 'You *do* see, do you not, how strange it might appear. . .should anybody begin to think of it? Should anyone perhaps suggest. . .well, after all, Luciana, we none of us were *there*, in the Peninsula. When Rory died. When Philip. . .'

Luciana felt a rage so elemental erupt inside her then she wondered that she did not strike him. She wanted to. For the first time ever, her gentle nature was overwhelmed with the desire to inflict cruel, neverending pain. As he was doing, knowing Philip's death was her greatest vulnerability.

But she would never let him see it. Her voice iced over with contempt for his words. 'Lysander, you are insane! Quite criminally insane if you imagine for one *moment*—'

'That anyone might. . .might, shall we say, be *encouraged* to think that perhaps my cousins' deaths were not. . .as we supposed? And yet we have seen, the whole world and his wife has seen how. . .*close* you and Lord Rivington are become for people supposed to be such strangers. Perhaps. . .it is just *possible* somebody might say that you are not so new to one another. Perhaps someone might, oh, so very carelessly, say how *strange* that Lord Philip's widow should seem so contented in her marriage to a man she never met before. . .perhaps she *has* met him. Perhaps. . .it *could* just be said. . .that your husband's—your *first* husband, that is—your husband's death was not so *inconvenient*.'

Luciana could not, no sane person could, believe that he was saying it. It simply was not happening. It was beyond all crediting that anyone but a man of so warped a personality could invent the obscenities he was suggesting.

Nobody in their right mind. . .

'Thing is—' Lysander turned the blandest eye upon the struggling peacock, trapped upon a rose bush by his tail '—rumours are *awkward* things. They may be scoffed at, they may be dismissed, nobody may truly *believe* them, and yet, what is it they say? No smoke without fire. . .what a vulgar expression that is! Just the same, I think it well defines the matter. And on this occasion. . .well, you heard it for yourself, my dearest Luciana—everyone quite taken with how like to Lord Rivington your eldest son appears.'

Luciana really did laugh then, a strange, exhilarating mix of anger and complete derision. If it was not so wicked it would be quite—'Wonderful! Oh but, Lysander, you have at last succeeded in impressing me! You really ought to take up your pen and write a novel for you are quite wasted upon this. . .now—' and she mimicked his affected manner quite ruthlessly '—what is the word for it? Yes, *blackmail*! What a vulgar little word that is!'

And she knew something very important then. She had Lysander beaten. She knew something else, much more important. She was going to give in. Lysander wanted something from her and she was going to give it to him. But in her way, for her reasons, not his.

'Let me have this quite straight in my mind, Lysander, so we do not misunderstand each other. If I do not—forgive me if I leap ahead, I know you will be coming to the point directly—if I do not do as you wish, *somehow* people will start to hear these ugly rumours. That Max is responsible for his father's death? For Rory's too. For my husband's? Because I have—despite all the servants in the world, with all the tongues to gossip—somehow kept it secret from the world that I have *known* Max all the while. Known him intimately well, indeed. Well enough for him to father Carlo?'

She could not help it. God knew, it truly was the funniest thing she had ever heard. And—she faced it squarely—the most damaging.

Lysander was right. People talked. And what people talked about most were those senseless, exaggerated lies that were the spice of social living. Where was the excitement in gossiping of new fashions when there was a character to be assassinated over the Madeira and almond biscuits?

No-one would believe such lies, but a certain shading, a question mark hung over those tainted with a rumour. Smoke stains. And while Max could take care of himself she had to think of Carlo.

Not even Lysander could be so brainless he imagined he could challenge for the Standish titles. That he could take Carlo's claim to the marquessate to court—and not

have a judge finally condemn him for the blackguard
that he was. It was not that. . ..

What Lysander could gain from this was not the
Standish inheritance. Only that stone-thrown-in-a-pool
ripple of unpleasantness to follow Carlo and Freddie
into their adult years, to set people whispering and
wondering. No doubt at all, Carlo and Freddie were
made of such stuff as they would laugh at it. But their
mother was not prepared for it to come to that.

So—give Lysander what he wanted. 'What is it I can
do for you, Lysander? Money?'

Yes, of course, money. Lysander had all the pretensions of the man-about-town he never could be. Brought
up to show off and to spend as if the inheritance were
his, he had done just that. Everything he had was
extravagance and show, with nothing to back it up when
it came to the reckoning with his creditors. Lysander
was a wastrel and a spendthrift, and had spent just too
much, now, for his lifestyle to be much longer indulged.

Lysander was puzzled. She was not reacting as he
wanted. He wanted money—dear God, did he need the
money!—but, most of all, he had wanted his revenge.
And he was not going to have it. He could not touch her.
She was beyond his reach; her children were. So why
was she agreeing to pay him?

'A few thousand pounds would be—'

'Very welcome. I can see that, Cousin!'

And at last she could. *Shabby morally and physically*—Lysander reeked of nobility in decay.

'And shall we say three thousand more welcome than
two?' She saw his eyes blaze against his will and
disappointed him.

'I should very much like three thousand pounds to

play with too, but I do not have it, Lysander. Are you suggesting that I should ask my husband?'

'The Standish are worth a fortune!'

'A fortune safely in my husband's keeping. He is the boys' trustee. Now do not tell me you had forgot it!'

It was the thrust that killed. She felt the fight bleed out of him and shocked herself just a little at her enjoyment of it. She had decided what to do. Lysander's views in the matter were quite irrelevant.

'This is what I will do, Lysander. I have my pearls, of a provenance so exciting no doubt I shall raise a thousand guineas or so. Some fool will pay that just to hold the Medici Collar.'

That they were her last link with Luciana da Montefalco must not matter now. She had her boys' future to think of, not her past. Lysander would never know how much it hurt her.

Head held high, she added, so very finally, 'What *you* will do in return, Lysander—why I am doing this at all, since your threats just cannot be taken seriously—is leave the country and not come back again. I have heard that America is quite a place for a man with a little money in his pocket. Or possibly some far flung colony—'

'*Leave* Somerton?'

'Oh, I think so, don't you, Lysander? Besides, you have nothing to do with Somerton at all. You will give me a week—' the week she had while Max was occupied with his father's funeral '—and then return here. I shall have sold the pearls. When you have the money, you will go. I am sure Max will be only too happy to see to Graveney's lease for you.'

She was so sure she was in control now, she even

managed laughter. 'And no need to trouble about poor Antigone, Lysander. I should be delighted to have another pack of puppies for the children.'

Over! It was over! Because Lysander needed the money so badly he would not risk another word. Not now.

Not until later. Lysander was new to this blackmail business, but not so green he would not, when he had time to think of it, realise it was not worth his while to be gone from England. His threat had been real—its menace continuing.

But Luciana would think of none of that now. She just wanted rid of him. To be inside her house, surrounded by her children, waiting for her husband to come home.

Soon. Max must come soon!

Then Luciana realised just what Max would be coming back to. A wife who was going to lie to him for the very first time.

She hated the idea. But she had to do it. To trouble him with Lysander's antics now, when she could manage them herself, was not for thinking of. She would not add to all his burdens.

Max would be coming home to a wife with secrets. The very thing she hated most in him, she was about to do in her turn.

Luciana dismissed Lysander by just walking away from him, drained beyond measure that she had had to waste her time, one breath, upon such a disagreeable encounter. She went into the house, calling for Freddie and Carlo and Catalina, needing their nonsense to lift her spirits.

* * * *

She was so subdued when Max walked into the morning room six days later that he went to her at once. He had hated being away. There had hardly been a minute he had not thought about her fainting at the cricket match, and no amount of Gabe's assuring him that women were always to be fainting to no purpose would allay his concern. He wanted to be with her, protecting her, not trying to read between the lines of her hasty notes of reassurance. He wanted to be home.

'Luciana?'

She looked up from the book she could not read and felt a terrible exhaustion. She had to be so watchful, so controlled, to have a hope of keeping anything from him that she had drained herself. The burden of keeping secrets was a real oppression.

And it showed. She understood the question in his voice and hurried to answer it. 'I'm better, Max. Truly. I think I must just have taken a chill. . .'

Her first lie, even harder than she had expected it to be because he did not for one second believe her. So she hurried to distract him from more questions. 'Did it all go well, Max? Was it horridly bad?'

And he let her get away with her lying. Because he was so glad to be with her again. So glad, he could not lie to her.

'I found it difficult.' He took the hand she held out to him and sat beside her, Luciana curling close against his side, knowing it was what he needed. Luciana laid her head against his shoulder and marvelled at this new stage in their friendship. He had not kissed her. She had not kissed him. Closeness of a calmer kind was craved.

'I'm sorry. What a mess it all is! I think. . .truly, Max, it has to be the end of our troubles for a while. So much has happened to us all. . .too much. There has to be a calm in every storm.'

'There is.' Max held her close against him, exchanging warmth for warmth. 'Here. I told you. Always here! How have the monsters been behaving? Has my own particular monster blackened anyone else's eye?'

'Not *entirely*, though she has rather damaged poor Freddie she is quite fearsome when she has a ball in hand!'

Strange that she spoke of Catalina as if she had always lived with the child. Luciana thought for the first time, She's a wild little thing, and it is not Max she gets it from. Her mother must have been. . . But she knew nothing about Catalina's mother. It bothered her but she could not ask it. Least of all now she kept secrets of her own.

'What amazes me most is that Freddie has the restraint not to thump her. She's a wild little thing. . .' Max disconcertingly echoed Luciana's thoughts. 'Strange to be finding out about my own child like this. . . I'm sorry my father could not know her. I think he would have been proud.'

'I know he would. She's a marvellous child, Max; she's going to be a very special woman.' Meaning, Tell me about her mother; please talk to me. Talk and bring us back together after this time apart. Tell me what is hurting you now.

But she had things she could not tell him. Wearily Luciana sat up, suddenly tense with guilt, scared that in touching her he would feel her unease. She could not face his questions. Lying by omission was so much easier than lying to his face. So she got to her feet.

'Come and see for yourself what the *monsters* are up

to. They've been asking hourly when you are going to come home.'

And Max just sat there, staring after her. Impossible—*impossible*! He felt excluded.

And was not standing for it! They were both tired, but there had been no argument between them. Anger stirred, born of his unfamiliarity with helplessness.

'Something is wrong, Luciana, and you are not telling me.'

Luciana could have cried. He was forcing her into what she could not bear to do. She had to look right at him and deceive him.

'Nothing, Max, truly, *nothing* is wrong. What could be?'

And because she knew he would demand she answer it, pretending she heard a noise, she fled the room.

Luciana wanted him so much, waited with such need for him to come to join her that night, and yet she was scared to have him near her. So scared she was becoming irrational, she knew it.

After all, was it so bad that if she did tell him about Lysander they could not laugh at it? But she knew Max never would. It would make him angry, most of all with her. She had begun to learn this. Of all things to make him rage at her, it was when he suspected her managing without him.

Only a week, a day ago, this would have infuriated her, for she had coped alone for years. But she understood now just how much this marriage, his care of her, was redressing the balance of his past. His chance to atone for whatever he believed he had done.

Luciana lay in the dark, needing him close, needing

him to love her, to make everything go away but their absolute connection. But—it struck her suddenly—what if he guessed about the baby?

Fool! It was not a month yet, he *could* not know. If she could feel it in the tautness of her breasts, see it in the shadows about her eyes, he would never know the signs. What man would? Yet he read her mind so well, so often. . .

Max remained downstairs in the library, doing just that, so wrongly. He needed to be with her. He could not stand it much longer, he had to go to her. But she had been different when he came home and he knew it was because he had been away. Distanced from him, she was beginning to really see just what she had rushed into. That she had been fleeing loneliness and grief into marriage with a stranger. Too much, too soon.

She had been so closed with him tonight; lied, rejected him. God knew what she could have to lie about, but she had. The suspicion that she was protecting him from something made him wild with rage.

He was still angry when he came into their bedroom. Luciana could feel it in him even before he crossed the room. It was unbearable. It reminded her of that night, not so very long ago, when he had been reaching through her for oblivion. As he was reaching now.

It did not feel like love—not love alone—that drove him tonight. There was something too demanding, not of her, but of her privacy, as if he could force her secrets from her with his passion. There was wildness in him tonight, and Luciana hated it. She felt his disappointment in her—her guilt told her she was to blame. He was angry. She was unreceptive. She wanted him so terribly, but she could not show it.

Max heard her cry, then heard her crying, and tried to comfort her. But Luciana, almost out of control with the need to talk to him, to tell him, to make him talk to her, turned away. She shivered close against him, needing the warmth of his arms as she always would now when she slept, but she felt worlds beyond his reach.

Luciana lay awake for hours staring into the dark, bleak with misery. She listened to his breathing, so close, so reassuring, and hugged her arms about her growing child in utter misery.

Tomorrow she would tell him. She had to. This must not happen again. She could not be estranged from him. This had to stop.

In the morning she would tell him everything.

Please, God, just let it not be far too late.

Max was gone from the house, out on the estate the whole of that day. When he was at Somerton only the children saw him. Luciana knew she was being avoided and her guilt rubbed in the reason why.

Guilt had choked her awake on a cry of misery, reaching across an empty bed to say that she was sorry. Guilt about it all, because behind her stupidity in hiding her pregnancy, hiding Lysander's cruelty from Max, lay a deeper guilt, unresolved and irrational and hurting. Philip. So much had gone wrong for her and Max. It was almost as if she was not meant to be happy with anyone but Philip!

Stupid, stupid superstition! Luciana would not let it damage her new marriage. Philip would never have wanted her to feel such utter distress. It was self-induced, she knew that. Luciana was going to find her husband and apologise.

She was as resolved to open up to him as she had been to marry him and make him happy. Luciana ran down the stairs towards the hall where she could hear Max talking. The early evening mail had come and all her resolve was broken.

It was a trivial thing. Several letters had come for Max, he was reading one as she came towards him. The moment he heard her he quite deliberately—it seemed to her pointedly—folded the letter and put it in his pocket.

Luciana was stabbed through with hurt. She hadn't been about to pry, only apologise.

Dear God, were they never going to understand one another again?

She tried. 'Is it Rivenal, Max? Do you have to go back? Please say you don't. . .'

Max heard the plea in her voice and felt more of a monster than he had felt even last night when he had made love to her, knowing he was so angry. The worst crime he could commit against her. . .she had wanted him, but he felt he had cheated her. Such urgent domination was not what his love for her should be about. Guilt made him cool with her. . .

'Yes, but nothing that need concern you, Luciana. Where are the children?'

He was avoiding the real conflict, as she had done in the morning-room yesterday. Dismissing her.

Aching with regret, and more than a little angry, Luciana turned away from him. She could not apologise now. She could not mean it.

'The boys have taken Catalina to play with Anthony at Deverham.'

'No-one told me.'

'You weren't here to tell. Besides—'

'Besides, I had something I wanted to say to my daughter! Do I need permission, Luciana?'

And they stared at each other, not believing they were doing this. Conjuring a fight out of thinnest air, because they could not face the real problem.

'Don't be idiotic, Max! You expect that I must run to you to approve my plans before—'

'Now who is being foolish? Dear God, I cannot think what has got into you since—'

'*Me*!' And she nearly screamed at him, *Your child*! That is what is in me, Max! But you do not deserve it that I tell you. He was spoiling everything. 'Oh, I'm too tired for this. . .' And she was far too tired suddenly, she could barely stand, and clutched the bannisters for support.

'Luciana?' He saw it and burned with shame at hurting her. She was ill—she looked really ill. '*Tell me*!'

And Luciana, overwhelmed by his need to help, his intensity, her own confusion, sank onto the bottom stair and said the last thing she ever meant—it wasn't true.

'Oh, leave me alone, Max. Go away! I don't want you!'

Even as he turned on his heel and slammed back out of the door into the chill wet autumn evening, she was sobbing after him, 'Oh, come *back*, damn it! *Damn you*, Max!'

It was going to drive her mad. Love was. It was a nightmare. It controlled everything. She had no control left in her at all. She was wild with distress, as she had not been even when Philip had died. Love was a punishing thing.

Her maid rushed down the stairs, nodding to herself—

so her Ladyship was expecting another, was she? Mary read the signs and dealt with them as best she knew how.

'You come with me, my lady. No, no argument. To bed with you. . . .'

Luciana, who had never showed anyone her feelings in her life, clung shaking to this old friend, no longer caring.

'I hate him! I *hate* him!'

Mary, born Maria in the Tuscan hills and married to Liam since the age of seventeen, knew all about love that was overwhelming.

'I know you do, *contessina*. Don't I just know you do!'

'Men. . .they are *monsters*!' Luciana gave herself gratefully into childish rage. He need not think she was coming after him again. Hateful! The very best man in the world.

It went on for days, this chilling stand-off as Luciana carefully avoided her husband and Max, furious to be shut out, avoided her. It was driving him mad to see her so hollow-eyed, to have no idea what he had really done. To know something quite dramatic was wrong with her and she would not tell him.

Would it make it better if she did tell him now? He really did wonder. He had never imagined it could become like this. The intensity of their hostility was stifling.

So Luciana was not surprised to be told that he had gone to Rivenal.

'Just for today,' Carlo added, with a distinct feeling he had got the message garbled. He had been so disap-

pointed, because Max had promised to take him riding
on the safe parts of the moor. Max must have forgotten
and had looked so strange, Carlo had not dared to
remind him.

Carlo resented it. He took one look at his mother's
tired eyes and resented it still further. Freddie was as
insensitive as always.

'He was horrid this morning! When I dropped my
milk on him. . . I didn't mean to. He was really cross
with me!'

And Luciana had a very unexpected surprise. *Good*!
She thought, good for Max! Because the Lord alone
knew Freddie was a careless creature and she was—she
could see it now—so very disinclined to reprimand him.
Because of Philip.

He was Philip's last gift to her, her idiotic baby, who
could never stay on his feet for more than a second at a
time, nor go near anything more fragile than a mountain
without demolishing it. Because Philip had died she had
over-compensated. Her boys could not have their father
and so she had spoiled them. A little healthy anger on
Max's part would do no harm.

And yet she was furious with him for it. Because he
had been angry at her, not really at Freddie, not entirely.

'Darling, you really can't be too surprised if people
don't want milk all over them!' She noticed Freddie's
astonishment at the censure in her voice. 'Yes, Freddie,
I am telling you off to behave more sensibly! A novel
experience, I think you'll find it!'

Carlo was stunned. Mamma had never sounded so
serious when they were in trouble before.

'Come on, Freddie, let's find Liam and Catalina.'

They would be safer out of the way, besides he was angry with his mother.

'Mamma's awfully cross,' grumbled Freddie, feeling the injustice of it, in his most carrying voice.

Damn Max for this! Freddie had what he deserved, but damn Max just the same. Life was so much more uncomplicated without him.

It could get no worse, at least she could say that.

She had forgotten completely about Lysander.

'Perhaps I was foolish to imagine you would sell the Medici pearls!' Lysander was triumphant, if confounded. He could not afford for her to change her mind with the duns so close upon his heels.

Luciana had so far forgotten him, cared so little about his existence, she had ordered him to follow her to the library, barely aware of what she was doing, she was so obsessed with her quarrel with her husband. With finding herself for the first time at odds with Carlo and with Freddie.

'You may think as you choose, Lysander, for I have not the patience to listen to it—'

Pearls. . . Luciana was so uninterested in Lysander's difficulties she could barely even think what pearls might be. Or where she kept them. She really did not want to cope with this. She was so shaky with the morning debility of her pregnancy, she almost *could* not cope with it.

Opening the library door, her only thought was to get the pearls and send Lysander on his way; Luciana walked in—and froze.

Max was there.

Carlo had said he was gone to Rivenal! It was the last

straw for Luciana, whose nausea rushed up to meet the blood plummeting to her feet.

Max caught her before she fell, in an iron grip of fury. But the rage was all for Mr Standish.

'Out!' It was all he said. One word, and Mr Standish was hastening for the door.

Max had forgotten him before he was halfway to his freedom.

'Luciana! Sshh! No, safe now, brave girl! Oh, you *stupid, stupid* girl!'

And with that he swung her up into his arms and carried her up the stairs to their chamber.

Luciana clung to him as best she could, dizzy and sick with relief, knowing he was going to shout at her, and not caring. He was shouting because just the sight of her passing out like that made him so afraid.

Max laid her on the bed and sat beside her, stroking the fallen hair. 'Talk to me! *Talk to me*, Luciana!'

And it came spilling out in a compelling mix of laughter and tears. 'Lysander—oh, I know it was the most foolish thing, but I saw the opportunity to be rid of him—'

'You did *what*?'

'I know, Max, but. . .oh, I wish you had seen it. . .no, I don't, I did not want you to have the trouble of it. He tried to. . .blackmail me!'

All of a sudden, it was so ridiculous a thing, Luciana was truly laughing, most of all at her husband's face as he just stared at her, words utterly beyond him.

Luciana lifted her hand to his face, smoothing his frown away. 'I know—the drollest thing imaginable. Max, he was going to tell everybody you and I were lovers. . . I mean *before*, that Carlo is your son and you—'

No, this could never be laughed at. This was sickening in the extreme.

'And I what?'

'Nothing, Max, it does not matter now.'

'If it did not matter you would tell me.'

She could not fight him. Even as he held her so gently she had to tell, he was forcing it out of her with just his eyes. 'Your father. . . Rory. Philip. He said. . .he said you were not sorry they had died.'

And her husband froze. No other human being could know just what those words had done to him. He would not have known himself until now. The appalling truth. If Rory and Philip had lived, there would have been no Luciana. No comforting her now, no swearing he would kill Lysander for her sake.

Now she was comforting him, calming him, knowing as much as anyone ever could the horror that had burst like a shell inside him. 'Max, don't mind him! He is an evil, evil little man, so insignificant. . .'

'Yet you were going to pay him—yes, you were! What with—*why*?' He could not let the last words out: If you did not believe him.

She heard them, anyway, and flung herself into his arms, to kill the thought before it began to live and to pollute their marriage more than any secret had done.

'Max, don't you dare! Don't you *dare* be such a fool! I wanted him to go—I just wanted him gone where he could never hurt us again. I didn't care what it cost—'

She was calming him, she could feel it.

'And just what was that cost, exactly?'

'My. . .oh, don't be cross, Max, please don't look at me like that! My pearls—'

'The pearls you wore for our wedding!'

It really mattered to him. Luciana looked at Max then, and knew he would remember every second of that day as she would, everything about her branded into his mind.

'I'm *sorry*, besides I quite forgot about them. I have not sold them—'

'I damned well hope not! I'd have bought them back! You really are the most unmitigated little fool, Luciana!'

'I know.' Her relief at hearing such lover-like words was absolute. '*I know*,' she murmured softly, at last as comforted as he was.

'And so am I! Luciana, what has happened to us the past few days? I can't explain—'

And suddenly she knew the time had come.

'I can. I can, Max. I am with child.'

Luciana never would know how long he stared at her, utterly uncomprehending and yet joy dawning even before he heard her repeating it with such intensity.

'I am with child, Max. *Your* child.'

And she felt the exultation, the triumph in him, and understood that all he had ever done for her, given her, she had just returned a million times over. This was something all his own. Something of her that belonged to no-one else. Not Philip. No-one. It was like the very first time they had made love so urgently, and he had heard her tell the truth, it was never like this! This was the most important thing she had ever said or done.

Max fought for words, not believing. Not deserving this, only asking stupidly, 'Are you certain?'

She was now. 'I'm certain. Here, give me your hand.' And she held it against her breast so he could learn for himself the subtle changes that had already started in her. 'See. . .can you feel it?'

Max cupped his hand about her, and felt it—infinitesimally heavier, fuller. Already? It shamed him that he did not know.

It had never been like this with Antolina. Simply, one day she had just told him. He had seen nothing new in her because he had not looked for it. Not as he looked now, searched with his hands across the softness of her womb and earned the teasing laughter he deserved.

'Idiot! Not yet. . .'

And Max stopped that laughter with a kiss so shattering, Luciana fell back against the pillows, her arms about his neck, knowing that all was mended. He was happy. They had fought, stupidly but terribly, because this love was all so new and all too much. They were two strong people not used to being the victims of emotion. Now feelings were all that mattered as Max kissed her again, then he panicked.

'I will not hurt you. . .it?'

Luciana's heart spilled over with tenderness.

'Fool!' she whispered. Then murmured so softly, 'You'll see!'

Late in the night, much later, when the children were in bed and Max had fussed once too often, as men seemed to have to do, about should she not have her feet up, and be drinking milk and resting, Luciana stirred beside him, restless with excitement as if another eight months anticipation were unbearable. She felt it communicate to Max, so abandoned in sleep beside her. His arms came about her and she felt the whisper she so craved against her hair.

'Sleep, angel. You cannot make it happen any sooner!'

And Luciana curled herself into his body which seemed to so exactly fit her own, tired, wanting never to move again, yet wanting him. . .feeling that he wanted her.

Some things he did know. . . She heard his indulgent laughter, heard him soothe her, coax her. 'Gently, Luciana mia! No, don't wake. Just let me in. Come to me. . .' And, so gently that it was but the barest easing of his body into hers, he was inside her. Luciana sighed, learning something that she had never known before. That even in absolute stillness, this joining could overwhelm her.

And him, as his voice became raw and the pleasure broke over him. 'Come for me, Luciana!' And she felt it beginning, and heard him laugh at her surprise as she cried out in amazement and he held her, and she felt the flood of his release inside her. Then heard his breathless laughter as he whispered, 'See!' And she fell asleep, holding him inside her, his hand warm against her heart.

This would last, was her final thought before oblivion overwhelmed her. This is how life for us is meant to be. This is stronger than any imaginable harm.

The last thing she heard was her husband's half-sleeping laughter.

Max was somewhere in the outer stratosphere and did not care who knew it. Luciana, unable to believe she could make any man so happy, watched him and had a moment of wondering—Is this how Philip felt? I hope it is. I want it to be how it was for him. I loved him so much. I hope I made him this happy. The memory of him pleased her.

Max was tossing a squealing Catalina up in the air, catching her as she fell, laughing to see her faith as she trusted him not to drop her, and giggled, 'More, Papa! Papa, more!'

Luciana, Freddie dozing in her lap, said it automatically. 'Don't you dare say "urrgh", Freddie!'

'I wasn't going to say—'

'*Anything*, I know!'

What would he say when she told him about the baby? Freddie was her baby—he was not going to like it at all. Carlo, still cool with Max, only half forgiving of the tension he could not understand that had so disrupted the past few days—Carlo was going to hate it.

Luciana wanted no more drama. Just for a while she wanted this quiet happiness. Just her and Max knowing about the baby for a while. She was no longer surprised to see him glance quickly at her when she thought of him—still connected. She smiled across the misting garden. Autumn could be a wonderful time of year.

Except when one was the owner of a thousand puppies.

Mud had collected on most; those that had not rolled in water-weed instead. There was a distinct whiff of the stables bringing up the rear. For all Lady Deverham had relieved the Standish household of three puppies, after all the place still seemed to be swarming.

And would soon swarm with more. Luciana looked back on this morning when Max, who had gone out before breakfast without a word, had returned with a lickingly grateful Antigone and told her that Lysander, after all, was leaving.

'Why in the world should he go now?' she had begun to ask.

'Because I told him to,' her husband explained, his eyes saying, Luciana trust me.

And she had, she did. Absolutely now. She felt free as a bird now she had revealed her secret and learned she never had need for them at all.

'Just promise me one thing. . .' Max had said, making light of what was the most serious moment of their marriage so far. 'Get *down*, Antigone!'

'I promise.' Luciana relieved him of the bouncing poodle.

'You haven't even heard what I was going to—'

'No more secrets. Promise me, too, Max. No more!'

'No.' He would tell her soon. He had known it for a very long time, really. He had to tell her about Antolina. He wanted the old life over with, now this new life had so hopefully begun. 'No more secrets, Luciana. I promise. Soon.'

'It's about. . .your wife, isn't it?'

'About Antolina, yes.' And for the first time the memory seemed far away and did not hurt him so badly.

'Thank you, Max.' Then she had lightened the moment because it wasn't yet time for revelations. 'Even if you have brought me this confounded poodle!'

Now the sun was sinking behind the wooded slopes of Somerton Rise and soon they must go indoors, all of them, children, Cass, Polly, the poodle and all! Poor Max, Luciana laughed at him as he chased his daughter across the lawn. He really should never doubt his courage! A lesser man would have deserted in horror long ago.

'I'm hungry!' Freddie brought everything back to earth with great decision and Luciana realised that she was, too. One more thing she recognised. Please, God, she hoped she was not going to develop odd cravings this time! She had demanded the most terrifying concoctions a month or so before Freddie was born.

Life did not get any better than this, as she brushed Freddie off her lap with, 'Well, go and round up Carlo and Catalina, then—'

'We can have our supper?'

'You can have your supper. Go and tell Max for me, will you?'

And Freddie scampered off to deliver his message. He was too young to hold a grudge, or even remember Max had snapped at him. Today Max was fun and Mamma was all warm and bright and happy.

Carlo saw it, resenting the fact that it was making up her fight with Max that had done it, not all the comfort he had tried to give her. Max was not forgiven.

He knew it, and had the sense not to make an issue of either talking too much or of avoiding Carlo.

'Did I hear someone mention food? I'm starving!'

'Starving!' chorused Catalina, with the vaguest idea it had something to do with her complaining stomach. Hungrier than any of them, she raced towards the terrace steps and just too late Max yelled at her.

'Catalina!' But she had fallen, hard, tripped by a puppy and her leg was bleeding enough to frighten any child.

Catalina was only four and Max could not bear a second of her pain. He was not yet used to parenthood; he had not learned to swallow hard and accept the minor accidents with at least an outward show of calm.

Catalina clung to him, sobbing, while the boys gazed at her, horrified and helpless. *Urrgh*, girls cry a lot, thought Freddie. Carlo just wanted to go to her, but Max was in his way.

Luciana sensed conflict and hurried to take charge. 'What a mess you're making of my step, you little idiot!' she teased in a voice so soothing that Catalina looked up and smiled at her. Max felt a jolt of rawest jealousy, wanting that smile for himself. Luciana knew him well now, as if she had known him all her life. She put her hand on his shoulder.

'But then, what can I expect if she must have another idiot for a father!'

It worked. She felt his laughter. Catalina did, too, and smiled, though her knee was hurting. 'Now, I think, before you stain the stones irrevocably, I had better take you into the house to find a bandage.'

Catalina understood no more words than house. Hearing this, she clung to Luciana, and this time Max was able to share her, though still wishing she had clung to him, but reminding himself, this is what I wanted for her and Luciana.

He had everything he ever wanted as he looked at them now.

Luciana carried her sniffing daughter up the stairs, talking nonsense to her all the while, until Catalina giggled in a hopeful fashion, calm enough to consent to her knee being washed and dressed with marigold ointment and wrapped in linen. But the child was upset still, it had been a cruel fall. Even an adult would feel the shock of it.

Catalina clung as Luciana settled her on her bed to rest a while.

'Pony!' She would never calm down until she had her wooden pony.

Luciana and Nurse hunted, but they could not find it. Catalina was getting more tearful all the while.

Oh, but what a wretch! Luciana turned out another box of Freddie's clutter, complaining to herself the way one does, I would swear she had it only yesterday. Think where I last saw her with it. *Garden*. Yes. . .*yes*, Max had put it in his pocket. That coat was surely cleaned by now. His dressing-room then. Luciana hurried from the nursery on her pony hunt, no other thought in mind but to find it and earn a little respite from Catalina's crying.

Max's dressing-room was so vivid with his presence Luciana lingered, breathing in the familiar scent of cedar wood in which his clothes were stored and touching the things he kept upon a tallboy in the corner. Private things, as she had private things. She was desperately curious, but it would not do to pry.

She found the pony. His valet must have set it on the tallboy, next to a small wooden box. It looked roughly made, Spanish. It was very battered. And the lid was loose, as she discovered to her horror when she picked up the pony and a hind leg caught the box and spilled the contents.

Luciana almost did not see it at first and then she did. Her own face, so young, so proud, smiling for Philip, all those years ago.

The miniature she had given him to take to war. The most precious thing he owned, he'd told her so. Philip's, no-one else's.

She was so bitterly hurt, so angry, so disappointed to find it here, she simply cried.

CHAPTER ELEVEN

'You found it, then.'

She had not heard Max enter the room, she had been so lost in her bewilderment. It was the most awful shock, she could not speak. . .

It was as if it were someone else's voice, ice-cold with accusation. 'Oh, yes, I found it!'

And Max at last saw that she did not mean the pony and could have kicked himself.

He had been going to give the picture to her. He had been waiting for the moment and decided this morning that the moment was come. He knew the shock it would be to see the miniature again, the memories it would engender, but she had been so secure in her happiness since telling him about the baby, he had felt at last that she could bear it.

Now he misunderstood what he was seeing and believed she could not.

'Angel, I'm sorry! I didn't mean you to find it like that.' Stained with Philip's blood.

'Oh, I know you didn't!' And suddenly all control was lost, as if it had never been. 'Dear God, do I know you didn't! It's mine, Max, *mine*! It's *Philip's*!'

And even though he understood at last, he missed the real point. 'I know that, angel, that's why I kept it for you.'

A lie. It was his in a way she could never begin to know. She had not been the one to take it out of Philip's hand when he was dead, out of his brother's hand while he was dying. He had thought he could never give it up, not even to Luciana, this talisman—not just Philip and Rory's, but his. But he had changed his mind, and her accusation hurt in a way he had never been hurt by her before.

So he punished her cruelly. 'I was waiting till the time felt right. I could hardly just give it to you! Damn it, Luciana, did you want me to thrust it at you, no explanation? Covered in your husband's blood!'

Dear God, it was! Luciana, whose hand had closed about the miniature as if she would never let it go, saw how the stains had seeped beneath the protecting glass. Her thumb was touching it. *Philip*. In some terrible way, she was touching Philip in the very last moment of his life.

She could not bear it. It came back to her in one drowning rush just how much she had loved him, how much she had lost. That this was *his* home, the boys were *his* children, she was Philip's wife.

Max's wife, carrying Max's child! For one brief, destroying moment it showed in her eyes. You wanted this! You wanted me! You are not sorry that he died!

And Max knew everything was over. Luciana knew his secret, all but the final shaming part of it. She knew him for what he was. It was as if love itself had died in her. He saw her face bleached with shock, rejecting him.

Oh, God help me, what have I said? she screamed inside. What have I done! She knew that somehow he had read her eyes, her stupid thoughts, so wickedly untrue, so unfair. She loved him, it didn't matter. It would not even matter if he had, for one brief moment of relief, been glad that she was free.

She knew without having to look at the other things kept with this miniature in the little wooden box, the private things that give away so much about a person. This had been precious to him and for only one reason. The reason he would not even deny as he watched her now, utterly misreading her silence, and said so bleakly, 'Think what you will of me, Luciana; all I ever did was love you.'

That was all. 'Think what you will.' And he walked away before she could run after him. She loved him—that was all she had ever thought of him. He had all her trust and care and respect. It had been a shock, that was all, finding the miniature. It was not Philip who mattered to her now. Philip had lived with her and loved her and was gone. It was Max who lived with her and loved her now. And was leaving—

The one thing he had sworn he would never do. She remembered, shaking, how she had made him promise it the first time they had lain together, and she had discovered such hope. 'Swear it you will never leave me!' He had meant it when he had said he never could.

Luciana broke from the grip of shock; she had to stop him. She had no care for anything at all, she had to bring him back. He is the bones that keep me standing, the blood that lets me breathe, she screamed inside, as she ran heedless for the stairs. She had to get to him.

He was only a few yards ahead of her and yet it was as if she ran in a dream, held back, backwards, standing still.

'Max. . .*Max*!'

He was gone—she sank onto the stairs in hopelessness, shivering with cold—wasting precious time. If only she could think. . .

Where was he going? Only one possibility. Rivenal. So. . .she would go there, too.

She took no cloak, she had only the softest indoor slippers, the most delicate of muslins, but she ran outside, racing for the stables. Not even Liam could stop her now.

'You cannot, *contessa*, you *must* not!' Mary had told him she thought her mistress with child.

Luciana did not even answer him. And, disturbed by their serene and gentle mistress's wild mood, the grooms disregarded Liam and obeyed her.

Luciana waited, trembling with impatience while they saddled her mare, then urged them to hurry, help her into the saddle. Max was so far ahead of her. . .

Of course, if she had stopped to think, she would have realised there was no need to hurry. He would be at Rivenal, no matter what time she got there he would be there, never far from Catalina.

But she was not thinking. Only feeling and knowing she had done him the most unforgivable harm. Luciana urged her mare out into the deer park and felt the drizzle of Autumn rain trickle from the clouds to meet her. Deep, penetrating damp, soaking through to her skin until she gasped with the cold, but she would not stop because of it. She wanted nothing, nothing at all, but to reach Max and run to him, beg for his forgiveness. Anything, just be with him.

She raced the mare the last half mile through the woods of Somerton Rise into the glade. And just as she began to despair—felt common sense raise its ugly head inside her, warning, too late, all this for nothing—Max was there.

Just as he had been that first day when he had come to

find her. Standing in the mist, where the rain could not penetrate the trees, as he had stood that day in sunlight, his mare once more drinking from the stream.

Luciana could not believe it, she dashed the rain from her eyes. No, tears. *Why* was he here?

He was here because he was a fool and he was going back to her the second he had thought through what he had to say. How to say it. Max could not believe he could be so irresponsible. And yet was that not the very heart of his guilt?

He had proved to himself as never before just how little he could be trusted. Luciana needed him, needed comforting words and a calm, measured explanation. I kept your picture because I loved it, I loved you. Rory gave it to me. The truth. Damn him, he should always have given her the truth!

Well, he would give it now. It must not be too late for it. They had too much, too precious, ever to lose. Through the chill of the mist came the memory of how close they had been only. . . Dear God, only an hour ago! Happy, looking forward, accepting there would be problems, yet driven by so much hope. Now. . .

No—it could not all be blown apart by something so easily explained! He had kept the picture because he needed it, but had grown enough through loving her to give it back where it belonged.

She had changed him. The man he had been before he came here would have walked away. Since the age of sixteen he had always run away from pain.

For a man who knew the world so well, Max knew nothing of himself at all.

Luciana watched him and saw it, blaming herself for the pain that was so physical, it seemed to weight his shoulders visibly. Shoulders so strong that she had known from the second she had first looked at him that she could lean on them and never be betrayed.

She never had been, in any way. He had meant to give her the picture. He had told the truth, kept the promise that mattered most. 'What I do say will be the truth, Luciana.'

He loved her. He had never hidden the fact. He had always told her.

And then she understood at last the thing that had always been wrong. She had loved him so much she had never said it, never put it into words. As if he did not need to hear them. She had thought he knew. . .

He *had* to know! Then she remembered all the damage done by his past and knew that he was not sure of her, and the knowledge calmed her.

She was calm until he turned and saw her, then she was running towards him as if running for her life. She was. And clinging to him, needing him just to stand as he needed her.

It came out like a prayer, a final absolving confession. 'I love you, Max—please, I love you so much! I'm sorry! Max, please, I'm so, so sorry!'

She meant that she had never told him. That she had never really understood how deep the damage of war, and his childhood had gone with him. She was sorry for every last thing that had ever hurt him.

He understood. Shaking with disbelief, Max believed. Max buried his face in her hair—miracles do happen.

'I *love* you, Max!' She was ablaze with the joy of saying it. 'You make me happier than I have ever known!'

She felt how impossible it was for him to speak and so

she fell silent, too, clinging to him, letting her body calm him, letting his calm her. They just stood, minutes passing, and they did not feel the rain as they made conscious contact with every atom of each other, so they knew it all, reached everything. Neither moved, neither even really breathed. . .

Until at last he could say, 'I was coming to tell you. You *do* know that?' And then he realised just what she had done and exploded at her, 'You stupid, *stupid* girl! To take such a risk—anything could have happened! You will have made yourself ill!'

Not lost the baby—he was not even thinking, as his father would have done, that she could have lost the heir to Rivenal. Only of her. And so she kissed him to silence with tenderest laughter.

'I am having a *baby*, Max, not declining towards my grave!'

'But all the same—'

'All the same, nonsense! Oh, you men are so ridiculous! As if I have not done this before!'

The surge of jealousy that stung through him astounded her. Yet her heart soared. She wanted him to mind, she wanted him to be so greedily possessive. She wanted any proof she could have that he loved her, for all her foolishness, her lack of understanding these past few days.

'Just the same,' he repeated stubbornly.

And Luciana knew the time was right. 'Tell me now. Please. Tell me everything.'

So much, where to start?

At the beginning. 'I always loved you. I thought I was mad, but I always wanted you. From the very first moment Philip talked of you. He and Rory and I met when they came into the regiment, just a pair of foolish boys who took foolish risks and scared the wits right out of their commanding officer. Who happened to be me! I was obliged to reprimand them so often, I soon found out who they were. Philip was quite delighted with me — the Rivenal scandal traced to his lair at last! I liked him. You know I did. He was a — magical person, everyone felt it. . .' This was so hard. Truth like this was never easy. 'But I envied him, God, but how that envy hurt, Luciana, you'll never know!'

It still hurt so much, he had to walk away from her. And serene as she had been when first he saw her, she let him go, knowing he would come back when he needed the comfort of her.

'I remember when I first saw your face. . .the miniature, I couldn't believe it. *So* beautiful, so peaceful! I *burned* for you. Imagine it — I loved those brothers like my own, but I would have killed to have you! Lysander. . .maybe he saw what even I don't want to know.'

'I said the *truth*, Max. That is guilt talking!' Irrational, punishing guilt was something she had learned so much about.

And he smiled, knowing it. Forgiving himself at last for natural feelings, as he had once taught her to do.

'I never wanted it this way. For Philip to die. I never really thought I'd ever know you. Except maybe one day as a guest in your house. It would have been enough. . .' No, the truth, he had owed it to them both. 'No, it never would.'

Luciana sat on the fallen willow and watched her husband begin his long journey into peace of mind. It was as if she could see a physical burden shedding. It was wonderful.

'Then, on the retreat towards Corunna. . . I thought Philip and Rory had died. It all went mad. In the snow and the rain, the French were harrying us from behind relentlessly and we were the rearguard. We took a damned fool risk—we had to take it—we charged them at a river crossing. I saw them fall, Rory and Philip. I. . . I don't much know what happened after that, I didn't care, I was just. . .wild with anger. I have never hated in war before, war isn't like that. But I hated then. It made me careless, of course. A sabre brought me down; it was the river that saved me, swept me out of reach. I knew I was dying. . .'

It was a nightmare story. Luciana could not bear it. But she would. He needed to tell her everything.

'I didn't, because of Antolina. She came down to the river for water and she found me. She somehow got me home to her village where she hid me, kept me safe. I owed my life to her. . .she was very beautiful. It seemed impossible I was alive, I needed to feel it. . .do you understand?'

'Yes. Oh, yes!'

'She needed it too. Her lover was killed in a skirmish with the French. We needed each other. It was good— but it didn't matter. Until she told me she was expecting Catalina.' Max remembered it now, his wish that he had been hearing anything but that. So far from how it had been with Luciana. 'I didn't love her, she didn't love me, but I married her.'

Of course, thought Luciana. And yet he still condemned himself for a selfishness he could never own.

'I left just a week later. I knew I shouldn't, the village

was in danger, all those villages were under threat, the French suspected they were helping us plunder their supply lines. I told myself it was my duty to get back to my regiment, that it was for the best to leave Antolina behind. She was with child, she needed her mother... I had a thousand excuses and made certain I believed every one of them! Besides, Antolina had told me the things her lover had spied out about the French troop movements. Things vital to the safety of our own men, I had to get to England if I could. I knew Corunna was too dangerous by then, we had been pushed disastrously out of Spain; I had to get to Lisbon.'

Portugal! Dear God, he had crossed half of Spain in the teeth of Napoleon's forces!

'I walked, it was the safest way. It was better to melt into the countryside, the most innocuous of travellers, than to risk being stopped by French patrols and never getting through at all. God alone knows how far I walked, but I did, and all the time I walked I went on lying.'

Here was the squirming, shameful truth at last.

'I told myself I was doing it for my country, for my comrades, but I was only ever doing it for you. Yes, Luciana, *you*! I thought your husband was dead. All those miles, never letting myself remember I had a wife of my own now, I was not free. I just had to get to you. Whatever. To tell you how Philip died, how courageous he had been, to offer what help I could. I walked day and night, hardly eating, barely sleeping, to reach a woman I could never, *ever* have!'

But he had her now. His wife. His redemption lay there. She had not, after all, been the longings of a man

obsessed, destined to come to disillusion. He had not
been wrong. He was born to be with Luciana now.

'Rory and Philip were in Lisbon when I got there,
larger than life and as irresponsible as ever. I'll never
forget how I felt when I saw them—they had thought
me dead, too. And all they could do was deride us all for
being unseated from our horses like babies from their
first ponies! I never could laugh at it. I had been in hell,
wanting you, yet desperately wanting Philip to be alive.
I just threw myself into the war after that and swore I
would never think of you again.'

Luciana just looked at him, humbled beyond measure. To be loved like that, by a man who did not even
know her. Luciana Standish. Luciana Rivenal now.

'I'd left what valuables I could with Antolina, gold,
anything she and her mother could sell for food. That is
how they knew at the convent that Catalina's father was
an English soldier, and maybe even still alive. My signet
ring Antolina had placed on a chain round her baby's
neck.

'And there were letters, too—I sent what money I
could spare, which was less than useless since even our
officers were never being paid. If Antolina got it I never
knew, I heard nothing. . .until one letter came, begging
me to help her. The French had caught one of her
cousins spying, she knew the whole village would be
punished for it. Bonaparte's revenge was always brutal.
She needed me.'

Even now, could he face this? His betrayal of the wife
who had called on him for help. 'I didn't go.'

How could he, Luciana thought, how *could* he have
gone to Antolina? Where had he been when this letter

reached him, how far away? How many of Napoleon's legions in between?

'Lisbon,' he told her, as if she had asked it out loud, and wondered if she realised—it had been the winter after Talavera. He had been rotting in Lisbon, restless for his hand to mend so he could get back to the fighting. Anything not to have time to think, because Philip really was dead this time and Max never would know, really, if his hesitation to return to Antolina was because Luciana truly was alone.

He could not remember ever having thought it, but he despised himself now, as he had then, just as much as if he had.

'I should have gone to her, Luciana. I should have deserted the army if I had to! I should have begged Rory to come with me. . .yet I had not even told him I was married! I felt so ashamed of having left Antolina at all, I believed he would despise me. He always knew, you see—he always knew I loved you, too.

'Do you see, Luciana? All I could think of was my own worthless self! I didn't go to her and Antolina died. My child could have been killed! Lysander was right about me. If I had cared about anything but. . .if I had cared enough about her, the woman to whom I owed my life, I would have done anything to try to save her. Even if it meant I would never have any hope of you. . .never, ever see you. Because if Antolina had lived—'

Which was when Luciana stopped him, she could not bear another second of such pain. His pain. She could barely even begin to see how he had ever imagined she would condemn him. Despise him, that was what he had said. This man who had done all any man ever could in the circumstances Fate gave him. She finished his story for him.

'You were lying half dead in an infirmary, because you tried to save my husband's life, and you ask me to accuse you of selfishness? Your hand was destroyed, the friend you loved was dead, you had to battle every authority and more to be permitted to remain in the regiment at all you were so hurt, so ill, and you think I would despise you!

'You could barely stand—Max, you cannot think Rory never told me? He told me everything you did. How you even taught yourself to write again with the only hand left to you just so you could send a letter of condolence to me.

'You were hundreds of miles from Antolina, you could never have got to her in time. For all you know, she was dead before her letter reached you. You did all you could, Max, if you had gone back you never could have saved her. You would have died beside her, then what would have become of Catalina?'

It was over for him. Just one word, Catalina, spoken by the woman he loved and trusted beyond all friends he had ever known. He believed her. It was the truth and this serene certainty of hers was absolution. There was nothing to forgive, when you looked at it Luciana's way. There had only ever been sin in the eyes of a man who expected the impossible of himself and, as any human must, had failed.

Exactly what his wife was saying now.

'Max, even now don't you see? A weaker man would never have punished himself like this. Never have asked the impossible of himself! You always do—you ask more of yourself than anyone else would ever dream.

278 THE STANDISH INHERITANCE

No-one who loves you would expect the perfection you demand of yourself. Oh, my love, even now, don't you know you are allowed to fail?'

Only mortal, too. Max remembered when she had said those words to him, lying in his arms that first long night together, and accepted everything she was saying now. This was all that mattered, all that was real. Luciana and her calm, redeeming words.

'Catalina was found alive, Max; that is all that matters. All Antolina would have cared about, please believe me! She would only have cared about her child.'

Suddenly Luciana felt very close to this woman she had never known, and had envied just a little, until now. She envied no-one anything any more. She had something no-one else could ever know—Max—the best man in the world. Most of all because he did not know it.

'Yes.' Max wondered if he would ever get over the moment he first saw his daughter; first believed something worthwhile had survived this evil war.

'Finding her alive. . .when I never even knew that she had been safely born! Not until the war was over and the Superior at San Bernarda's felt it safe to send for me at Toulouse. If Antolina wrote to tell me, I never got that letter. I never knew. . .and then I found her!'

Catalina, the responsibility that had given him the courage, the urgency to come home and seek out Luciana, however unworthy of her he felt himself to be. He did not feel unworthy now.

Luciana's heart stopped beating as at last he came back to her, walking away from his past, taking her into his arms to lift her from the fallen willow.

'Luciana, all *that*—all that *suffering*, for all of us, and it was only now, when I believed I had lost you, that I knew what hell most truly is!'

Luciana curled her arms about his waist and held this man who had brought life back to her—her own and this new life inside her—and was able to laugh a little at him now.

'Oh, Max, you never came even close to losing me! I would have come after you on my knees if I had had to!'

But he could not yet laugh at it. The chill of fear was still inside him, not quite warmed away. She had to hear it.

'No, Luciana, *listen* to me! Listen until you know, until you never doubt again. . . I never want to be alive without you. I never would be! I would never know laughter or sleep or hope or peace again. . .*never*! Oh God, Luciana, hell is what *isn't* there!'

A hell far behind them now. She had the words to say so at last.

'I know that. I knew it from the moment Philip died. I thought I would never live again. . .never do, *feel* anything. I was thinking about it, just a little, when you came and found us that first day. Remember, Max? Do you know what I thought when I first saw you? No—no, you never could! I just *knew*, the second you first spoke to me, I knew my hell was over, I was free. The first thing I thought, Max, was, I could trust this man with my life, even with the lives of my children. And I never will be proved wrong. One day, Max, you'll see! Just how you appear to other people, just how easy it is to believe in you and love you. Just as your mad Irish mercenaries loved you. . . Liam does, not only because you saved his life. And Freddie, Catalina—'

'Carlo?'

'Yes, Carlo too, though he will be a little unbending for a while. He will resent you. You understand better than most how he's feeling; it is not always easy to relinquish a burden one has carried for so long a while.'

Guilt, grief, adult responsibility come too soon; they were, the three of them, new-born into a life free of such oppressions. Another change, however good, was hard for so young a child. 'Max, just give him time. He likes you so much. He only just stopped himself calling you his Papa at the cricket match, he was so proud to be giving you that confounded bacon!'

'He did?'

And Luciana hugged herself closer, loving his incredulity, his pleasure.

'Yes, and Freddie too. You were quite the hero! So please, Max, just wait and see. Don't try so hard. Don't blame yourself when things go wrong; Carlo can be merciless when he is being troublesome.'

She could see this now, and accept it much more comfortably because Max was here.

'I've over-indulged them, but they are good, kind-natured boys, Philip's sons to the heart. They love you already.'

'As Catalina loves you.'

'I hope she does. I want her to. Max, will you mind it if she one day calls me her mamma?'

'*Mind*!' And at last Luciana heard the laughter she had had such faith in from the very start.

'Luciana, you give me everything I ever came home for, then you ask me if I *mind* it!'

Impossible she could not see. . .how alike to one another they were! She no more saw just how truly she was loved than he did.

'Shall I tell you what *I* first thought when I saw *you*, my lady? I just looked at you and thought, Luciana, named for the light. *Ad lucem*—yes, Philip told me the Montefalco motto—towards the light. After all those years, and all I had to do was walk across a stretch of grass. To you, Luciana.'

He had walked towards the light and it had let him in.

Luciana had the strangest feeling then, as she looked across the glade where so much that had been good had happened. Her special place, where, since childhood, she had come looking for peace. Where, in Max, she found it. It had been Philip's place, Rory's too, and it was again.

Quite simply, she knew she and Max were not alone here. She could almost hear her lost husband, his brother who had so loved her, laughing across the years. She could hear what they were saying.

'You see now, don't you, Luciana? *This* is what we left to you. *This* is the Standish inheritance. Not land, not bricks, not fortune and security. Peace.'

Fleetingly Max tensed, she felt it beneath her shaking hands. Shaking with joy. He felt it, too.

'They loved you so *much*!' It was the most raw of whispers as he took her hand in the ruin of his, no longer even aware of its destruction.

Luciana curled her fingers into the remains of his. The greatest gift the Standish had bequeathed her was that she could tell him so simply now. 'Yes, to have left me the chance of *you*, Max. . .'

'And me the hope of you.'

When she opened her eyes again, barely withdrawn from his kiss, the glade was still. Only the stream and the mares and the sun breaking through.

'Come, my lady, it is time to take you home.'

He had said that once before. That very first day. But it meant so much more now.

Home, to both of them. All of them. The children they had now, the child to come. Hand in hand, not able to let go of one another, they turned to go home from the glade of Somerton Rise. To tell the children about the baby. . .or maybe not just for a while. . .

All the time in the world, for anything they wanted.

The bequest of the other men who had loved her was this, that she faced her future with such glowing eyes.

EPILOGUE

RORY PHILIP FITZGERALD CAVENDISH, Earl of Rivington, was born on the eve of the battle that ended the war and brought his father's comrades home in victory.

Far away, across the water, men danced for a duchess and wondered, those who were young enough to be excited, or old enough to be afraid, about an unknown place beyond the forest called Waterloo. But here in the sun-scented evening at Somerton there was only silence and hope and peace. The heir to Rivenal slept in his mother's arms.

Three hours old and still so impossible to believe in! For his father this child was almost a thing unreal, for what bonded mother and son in this moment could never be shared. And yet it felt it was, *so* shared. Luciana always made him feel like this; drawn close, wanted, part of every emotion that soared inside her. Yet he could not—how could any man?—really know what she was feeling now.

Could she have said? Luciana gazed down at this new life in her arms and knew she never could. Yet one more miracle had happened; she would never have to. No need to say to Max, this is yours, *ours*, I love you, *thank* you, all those things she so longed for him to know. He knew.

She could feel it in just the touch of his hand as it closed so securely over hers, their son's, loving him absolutely, loving her. She felt it, heard it in every breath, her husband's shock, joy, disbelief. . .that he was fascinated and humbled and a little scared.

Luciana laid her cheek against his broken fingers, to lay that fear to rest, wanting only for Max to feel as she was feeling now, a contentment rooted more deeply than any she had ever known.

It had taken hold of her from the moment she first began her labour, this quiet conviction that all was well, all safe. She was lost in its all-pervading languor and yet she was excited too, and dazzled. Surprised almost to shock as she smiled at her baby's closing eyes, fluttering between sleep and wakefulness, as he began to suck her finger.

It all felt so new. Raw, unimaginable, unrepeatable. Then she looked up at Max, understanding at last, it *was* new. It *was* different. This time she was not alone with her achievement. The man she loved was here.

Their children too, creeping so theatrically into the room, Liam's warnings that they be silent and go sensibly ringing unheeded in their ears. Freddie had his fingers over his lips and was shushing Catalina and Carlo so noisily that the baby stirred and Luciana started laughing.

Crying too, but then surely if there was a time for such depth of happiness it was now, as Max lifted Catalina onto the pillows beside her because the bed was so high and Catalina could not see her tiny brother.

Freddie bounced over at this, sensing unfair advantage, but Max stalled him before impact, casting a look at Carlo which said, Curb the little monster. Luciana smiled as Carlo nodded and—rather too literally—

seized control of Freddie. Max and Carlo had reached a very optimistic understanding.

Freddie, too intrigued to waste time squirming free of older brothers, tucked against his mother's side and peered at this strange new being she was holding. Very unsure of it—Luciana smiled at his wrinkling nose—for Rory was so small, besides ignoring him which Freddie was not used to.

Carlo came closer last of all, too grown up for Freddie's puzzlement or Catalina's murmuring curiosity. At least he tried to be.

Luciana held her breath, knowing what was coming. So many changes, but some things would always be the same.

'She's all *shrivelled*!'

'*He*!'

'*He*, then! He's all *red*!'

'*Bonito*!'

'Pretty! *Pretty*!'

And Luciana smiled up at Max, both laughing, both so calm with certainty.

'Don't you *dare* say "urrgh", Car—' they began in unison.

'I wasn't going to say *anything*!' said Freddie.

LEGACY of LOVE

Coming next month

DARING DECEPTION
Brenda Hiatt
Regency

Gavin Alexander, sixth Earl of Seabrooke, needed an heiress—fast! His newly acquired title came with a mountain of debts, and he was fast losing face with polite society. So when Thomas Chesterton offered his sister—and her fortune—to him, in repayment of a gaming debt, Seabrooke thought his problems were over. But his betrothed, Miss Frederica Chesterton, was not one to go meekly to her fate!

In desperation, Frederica infiltrated Lord Seabrooke's household, posing as an assistant housekeeper. While there, she unearthed two disturbing discoveries—Lord Seabrooke was guarding a secret, and Frederica was close to losing her heart in spite of it!

THE OUTRAGEOUS DOWAGER
Sarah Westleigh
Regency 1814

Lady Alexia Hamilton, Dowager Countess of Amber, had been given little choice in her first marriage, though she had come to love her kind, elderly husband. But, having lived the past few years immured in the country, Lexie intended to enjoy her return to London, a city en fête. A fact which got her into trouble, from which she was rescued by the Marquess of Stormaston. Storm was entranced by Lexie, and determined to make her his mistress—but Lexie wanted marriage! Who would win this amusing battle of wills?

GET 4 BOOKS
AND A MYSTERY GIFT

Return the coupon below and we'll send you 4 Legacy of Love novels and a mystery gift absolutely FREE! We'll even pay the postage and packing for you.

We're making you this offer to introduce you to the benefits of Reader Service: FREE home delivery of brand-new Legacy of Love novels, at least a month before they are available in the shops, FREE gifts and a monthly Newsletter packed with information.

Accepting these FREE books and gift places you under no obligation to buy, you may cancel at any time, even after receiving just your free shipment. Simply complete the coupon below and send it to:

MILLS & BOON READER SERVICE, FREEPOST, CROYDON, SURREY, CR9 3WZ.

No stamp needed

Yes, please send me 4 free Legacy of Love novels and a mystery gift. I understand that unless you hear from me, I will receive 4 superb new titles every month for just £2.99* each postage and packing free. I am under no obligation to purchase any books and I may cancel or suspend my subscription at any time, but the free books and gifts will be mine to keep in any case. (I am over 18 years of age)

1EP6M

Ms/Mrs/Miss/Mr _____

Address _____

_____

_____ Postcode _____